THE MAN WHO THE SEA WOULDN'T DROWN

The Ballad of Timid Stormwind

THE MAN WHO THE SEA WOULDN'T DROWN

The Ballad of Timid Stormwind

BOOK 1

R.P. Ashe

The Man Who the Sea Wouldn't Drown

This is a work of fiction. Names, characters, places, and incidents either are the product of the author's imagination or are used fictitiously. Any resemblance to actual persons, events, or locations is entirely coincidental.

Paperback, First Edition, 2020
ISBN 978-1-7358193-0-3

Contents

TO MY FRIENDS,
WHOEVER YOU ARE.

A NOTE FROM THE AUTHOR

I have a story that I'd like to share with you. It's not a short story, but it's not extraordinarily long either. It's not the greatest story ever told — that's for sure — and it's not real.

But that doesn't mean that it's worthless. In fact, I believe that all stories have value. Before they can ever be told, they must be planted inside someone. Then throughout the years, as they are retold — if they are retold — they change. It is these stories that have the most value and the most to give. Because if someone hasn't yet heard it, a good story can be shaped and molded to fit new ears perfectly — and that makes them worth almost anything.

I've had this story inside of me for a long time — bubbling up, brewing, and fermenting. Percolating, even. And I think that it's just about ready to be pulled off the stove and poured for the first time.

My hope is that you find this story delightful enough to share with others, and it is not so precise or fragile that it cannot withstand the stretching and shaping that comes with an abridged retelling. And maybe someday, if my dream comes true, I may meet it again and recognize my old friend — and hopefully I will be wise enough to sit quietly and listen, eager to learn what new adventures it has to share with me.

PROLOGUE

THE MALACHAI

CHAPTER 1

To start, imagine yourself in a near-black void. You hover over a hunk of rock.

Viewed from far away, and far above, this little floating rock is like any other. There is sea, and there is not sea. There are high places, and there are very, very low places. But most everything is in the middle — where sea meets stone, where people can enjoy some of each whenever they want.

Look behind you, however, and you might see some things harder to understand. Little dots of light, a giant ball of hot flame, and another, tinier, floating rock — shiny and dark at the same time and in equal parts. All these things, too, have stories. But the story we want is much, much smaller.

Look down a bit more closely at the rock below and you'll see an island. A rather large one, actually. The one with a broad, soft edge on top and a hard, pointed tip on bottom. This is the Shrieking Isle, a land of golden opportunity and foggy misery. If you watch it for long enough, you'll witness a patchwork of white melt away into fat brown splotches and thin blue rivers. Swaths of green will sprout here and there — but those eventually disappear too, this time into yellow.

And then, for whatever strange reason, it puts on that patchy white coat again.

Squint just hard enough and you'll see things moving around where they probably shouldn't be. They aren't even on the island — they're miles off the coast in little wooden ships, braving crashing waves and thunderous winds. The story that we're looking for begins on one of those ships, the Malachai — because the people on it have just done something that they really, really shouldn't have.

Teetering out over the Malachai's edge, a young man watched wave after wave crash against its hull. Timid Stormwind, they called him — and that most definitely was his name. You might think it cruel to plague someone with so much tension in their name, but seafolk are a different lot. You see, the ones who do survive to old age are usually cut from the same humble cloth — do too much risk-taking in your younger days, and well, let's just say that calling someone shy or calm is actually a pledge of confidence.

Timid read the lines of wind on the water. "And I used to think the world was small," he thought out loud. The horizon was there, yes, but nothing else. Even if he stared over any other railing on the ship, still just horizon.

"It is, boy." The graveled voice came from Brawlin, a large, muscled man with bits of sun-dried skin peeking through his burlap shirt like blue sky through incomplete clouds. "Sorry, Timid," he continued, "forgot you don't grab the net anymore. But the world is only big from a boat."

Brawlin turned and strode away, path as straight as a tightrope — as if the sways and sags of the ship were merely a pleasant breeze in some other, sturdier place. Timid wondered how long it must have been since Brawlin had outgrown the net. Maybe decades.

Birds had returned to the ship earlier that morning, a sign that although the crew couldn't see it, they closed upon land. For the first time — or at least, so he told himself — Timid had not longed for it. During the last storm, he had kept his feet planted on the deck without help from the net that crisscrossed the Malachai's railings, and now the crew treated Timid as one of their own. As an adult. As a sailor. *As a pirate.*

And the birds brought another welcome sensation to the ship — noise. The sloshing of waves seemed to drown itself out after a few days, and the sounds of the ship all felt artificial — but birds, they were of God.

A ship always has needs to care for, but heading to port gives the crew a little more flexibility than they get when hauling nets. Even better, time on the wheel was quite leisurely. Nothing like spotting or pulling lines — not to mention the deck swabbers who were always swabbing. Timid had swabbed for years, and his knees still wore rugged calluses and pieces of splintered wood — unlike a number of the other dozen crewmembers who picked up sailing later in life with more marketable skills. And yet, Timid was one of few with steering privileges. Captain, first mate, second mate — and Timid was second mate. Longer tenured than anyone on the Malachai except for Captain Ezira, the fact that someone else was first mate was a testament only of Timid's young age. He couldn't be first as a matter of politics. Employing even a second mate who still grabbed the net was enough of a hubbub, but at least that was over.

Timid spent his extra time daydreaming on the railings or in the nest, but right about now he was due at the wheel. If left to do too much daydreaming, Timid would wonder whether he was actually first mate now that the Malachai was a few hands short. He didn't let himself stare out over the sea for too long, lest he came up with an answer to that question.

Timid turned and walked towards the back of the ship, trying his best to look as suave as Brawlin had. But because his sea legs were measured only in years — not decades — his path snaked across the busy deck as the ship swayed from side to side with the colliding surf.

And with a busy deck, comes song — always. As much a part of life aboard ship as wooden boards and translucent fins, every sailor fills a role in the constant choir ringing out over the ocean. Some songs — the long-haul chants — force rhythm and teamwork onto tasks incompletable by a lone worker. Others are mere limericks or whistle-tunes that breathe life into an otherwise lonely task.

And because always includes today, today was no different. Davin, a young one-handed man they kept around out of a sense of loyalty, called out the chorus to five sailors hauling a rope.

O' high on the watch, abandon yer reckon.

And the multi-man chorus boomed out in an off-key response.

Way, ay, sail the Fool's Wind.

Timid mumbled along to himself, as the call-and-response mimicked an echo behind him.

O' low below deck, abandon yer mutton.

Way, ay, sail the Fool's Wind.

The Malachai was a peculiar boat in several ways, none of which were due to the crew. First, it wasn't fit for whaling — the new craze that emptied harbors and turned captains into prospectors. Second, it wasn't that big — only a dozen crew and one fish hold. But what the Malachai lacked in cargo capacity it

made up for in speed, and so it still got hired. Its lateen sails —
large triangles falling from slanted crossbars that nearly touch
the deck at the front — allowed it to chase the wind, rather than
just follow it. And lastly, and for this the Malachai was a modern
ship, it had a wheel and a rudder. No oar hung from the stern
down to the water on a long handle. Rather, the ship was steered
by a movable piece of wood and iron, affixed on a hinge to the
back of the keel.

As Timid passed the belly of the ship, he again realized that
the fish hold smelled empty, even though it was not. The ocean
supplied its usual saltiness, which all seafolk knew as closely as
their own odor, but the smell of fish typically overpowered the
deck with its own unique stench — the one that there was no
mistaking. Today, nor in the last three days, no smell came from
the hold. Sometimes, Timid could imagine one. He imagined
a metallic smell. Like gold, from coins and the jewelry. Like iron,
from the knives and the blood.

Nobody else appeared fazed, and the symphony continued to
populate the air.

If I don't come home, my mistress will kill me.
Way, ay, sail the Fool's Wind.
And stay away from my wife, she thinks I'm with ye',
Way, ay, sail the Fool's Wind.

Timid reached the stern, climbing the portside stairs to the
aftcastle. His shift had been called out a few minutes ago, so the
wheel was unattended. A thick, frayed rope looped around one
of its pegs, fastening it to the floor so it didn't get a mind of its
own. His clothes were damp in patches — ships are wet places,
after all — but on this hot summer day it was mostly sweat.
Timid went to the stern's water barrel, submerging his hands
and ignoring the small mug tied to its rim. He cupped some out

and fed it to his lips. A little salty, but some of that was probably from his own hands. His brain imagined the metallic smell again, making him sick to his stomach. With a refreshing disregard for portion control, he downed a few more handfuls to quell the feeling. Birds were back, after all.

Using this much water for cosmetic hygiene really would not have been allowed if there were no birds. It was the ship's second to last water barrel — another reminder that this trip had taken a few days longer than expected. Two barrels for a dozen sailors wouldn't last long. And they never, ever broke the seal on the last barrel. The understanding among sailors and fishermen was that if you were desperate enough to open your last barrel, you'd never need to open another. Dead men don't drink.

"And not a dozen, Timid," he said to himself. "Only nine."

Timid threw the guide rope off the wheel and was thankful to see that it had been tied to the king's handle, the one with notches at the top so you could tell when the wheel was set to straight. They were without a first mate, so when they needed another crewmember to take a shift on the wheel, they chose Yarly — experienced, loyal, and dim. Yesterday, he had left the wheel tied up off center, meandering them west a few extra miles before Timid started his shift and noticed.

Timid stared out, surveying the flat, calm sea. Captain was probably asleep, since he insisted on being nightshift. And the rest of the night crew was sleeping too. That left six on deck, including Timid. Since most of the work happened during the day, they were fine with three at night if Captain was one of them. And a ship with no captain on deck suffers from the occasional daydream of its helmsman.

When night lays its shadow across the Shrieking Isle, it is better to be in your bed than out of it. So as the crew affixed a new canvas cover for the fish hold under a budding darkness, Timid wasted no time in retiring from his post. Some others, too, looked forward to the shift's end. Yarly had pulled scrubbing duty for his second shift today — which was not a coincidence — and scrub he had, removing the last bit of red stains from the deck and the stairs. Timid was happy for it and now walked without his stomach turning at every other step.

Timid descended the aftcastle steps down to the main deck. They each creaked in a different tone, reminding him of the evenings spent in Shrieksport taverns listening to terrible, local musical troupes. He turned and faced the doors that stood tucked away in the rear of the ship between the top two decks. Rather flimsy after suffering a decade of weathering, they offered no real protection from the cold. But they meant something. And they looked good — painted recently, actually. A large squid, with an arrow shaped head and six long and swirling tentacles, adorned the center at eye level with Timid. The door was blue, but the trim, carvings, and squid wore a rough coat of yellow. He cut the squid in half by pushing the doors open.

Captain Ezira lounged in a chair, head tilted back and mouth open. His arms hung at his side and a half-empty bottle sat on the floor at his fingertips. A large blue hat, adorned with a familiar yellow squid, lay upside down behind the chair and an old, outdated map covered the table. Timid grabbed the hat, set it on the Captain's chest, and rolled up the map. Such important charts belonged in a closet, but he let the map stay there for now — maybe Ezira was using it for something.

The Captain was a notoriously difficult man to rouse from sleep. Timid walked back to the open doorway, turned and faced the room again as if he had just entered, and knocked on the door frame loudly. He had his own special way of knocking, and it worked this time just as it always had.

The Captain clamped his mouth shut and wiped his lips with the back of his hand. "Ah, Timid." He yawned and stretched his arms and legs, shooting his bootless feet out under the table. "Where's the day gone?"

"Not to waste," Timid answered, "we should port around dawn. You know, with how little you sleep in your bed, you might as well let me have it." Timid didn't feel humorous today, but that's what always got through to Ezira, who harrumphed and gave Timid a dismissive, tired look.

"Miss it that much, do ya'?" Ezira joked. He enjoyed reminding Timid of the year or so that Timid spent constantly on the Malachai. When the ship was docked in harbor and the crew and captain were off for the night, Timid was allowed to stay on the ship and — in exchange for cleaning and keeping watch — sleep in the captain's quarters. He wasn't technically allowed to at first, but he'd been caught by tidying up after himself a little too well. Ezira had struck up a deal then.

Timid closed the door behind him and walked up to the table. He hid his hands behind his back. Sometime in the last hour his fingers had begun trembling with an agitation that had been built up over the last three days. Especially now that he'd made up his mind on what to say and was now only searching for the courage to let the words slip past his lips. Looking down at Ezira now, seeing the old man physically beneath him, he found it.

"After we port in Shumain," Timid said, "I'm going to collect my things and charter a ride to Shrieksport. That's my decision and I won't hear anything else on it."

Ezira sighed and ran his hands over his scruffed face. After a few moments, he sat up straight and set his hands back down on the chair armrests. He looked like a king.

"Aye, Timid. I won't stop ya'," Ezira said. He chewed on his lip for a moment before leaning forward and resting his elbows on his knees, twiddling his thumbs together. "But it's my duty to make sure that you won't do nothin' to hurt the crew."

"Duty?" Timid blurted out, unable to stick to his plan of remaining calm. "Now you care about duty? There's only nine people on this boat, Ezira!" Timid turned sharply towards the door and walked away.

Maybe he had pounded on the table. Maybe he had stomped across the room. Maybe he had pulled the doors open hard enough to make them swing and clang against the wall. Whatever he did, the five men staring at him from the deck had noticed. Even the birds seemed to stop and peer down as well, hesitant to pierce the silence.

Timid took a few steps toward mid-deck, heading for the stairs down to the crew quarters. Brawlin stood still at the top of the stairwell with a full sandbag on his shoulder. Timid stopped a step shy of running into Brawlin's chest. A few breaths passed, and Timid finally looked up to meet Brawlin's eyes. They were big — like Brawlin — and wide open, like he had just seen a peg-legged ghost from one of the seafolk tales.

Slowly, Brawlin pivoted himself out of Timid's path. Timid descended the stairs and entered the crew quarters in the steerage. As if the ship had permission to breathe again, bodies resumed their motions and the birds called out again.

Timid sat on the edge of his hammock and removed his boots. He rolled his wax earplugs between his thumb and forefinger and fit them snugly into his ears. In a few minutes, he was asleep to the muffled sound of planks being scrubbed. In a few hours, he was awake to the feel of water on his face.

CHAPTER 2

Seawater. Cold and briny. The sound of creaking boards, stressing until they snapped, gargled through Timid's earplugs. Water gushed in from a hole in the hull and drenched the lower deck. Timid removed his plugs and sat up, plopping his feet onto the ground. More water.

He struggled to put his boots on. The ship listed starboard, forcing him to hold tight to a post that supported his hammock. Water flowed down towards the hole, carrying debris and loose objects against his shins. Shouts filled the gaps between cracking planks. Violent waves lapped at the ship's hull near him, proving that the list had gotten severe enough to dip the lower deck down under the ocean's surface.

The steerage was empty apart from Timid. The rest of his shiftmates had woken before him, maybe to the sound of whatever had made the hole. Using his hands, Timid climbed up the awkwardly slanted stairs, which — while not very steep normally — were difficult to get his footing on.

The dark air, filled with motion, was a confusing mess. Some sailors carried torches, but most had thrown them down to help with something more pressing. Captain Ezira stood on the aftcastle balcony at the rear of the ship, barking orders for someone to save someone or secure something. Strangely, Ezira wasn't wearing his captain's hat. "Did he fall asleep and ground us?" Timid first thought.

Timid scuttled upward across the sloping deck. The tipping had corrected itself enough that the crew could still walk on the deck, just not very well. Brawlin threw crates and barrels overboard, often barely getting it high enough to go over the railing. Timid rushed up to grab one end of a crate and helped Brawlin launch it into the water, but lost his footing on the wet, angled deck and began to slide down. Brawlin quickly caught him with one arm and grabbed the railing's net with the other.

"Still grabbing the net, eh?" jeered Timid when he had stood back up.

Brawlin smiled and shook his head. "Don't tell boss."

A shout cut through the darkness, louder than the rest and filled with the unmistakable urgency of fear. "It's back!"

"What's back?" Timid asked Brawlin, but he didn't get an answer in time.

Specks of water soared into the air, spurting up from the sea behind the upturned hull of the boat. A dark silhouette rose out of the water, featureless and slender. Then, more splashing as similar shapes lifted up, high above the deck. Seawater rained down on Timid and Brawlin as the things moved towards the Malachai's exposed flank.

Torchlight glistened off the shapes as they inched closer. They were dark, but not black. The tips, flattened and pointed like spearheads, were lined with a rigid flange along the edges. The main shafts were more rounded but still slightly flat like a blade of grass.

"It's a tentacle…" Brawlin muttered slowly, still trying to process what he was seeing.

Another crash from below, in front of Timid and Brawlin. Water appeared to tumble and churn at the edge of the upturned hull, like a wave crashing over a large rock. Timid tore his eyes away and looked back towards the aftcastle. Ezira still stood there. Not helping, not unloading the deck, not securing the sails. Not even yelling out orders anymore.

Timid's mind darted to survival — to the dinghy, a small boat held up over the back railing of the ship. The Dangling Dinghy, they called it. He turned and took a step towards the stairs leading up to the aftcastle. Again, Brawlin grabbed his arm.

"Where you going?" Brawlin asked. "You need to stay topside."

"We need to abandon ship," Timid rebutted. The words stuck in his throat. To sailors, speaking those words was a curse in itself, separate from the situation that sparked them.

"We have to stay here and ride the ship down," Brawlin responded. "There's no dinghy, Timid. Remember?"

In fact, there hadn't been a dinghy for three days. Not since they lost it while boarding that other ship. Not since the ocean pinned them to this fate and sicked this creature on them as punishment.

Timid stared daggers at Ezira. The Captain didn't move, eyes transfixed by the tentacles and steeped in helplessness.

Hatred boiled out of Timid's mouth, frothing over his open lips. "You cursed us to this, Ezira! You've dragged us all to the pits with you!"

For a third time, Brawlin grabbed Timid. This time, the large and hulking man said nothing, only pointed down over the railing towards the source of the tentacles. But now, where the water had just been churning, a wide-open jaw thrust upward.

Two halves of a curved beak closed on the exposed hull with a crunch that shattered boards like straw in a horse's mouth. The tentacles slammed into the top of the deck and the people on it, throwing Timid backward and sliding down the deck headfirst. More boards splintered as the ship's mainmast wrenched loose from its roots and began to fall.

Timid slid, his wet boots and bare hands unable to get a grasp on the slick wood. Torches littered the deck as the rest of the crew ditched them to grab hold of anything still attached to the ship. The back of Timid's head, like the tip of a dull arrow, hit a post on the railing at the bottom. His body crumpled against the netting, lifeless. Seawater curled over his back as the ship sank below the waves.

Steady thee, Stormwind, and float.

The words shook Timid's skull like a plucked string. Encased in an icy cold, his limbs felt weightless. His eyes burst open to find nothing but blueish black. A sharp pain hit his lungs — the need for air.

Right yourself. In my waves, find lasting breath.

A calm warmth washed over Timid's skin and buzzed his spine. Unable to control his instincts any longer, he opened his mouth and water rushed down his throat. The pain relented like a popped bubble as water forced its way in and out of his chest as his body mandated.

Your crimes hang heavy as chains.

Timid was suspended, neither sinking nor floating. Below, pure blackness swallowed his feet. Above, blue faded in until it met a translucent layer of red torchlight and blood. To his sides, bodies sank past him — limp and only parts of the whole. Gold rain fell fast all around him, blinking out of sight as they slipped into shadow.

In my mercy find a buoy.

Movement in front of Timid caught his attention. A series of long, slender silhouettes swayed in concert and stretched out towards him. They approached, just out of arm's length, before turning broadside and revealing a body. The tentacles weaved together in a bundle at their source — a large shell that curved in on itself like a spiral. At the center of the thickest mass of tentacles was a giant, primitive eye wider than Timid's wingspan. He fought the instinct to thrash his limbs against the ocean.

Steady thee, Stormwind, and float.

The voice was not audible but instead sprouted from inside his skull at his brainstem. A current of water flushed against his body, slowly rising him up and away. The creature became black again, shadowed by the ocean, and melted away into the dark.

He looked up and saw that he approached the surface. His body still pushed water through itself in a cycle, and he felt afraid of the open air. Like it would choke him. After only a moment, red flooded his vision, both from the mass amount of blood in the water and from the firelight above it. His mouth and throat tasted a metallic twinge.

Timid spewed out a lungful of water as his head crested above the surface. Torches gleamed across the top of the water, still holding a flame with the help of stinking, sturdy whale oil. Pieces of wreckage dotted the surface every few yards, but no large chunks of the ship — only debris of planks, crates, barrels, and rope. And no bodies, either.

Timid managed his way over to a large beam of wood that could support his weight. The air stung his lungs, and his mouth noticed the overwhelming taste of salt that was seemingly pleasant for once. The sea's surface sat calmly, with no sign of the violent waves that had terrorized the crew in their last moments. The next hour brought the sunrise, coating the ocean waves in a calming yellow.

And on, Timid floated.

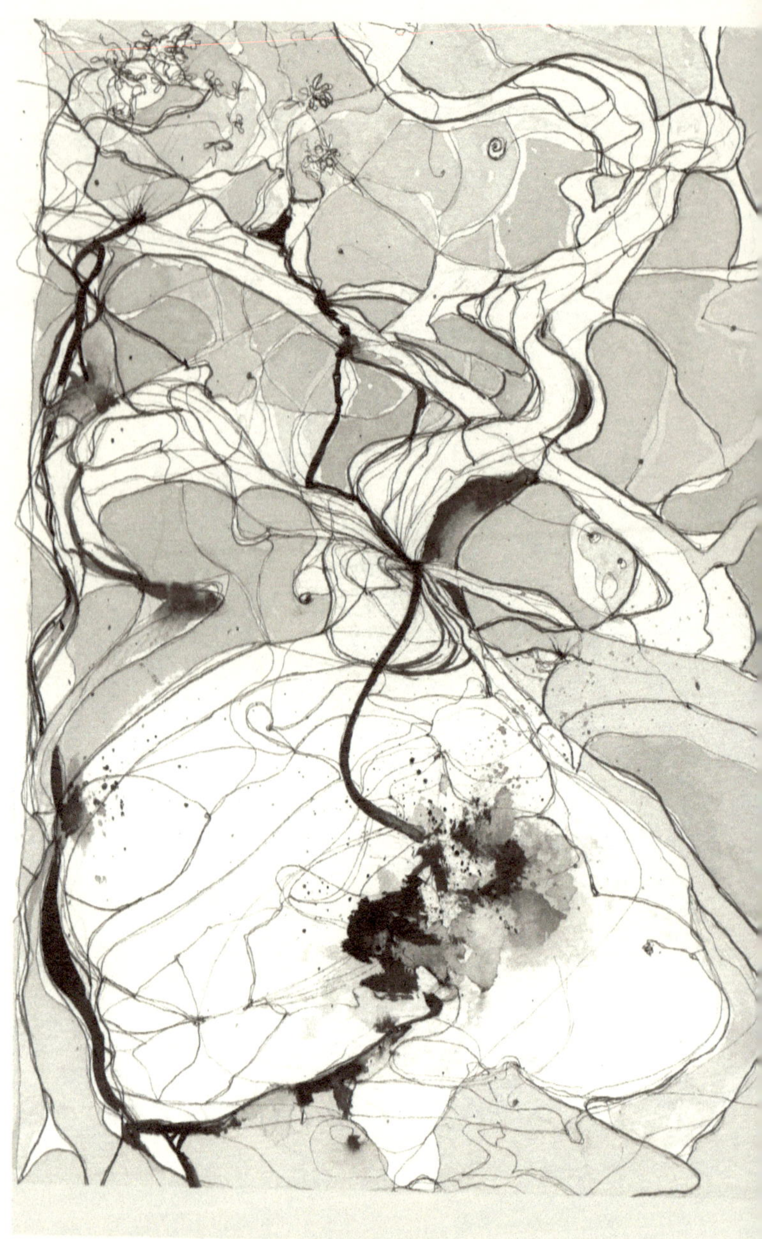

PART ONE

THE FOREST THROUGH THE TREES

CHAPTER 3

"Many songs are sung and many tales are told of the city of Goodhaven, though most consider it a myth. When no person has been known to reach it and be seen again in the same lifetime, myths start to spread. Every so often, a traveler on the North Road will claim that a squirrel or bird told them of the place where the trees walk and the grass listens."

Grenbo paused for a few seconds to make sure his audience felt the weight of his words. A dozen pairs of small eyes held themselves wide open at the prospect of new information. Grenbo glanced towards the front of the cafe, and thankfully saw the hostess still eavesdropping.

"What mortals know for a fact is this: far north in the Shrieking Isle, as the mountains slope down and stretch into the plains that border the sea, there lives a forest. Just about everyone in the isle knows of it, and knows it as the Living Forest. You see, not everything in the Shrieking Isle has been mapped and charted, including this forest. The North Road, the main road in that part of the world, attempts to skirt past it barely with brush on both sides. But it travels close enough to hear voices and feel eyes."

He had them right where he wanted them. Each had leaned forward about a foot since he began, some taking off their caps and others forgetting about anything else in their lives. The hostess, too, began to make trips to clean nearby tables that no guest had sat at in hours. The floor of the entire rear corner of the cafe was now occupied by quiet children, who had been told by someone or someone else about the man who had just returned from the Living Forest.

"So that night, as we crowded in a circle around the red whips of fire tangling at our feet, I told the two mercenaries this: 'The forest which surrounds us has been growing each season, expanding like the rings of a tree, and overtaking some sections of the North Road — this place included, as you can see. This is what remains of a small meadow where trade caravans used to rest along the road. Now, we're the only ones who dare to sleep here. See the small path that leads into the thick of the forest? Past the iron bars of the gatehouse and just out of the firelight? That's your path.'

"That's what I told them: the truth."

For once, the children all sat still. Some mouths clenched shut, others were left wide open. Grenbo basked in the attention. It was more than a city guard usually received — most of his time on duty was spent being ignored, and that was doubly true in the poorer neighborhoods like this one. This was his time, his claim to fame. After all, he had been sent on a *special mission* by none other than King Hallond himself. But though Grenbo didn't know it, that story was made up by the Boars, the organization that hired him as an escort. The Boars had asked the City Guard for help and received two armed guards from a district that could absorb a loss if there happened to be an unsavory accident on the road. But even if Grenbo knew all that went on behind the scenes, he wouldn't have inserted any disparaging facts into his story. Why would he? Nobody else ever seemed to. For that same reason, Grenbo had conveniently left out that he wasn't the person who really told that story to the two mercenaries. Until now, he was no storyteller. He was merely an extra body. But nobody else here had to know that.

"The junction had a guard post in the gatehouse, which has long been abandoned ever since the forest overtook it. Neither the post nor the gatehouse holds a guardsman anymore, and instead remains a tilted sign hanging by one end rope. It reads: 'No man shall travel this path to Goodhaven and return.'

"So with that at our backs, we sat around the campfire, engulfed by the edge of the forest. The junction kept us safe, it was wide enough that we could see the stars through the hole in the canopy. They say that when the canopy closes you in and you can't see the stars at night anymore, that's when you know that you're in the depths of the forest and that you'll never return.

"From there, the trees grow taller and the branches grow thicker, enclosing you in like a giant cathedral with a fifty-foot ceiling for as far as you can see. And if you're lucky, you can catch a glimpse of an Essai tree in the darkness. A tree with a trunk as wide as any of your houses, sitting out in the blackness alone."

One of the children piped up, "Did you see any?"

Grenbo smiled. "No, little lad. I didn't."

"Well, why not?" Another one chipping in. They were getting a little too excited. Maybe mentioning the Essai trees was a bit over the top for someone who hadn't actually seen one.

"Because there weren't any where I was. But down the path…" Grenbo tried to select his next words carefully.

A small girl cut him off, "You di'n't go down the path? I thought you went into the for'st!"

"I did, I told you," Grenbo insisted. "I went to the junction that the forbidden path starts from!" Maybe the path wasn't exactly forbidden, but surely these children wouldn't know that.

"He's just a fibber," said a fourth child now brave enough to call out Grenbo, his authority waning enough to lose their mass attention.

A fifth, "Everybody knows someone who's been to the junction. It's on the main road." It was over. The hostess began to walk back to her post at the front of the cafe. Not out of earshot, but the message rang clear.

Grenbo tried to save face and cried out, "But the forest has grown! There's trees on both sides now! Big, tall trees with branches as thick as your legs!" He was practically yelling as the children stood up and began to walk away, some holding the hands of younger brothers or sisters.

He could overhear one or two saying, "Bunch of bushes, I bet." And another murmur, "I bet he didn't even go."

The cafe cleared out for the most part, with some remaining children tugging at their parents to leave, who in turn were upset that Grenbo hadn't distracted the little ones for nearly as long as they hoped. The hostess never returned to the back corner to reset the chairs and tables the children had pushed aside to make their seating area.

Grenbo sat for a few minutes, finishing his tea and wondering what the mercenaries he escorted might actually be up to around this time. He got up and placed his cap on his head. Getting a little too close to the hostess, who wasn't trying very hard to suppress a laugh, Grenbo walked out the front door.

Like most streets in Corical, the avenue was dusty. The city only paid to water down the streets in the quieter and nicer sections of town, which he thoroughly relished whenever he got lucky enough to get stationed in one. And the buildings there were built out of wood, not stone, so there was much less dirt and dust to begin with. Plus, their cafes were actual restaurants, too, with more than ten tables and more than one hostess to try your luck on.

The sun beat down like a hot brand and Grenbo could feel the heat radiate from the stone street through his thin day-off shoes. A surprisingly hot day in one of the coldest springs he could remember. Maybe that meant a storm was due. He moseyed around the corner to his home, just two blocks, disappointed that the mercenaries wouldn't require an escort home from the Living Forest. Because they wouldn't come back. Nobody ever does.

CHAPTER 4

The crisp morning air greeted Timid's toes as they stuck just a little outside his tent door. A toad's groan leaked out from somewhere in camp, followed by a symphony from its cousins. Timid was getting used to sleeping like this, but his bedroll was on its last leg. He pried himself up off the ground and ran his hands through his tangled mass of hair to force out a yawn. He hadn't shorn it all winter and so he tied it up above his head into a bun, embarrassed that he couldn't afford the oil to slick it back in the fashionable city-boy style. At least he was blessed with a scruffless face — or else he'd have revealed himself to his new mercenary friends as nothing more than a common street rat.

The sun rose quickly in the eastward sky above camp and poked its fingers between the horizon and the bottoms of the trees, split apart at the knuckles by a forest of trunks. He liked to be up by now and sunrise was the time to get dew under his feet — one of the most satisfying sensations for weary, road-traveled soles. Plus, the brisk morning air was a rare treasure during the warm months this far north.

Latitude matters on the Shrieking Isle. The northern lands above the mountain range — that's the one that these men just crossed — enjoy bright summers and snowless winters. But winter locks the southern tip of the Isle in storms that force even the hardiest vessels to move to fairer tides. In summer, fishermen can access the South's newly-thawed waters and more bountiful takes. But the northern catches pick up something by going over the pass in summer — glacially-locked ice. Starting in spring, fish from the northern villages are transported to the pass as fresh as possible — sometimes live — where they are buried in chopped-up chunks of glaciers before being transported down to the hungry mouths at the mountain's foot in Corical.

The rest of the camp wasn't up, so Timid walked to the other side of the clearing and sat on a large flat rock he'd found the night before. If he were the praying type, this would be the spot to do it. But seafolk and other followers of Eadron — the god of the seas — didn't really pray in the normal sense. Instead, Timid typically woke up early and imagined himself surrounded by ocean, rocking in the surf. He felt so far inland now. So far away from the cold spray washing over the decks and across his face. So far away from having a deep dark abyss under his feet. Nothing under his feet now — nothing but solid ground.

A tent rustled behind him. Swait, his traveling companion and fellow Boar deputy, emerged and walked to the edge of the clearing to relieve himself. Timid didn't think of Swait as his guide, although it might have been accurate. He was a mercenary — they both were — and they were both paid for the same job. Swait had been this way several times before and had spent a considerable chunk of his well-seasoned life north of the mountains. He acted like a guide at times, but he was the same as Timid — someone willing to do something for money that nobody else wanted to do. And that's why the pay was so good.

But hey, a child was missing. Sure, kids go missing every day — especially on Black Tide — but someone was willing to pay for this kid, and that's the difference between having a search party and being forgotten. And, well, the King has an interest in prosecuting child-killing — a crime punished with something worse than death. That is, if it's committed by a person.

And what better way, Timid thought, to atone? In the same way that someone is responsible for sinking a ship if they eye a leak in its hull and decide not to fix it, Timid carried the burden of betrayal. To be truly free, he needed to cast it off. Unfortunately, that meant stepping into the icy chill lurking everywhere outside of his comfort zone. And this damsel in distress seemed particularly isolated and difficult to find.

They had already taken three full days by horseback to get here. Snow was still lightly dusting the pass every few days as winter held on by its fingernails. Trekkable by travelers on horseback, sure, but not by caravans — or else Timid and Swait typically could have hitched a ride in exchange for providing protection.

And because their early trek meant few other travelers, the group hadn't seen a soul since leaving the ice-packing camp in the mountain pass. But depending on who you asked, though, that might not be true. Various religions claim that trees and plants, or even rocks, have souls. And when Timid was surrounded by the mountain peaks and the ice that had clung to the cliffs for centuries upon centuries, he could sort of believe it. The people who first colonized the isle must have looked up at the same millennia-old chunks of rock and ice, and he could feel some sort of peace from that. Though maybe it was Eadron watching him from the water locked away in the endless valleys of snow.

The four men — Timid, Swait, and the two guards — gathered around the remnants of last night's fire. Swait crouched down and started a new flame with a skillful ease that disclosed his deep experience. It seemed that in each hour of each day, Swait utilized a skill that Timid poignantly lacked — skills needed if you're going into the forest where nobody goes. The guards huddled so closely together that they seemed afraid of the cold air, like they were hiding from the thought of winter lurking just out of sight. Timid sat and chewed on his breakfast, an unimpressive strip of cured meat. His boots became fond of the heat as they tried to rid themselves of any remaining water that they carried with them from yesterday.

Timid patiently waited for another story like the one from last night, too shy to ask for one outright. He had never really heard about the forest, at least not like that — cathedrals and gargantuan shadows. A week ago, the story might have frightened him off of the bounty altogether, but now it was a comforting way of figuring out what he was getting himself into. He imagined that the fables surrounding Mount Harbinger were also told by those who set out to summit it. What fools they were, ignoring a name like that. On the Shrieking Isle, some stories swallow their victims and others only chew them up and spit them out. Timid was not excited about the prospect of getting stuck between something's teeth, but it beat the other option and at least a story would come out of it.

Every sailor wants to be a great storyteller, and Timid was no different. He appreciated a well-told story more than any drug or vice he had yet found. Sailors used tales of storms, superstitions and accidents as the main way to keep from going insane at sea. A calm, deep voice and hands that could draw in the air were just as valuable to have on board as any net or line. But Timid had found storytelling circles to be much rarer on land than at sea. And being the youngest, he rarely had the ability to contribute to a storytelling circle when they did form.

The two guards couldn't be more different from each other. The lead guard was older, maybe in his forties, and acted as the expedition leader for the most part. He was also the nightly storyteller, and had quite the knack for it. He was a bit rugged, with worn-in clothes and a long, tired face. He looked most similar to Swait, in both demeanor and probable experience. The other guard — Grenbo was his name — was much younger than the veterans. Grenbo and Timid were definitely of the same generation, and this seemed to be his first trip of this kind, too. Even so far, this adventure was obviously the most exciting thing to ever happen to him. No wonder he didn't have any stories, Timid thought, but maybe this could be one — if he ever found out that he had been paid to escort a fugitive. But at least, with being out here, Timid didn't have to worry about anybody riding up and delivering a fresh list of bounties with him at the top.

The group pulled down their tents and made their packs ready for the road again. Timid had to reorganize his to make it fit for traveling on foot. The horse had done most of the work up to this point — nobody ever really got much done without a horse. But now he'd be without one, as the guards would lead the extra two back with them.

Timid wandered over to the abandoned guard post at the edge of the clearing. The path that they were supposed to walk was straddled by a gatehouse, wide enough to let carriages and trade wagons through. It must have seemed so out of place back when it was in use — a pure stone structure abutted by wilderness. Now, a few years out of service, it was encased in the grasp of vines, overgrown shrubs, and piles of leaves from past autumns. The gate lay on the ground completely to the side, rusting away into the dirt. The trees behind the gatehouse loomed larger and more closely together than they did in the forest's fringe.

The path itself obviously had not seen much use in the last few decades. After all, the way the stories go, anyone using it had only gone one way. But that included no organized groups and no professionals. And as far as Timid was pretending, he was a professional.

So he acted the part. He put his hand to the ground and awkwardly shuffled down the path, trying to find any grooves that could be from human feet or thin, wooden rails. When he found nothing, a seed of anxiety sprouted in his stomach. The trail was cold, as the other professionals would say.

He had hoped for something simpler. Maybe a small, living child waving at him from the edge of the underbrush. Or a sign that said, "She's dead, go home." Really anything other than stepping into the forest from which no one returns. And although the girl they were searching for had allegedly been pulling a wagon, it had also never been found. Timid and Swait were tasked with looking for signs of it, too — perhaps as a signpost of the girl's fate or whereabouts. And that was about all they knew, other than that her name was Cherry and that she had been trying to go from one town to another and must have taken a wrong turn towards the mountains — if she was lucky. And if she was unlucky, well that probably meant bandits. They like to hole themselves up in the cracks and valleys in the unsettled foothills. But even fugitives didn't go in *this* forest.

Swait walked over to Timid. "Good work, deputy," Swait said. "I guess you've officially entered the forest and lived to tell about it."

"I don't think the Boars would consider the same," Timid said. "We've got to actually go in. I can't tell how recently the path was used, but it's wide enough for a wagon. I was hoping we could get away with just traveling north to the next village and asking around. But she could be in here."

"Aye," Swait affirmed. "Want me to take the lead? I've got the bigger sword." Swait smirked and turned his hip towards Timid — as if Timid wasn't already aware of the monstrous thing. It dwarfed what the guards carried, and to speak of it in the same sentence as Timid's old, spindly fish carving knife would cause it dishonor.

Timid gulped air, his collar seemingly shrinking around his neck as he imagined what hid in the forest's dark belly. Surely nothing that would be afraid of his filet knife. "Well, I don't know how I feel about being in back," he said.

Swait laughed. "Better than being alone! You'll be fine, lad. Just stay within talking distance, I don't want you to have to yell if you hear something. I also don't want to turn around and have you gone, so if you get nabbed please let out a yelp or something." Swait smiled at his own joke. He was obviously comfortable talking about death and at peace with believing they wouldn't come back alive.

And, with all the stories about this place, that was the right sort of thing to believe.

CHAPTER 5

Here, twice now, we have met a man. The ruins of his past, as you may recall, put him at odds with the moral code of the world. And on the Shrieking Isle, that code is largely written by seafolk — the ones inextricably linked to all things saltwater. They believe that when a man or woman sets sail on the high seas, they pledge a solemn swear. Part of it says that you never wash your feet in the water barrel, but the more important parts mandate that no one cause harm to another sailor's ship, their catch, or their connection to the living half of the universe.

There are curses laid upon those who break their oath to the ocean — that much you have witnessed. But do not envy the man who escapes an early, watery grave. Because though he is given a second chance, the world has much more — and much worse — in store for those who do not repay their debts.

The canopy cast a surprisingly dark shade, but Timid's eyes adjusted to it within minutes — perhaps trained by frequent shifts between lower and upper decks. The farther in the two men went, the larger and more spread out the trees became, until each tree was separated from its brethren by a half dozen paces. Soon, it was more like the inside of a building or cave than a forest, as no more rays of sunlight dotted the dirt and the ground was void of shrubs or grasses. Eventually, true to the stories, the forest opened its doors like a great cathedral as its lowest branches lifted up higher and higher, and higher and higher.

Since the forest floor here was open and free, Timid felt that he could walk or even run wherever he pleased without fear of a stray branch or toad — a real hazard on most of the isle. In some coastal cities and towns, toads grew large enough to prey on cats — and, if the stories were to be believed, even babies and small children. But Timid hadn't seen a single toad since entering the forest, which came as a relief knowing that their annoying groans wouldn't keep him from sleeping peacefully tonight.

The forest city was supposedly due west of the junction, and they couldn't get their bearings easily in here besides from the path. Other than providing navigation, the path here was not helpful in itself — as they could easily walk openly among the spread-out trunks. Leading a wagon or cart off trail would be effortless, the only sign of meandering wheels would be a bump or two from a few extra roots. And in turn, getting back on the near invisible path would be hard, likely crossing over into the other half of the forest without even knowing it.

Slowing down and watching Swait get almost uncomfortably far off, Timid closed his eyes and took a deep breath. Stress grew around him as naturally as the trees. He felt his nerves overworked and his mind stretched too thin by constantly being on alert. So, for a moment, he let his guard down and tried to slow his ever-racing thoughts. And right then, within that single moment, he knew that something had started sneaking up on him.

He whipped his head to the side, his right hand jolting back to his belt to grab his filet knife. He spun around and braced himself against the tree trunk with his left arm, stumbling on the uneven ground.

Nothing. Only faint light and the quiet, natural order of things.

His eyes scanned the darkness quickly, trying to find the horizon so he could check for movement against the black background. He knew that something had been right behind him, so surely that his lungs and heart hadn't had the time to catch up to his head and his hands. He noticed now that the larger-than-man trees provided a perfect cover for someone or something trying to inch closer and closer without being seen.

Timid finally stepped back into line with Swait after a quiet hustle to catch back up before his partner noticed. He'd been gone for about half a minute, and Swait likely had no idea — which wasn't a great sign for the person in the back of the line. They were hours and miles inside the real forest now. If they wanted to leave they'd likely have to camp at least once or walk through the night until they were out. Neither option eased the growing, nervous pit in Timid's stomach.

Night arrived on the same slow, constant march that it uses to get everywhere. Timid noticed his breath begin to fog in front of his face. The blackness felt thick — like you could reach out and get a handful of some — and it cooled the air like a stagnant cavern. Like it was smothering the life out of the forest floor. Like it was watching you.

Not much wind made it through the leaves, but Timid could hear it rustle above as if a river flowed across the sky-scraping treetops. Timid was caught looking up, and thus didn't notice Swait until he was only a few steps away. Swait had stopped, staring out into the forest. At his feet lay a shard of wood. About a foot long, it looked rounded and worn like the outer edge of a large wheel.

"Look," Swait whispered, nodding in a direction off the path and reaching for his sword. But Timid didn't see anything. Swait pulled his sword an inch or so up out of its sheath, breaking the seal so that he could draw it faster when he needed to. A bit of steel showed out, bright among everything else. The whole thing seemed unnecessarily oversized, hanging all the way down to the bottom of Swait's shin.

"I'll go," Swait said. "Stay and watch my back." He left without waiting for a response.

"But..." Timid whispered to no one, "who's going to watch my back?"

Timid glanced over his shoulders repeatedly. Their isolation was painfully apparent now, creeping up on him as soon as Swait left the path. Timid had felt relatively safe as long as he was within a few yards of Swait — but now thinking about it, he wasn't sure if he gave the same comfort in return.

Timid tried to find where Swait was heading, but his eyes weren't sharp enough to pick out anything but Swait's shape and the tall forms of the trees. Sometimes Swait would stop and reach to the ground, before continuing a short ways and doing it again.

"Maybe it's good Swait is in front, with eyes like that," Timid thought to himself.

After a few minutes, Swait emerged from the dark, fingers still wrapped around sword hilt.

"It's a wagon, all torn up and dragged around," Swait said. He spit on the ground and moved his tongue against his cheeks while he thought.

"Damn," Timid cursed, more at the entire situation than anything in particular. "Any sign of anything else? Like a body?" Timid wanted any reason to go back now. A reminder, and now possibly evidence, that nobody ever made it out of here burrowed into Timid's brain.

Swait bent with his hands on his knees, taking big breaths and thinking. For the first time that Timid had seen, Swait looked frightened. His beard had started to come in over the last few days and Timid realized that Swait was his senior by more than a few decades. Gray hairs peppered his chin and his short hair faded to receding wisps in front. The lines of age and experience crossing his face reminded Timid of all the old sailors he'd met, but with much better teeth and hygiene. Swait's exposed hands bore numerous scars, mostly across the back of his rugged knuckles and thick fingers. Several of his nails were bloodied or torn, apparently permanently. Obviously, years of doing this kind of work had taken a toll on Swait in a way that Timid didn't know anything about. Swait most likely had dozens of jobs under his belt — but for Timid, this was number one.

"Yeah, there's something else," Swait finally answered, spitting again. "But you're gonna want to see it. Get your knife out, too."

Timid obeyed and followed Swait out to the wagon. Timid didn't let his eyes rest, always looking over his shoulder or probing farther back into the darkness, looking for something that he knew was there.

The wagon's remains rested still and silently. Timid saw the trench etched into the ground from when it was dragged. Parts of it had been broken off, so much so that it couldn't do anything but lie on its side. The metal axle was exposed and partially broken out of its slot on the wagon's underside. Timid crouched down and felt numerous large grooves scratched into most of the wood.

"Scratches and bites?" Timid observed. "But from what?" He ran his hand down the length of the wood. The same sort of markings were also on the side facing the dirt. "At least some of these were made before it was dragged here," he said. "Maybe all of them."

Swait whispered for Timid's attention from a few feet away. Timid turned to see him crouched and looking at the ground, gently sifting grains of soil between his fingers.

"See this?" Swait asked. "I've never seen anything like it."

Timid circled around to get a look over Swait's shoulder. From what Timid knew about such things, it appeared to be a very large animal print. Four toes, each with a deep claw print at its tip, came together at a set of rounded pads. A dog's hind print, it looked like — but grotesquely stretched out so that there was a human-like heel at the back end. Timid could probably have fit both of his feet inside of it without touching the edges.

"What in the hell…" Timid found himself at a loss for words. The isle was supposed to have giants and magical creatures, but rarely. The best storytellers might only know enough tales of them to count on one hand. And those were usually of hill giants or stone-gazed basilisks, or even the occasional tribe of toad savages. Timid had heard no stories of what actually lived here, in the heart of the Living Forest. Perhaps it was something worse than tribes of toad savages, if that was possible.

Swait tapped Timid on the shoulder, startling him. Swait pointed into the forest, farther away from the path. "There's about a dozen of these coming from that way, but they stop."

Swait leaned hard on the last word, as if it was apparent to Timid what that was supposed to mean. But it wasn't.

Then, as Timid was busy thinking, he felt it again — the knowledge that something was sneaking up behind him. He whipped his head around and brandished his knife. Swait, noticing Timid but unsure of what he was looking for, took a quick step back and drew his sword. The air turned to fog in a cloud around them as they huffed.

"You hear that?" Swait turned his head to the side, pointing his ear towards somewhere. Swait gripped his sword hilt with both hands, the blade reflecting light as if it thought there wasn't total darkness around them. He stood motionless, appearing quite like a statue that Timid had once seen of an imaginary great protector of the isle. The sword's tip towered over their heads. It must have weighed more than one of Timid's legs, but Swait held it steady.

"Should we get back to the path?" Timid asked. The wagon provided a small amount of cover for their backs, but it only came up to their chests. Timid thought of the prints they saw, and the creature that had left them. The wagon wouldn't protect them against that thing — if anything, they could be pinned here.

"No," Swait answered, "but keep your knife in front of you. If you have to get away, walk backwards."

The forest around them shed its silence. An assortment of dull noises came from all directions. Rustling leaves on the left. A stick breaking on the right. A patter of footsteps, closer now. A flash of movement between two trees, low to the ground. Near enough that Timid saw more than shadows and shapes. A group of animals — wolves.

Timid counted three. They crept closer and closer, hiding whenever Timid or Swait looked at them and darting out when unwatched. Timid gripped his knife, harder than he ever had. He had never really used it, at least not like this. Carving the flesh and skin off a fish was a lot different than stabbing to kill. He'd only ever done it once, on an especially pesky toad. But Swait didn't know that — he thought Timid knew how to fight.

So Timid spoke up. "What now?" His voice cracked, broken apart by adrenaline. "Can we run? Damn! We should have run."

A growl rumbled from behind one of the trees as a wolf stepped out and bared its teeth. Confusion replaced fear when Timid looked at his traveling companion, whose eyes were closed.

"We never could have run," Swait answered. "They've been here the whole time." Swait took one hand off his sword and held it slightly to his side. He turned his palm upward and muttered something under his breath that Timid couldn't hear.

Their breaths stopped fogging. Warmth rolled across the side of Timid's face and a dull light scattered across the trees and ground. A dot of deep red glowed in Swait's hand. The rest of the family stepped out of hiding — all teeth.

A wolf stepped forward. Swait's eyes snapped open and his hand shot up above his head. Shadows grew short, as Swait's red dot flashed up to the canopy.

Timid's eyes darted up, drawn to the red trail shooting into the sky. It hit the canopy's underside and spread a rush of fire on impact, like a fallen drop of water smacking the ground. A sun-like intensity illuminated the forest floor, forcing Timid's dark-adjusted eyes to squint. The wolves, too, hid their eyes from the flash.

Although he'd likely met many people who could do it, Timid had only seen magic twice before. Once from a drunkard in a tavern winning bar bets, and the other from Ezira — when he had burned that ship and the men stranded on it. The gravity of the situation fell hard on Timid. Here was an experienced adventurer worthy enough to be granted magic, and who felt it necessary to keep it secret. Now, he was scared enough to reveal it. And if Swait was afraid, Timid wondered how afraid he should be. He thought of the mostly-fictitious tale of Sir Halibut and the Four Horsemen — in which a gallant knight sailed to each corner of the world and defeated a different ghastly monster each time, while his worthless squire watched from the sidelines and took notes.

Trying to be worth something, Timid probed towards the fur with his knife — but not well enough to prevent the wolves from inserting themselves between him and Swait. Two faced Swait — the more dangerous prey — and one faced Timid. He fell for its feigned attacks and provided sloppy slashes, which hit only air. Swait forced the other wolves to stay in front of him by backing up to the upturned belly of the wagon.

Timid had seen wolf packs several times before, they were a common nuisance throughout much of the isle. And, as typical, all paws here were ordinary — incapable of leaving those monstrous tracks.

Arms of fire spread out over their heads. Bits of burning leaves and branches slowly fell around them, dotting the forest floor with little specks of candlelight. Shadows danced across the ground and created dozens of flickering wolf shapes.

A wolf lunged at Swait. His fire-breathing hand rejoined the other on his sword's grip and he swung it downward like an axe. It glanced lightly, leaving the skin unbroken. But Swait followed through and brought the sword across again, swinging too quickly for the wolf to regain its balance and dodge. It hit hard across the wolf's collar, with a squeal and a crack as flesh and spine severed. Its legs collapsed, instantly lifeless. Swait pulled his sword out from the middle of the corpse, dripping blood down onto his hands as he held it back up in front of him, pointing the tip towards his single foe.

The piercing screech prompted Timid to look over, allowing his wolf a window to leap on him and push him to the ground. Clenching jaws shoved teeth through the thin sleeve covering Timid's left forearm. Timid yelled in pain and reflexively stabbed his knife into the wolf's side. The creature recoiled and thrashed its head, ripping a chunk of Timid's arm muscle away. A howling scream peaked then faded to a whimper as the wolf shook in the throes of death.

Timid scrambled to his feet, woozy either from the excitement of things or from smacking his head on the ground. But that distinction wouldn't matter for now.

Timid stared at Swait — the tantalizing presence of magic fresh on Timid's mind among all the pain and noise. But the remaining wolf turned to the bleeding Timid and threatened a lunge. But Swait, too, stepped forward. He extended his arm and fingers out straight, quickly gathering another dot of light at his palm. Before he could let go — before he could cleanse the wolf with fire — it stopped in its tracks and a set of nails scraped against the wagon's back.

A new, larger wolf leapt onto Swait from above. He rerouted his flaming hand upwards, and the fire engulfed the wolf's face. They fell in a heap, and the burning carcass came to rest on top of Swait, sizzling his skin as he lay pinned. His sword lay on the ground out of reach, reflecting the firelight peppered all around it.

Smelling easier prey, the lingering wolf eyed Swait now.

Timid's left arm hung almost lifeless at his side, dripping a decent amount of blood onto the ground. Sometimes, the drops audibly fizzled as they fell into smoldering leaves. The fire in the canopy crackled with deeper booms now, sending down larger chunks of branches. It reminded Timid of snow in a way, but more similar to a campfire turned upside down, sparks falling. Warmth gathered around Timid, building until it fought off the cold's biting teeth. He felt a bit of Swait's magic in each little speck of the fire.

With Timid out of his depth, Swait furiously elbowed his way free of the carcass. He had only risen to one knee and had not regained his sword before the wolf rushed him, too quick for him to do anything but extend an arm and summon another dot of fire. A steady stream of flames erupted from Swait's hand into the wolf's chest, burning away most of its skin and hair in an instant. The body landed in a crumpled heap.

"Timid, you must go," Swait said, talking through teeth clenched by pain. Blood leaked down Swait's face from a gash Timid just now noticed. His skin and hair were even worse, matted with globules of blood-wetted dirt. His clothing had mostly burned away, showing large patches of melted, bubbling skin. A rancid smell — animal guts, burnt hair, and molten flesh — hit Timid, filling his nose and throat. Timid's stomach turned and he threw up in his mouth but swallowed it again.

"Aye," Timid said, "let's get going. Think you can walk?" Timid stepped away to grab Swait's sword, keeping his eye on the remaining wolf watching from a distance.

Swait didn't respond for a moment, until Timid looked back and met his eyes. "No, Timid. My leg is broken."

Timid looked at the leg that Swait was kneeling on. His foot twisted sideways underneath itself, like the boot hung from an empty sock.

"You have to go," Swait said, "alone. Keep going, don't stray from the path. You've seen what's out here."

Timid's brain finally caught up to what had happened. "I'm not leaving you," Timid said through tears. "I can carry you. We can make it out by morning and we can get help on the road."

"No, Timid!" Swait yelled, blood and froth spilling out over his lips. "There are more!"

The last words rung Timid like a bell, freezing him. He scanned the dark edges of the firelight, watching shadows jump across the gaps between trees.

Swait grabbed his sword from Timid's hand. "Walk away and they shouldn't follow," Swait said. "They'll settle for me. Now go, Timid." Swait pushed him in the chest. "Go."

That was a command, and Timid obeyed it. Because he was scared, because he was relieved. But mostly because Swait was his guide — if only for this day.

Timid backed away farther and farther. The canopy fire had stopped spreading but had burned upwards through the first layer of branches. They were all falling now, surrounding Swait and sharing their firelight with the rest of the forest floor.

Timid reached the path and gave the scene a parting glance. He saw the silhouettes of a man on one knee, a sword at his side, and a dozen shapes darting and twisting between the trees. Another silhouette of another dead friend — add one more to the list. Turning towards the heart of the forest, Timid left the storm of light behind.

CHAPTER 6

Sunlight provides its main relief to the mind. Day may not truly be any safer than night in a place like the Living Forest, but as a cell with a window is different than an underground dungeon, sunlight brings a certain comfort. And some nights on the Shrieking Isle are safer than others. For nine out of ten nights, the moon lights up part of the sky for at least a few hours, usually enough to see by and get your bearings. That is, unless it is the tenth night — a Black Tide. And not many go out under the moonless Black Tide anyway, except for sailors on month-long voyages who don't really have much choice.

Luckily, for this land-locked slice of Timid's life, the next Black Tide was not for two more nights. Until then, the creepies and the crawlies would be only of the ordinary sort. Unless that whole superstition was just made-up poppycock.

Looking up, Timid waited to see any sign of daylight piercing the lower branches of the canopy, but each moment left him sorely disappointed. He trudged on and on, through the fatigue and the sleepiness. Soon, either the fog in his head or the blisters on his flesh would stop his feet from taking another step. He felt every inch of the winter spent running from his past — from anybody who might recognize him and ask questions about that last night on the ocean.

Once or twice he spotted a few larger shadows in the distance, away from the path. At first, they looked like houses, but with no windows, no lights, and no doors — built up story after story as they sank into the leaves above him. In a way, they were houses. Just not in a way that he could understand yet.

But mostly they were just big trees. Eventually, one grew so close to the path that it disappeared and resumed on the other side. The trunk crumpled under its own weight where it connected with the ground, ruining the bark's seamlessness. With his arms stretched out, Timid could barely find a curve. The trunk sloped out farther and farther as it approached the ground, smoothing out so much that Timid practically stood on it.

He tried to look up to see the top, but the trunk reached the canopy and punched straight through. Timid imagined a fish wondering whether dock posts continued above the water's surface. Looking up like that made Timid feel like he was falling backwards, straight through the ground and into an endless pit of dark earth and worms.

This tree provided another oddity, too. Here, the forest couldn't sit still. Timid might not have noticed it if he hadn't spent the last twenty hours in stark opposition, feeling alone and cut off from all he had known in the outside world. But now, he was surrounded by the cool breeze of a flurry of songs.

"Birds," he said aloud, pleasantly startled as he realized it.

Songbirds, probably small and colorful, refused to let silence come to rest. Their quick and fluttering chirps were much unlike the drawn-out caws of the larger predatory birds that grazed over the entire isle and its shorelines.

"Birds are of God," he remembered.

The tangled mess of worry in the front of Timid's mind melted away. No more analyzing if he should turn back, or complicated feelings about death. No more scary things, no more wolves, no more hairs on his skin sticking straight up, and no more breath hitting the back of his neck.

All under the limbs of the Essai tree.

Now that his brain had some space to operate, he turned more attention to his body. He had stopped the bleeding on his arm with a makeshift bandage made out of the bottom of his shirt. And checking it now, it wasn't as bad as he first feared — only a few surface cuts and a chunk of skin missing from the underside of his forearm. Luckily, he never minded blood too much — there was a lot of it on a ship. Even a fishing ship, from splinters, foul hooks, and rope burns and such. Drownings, however, he found hard to stomach. The first he saw was another boy his age, new on the ship and years away from not needing to grab the net. The next eight drownings weren't any easier to watch, but they all happened at once. It was like ripping off a bloodied bandage dried to a wound — which, coincidentally, was what he needed to do right now. He did it just to get the image out of his mind.

Timid sat with his head against the tree, closing his eyes. A memory flashed in his head — a silhouetted man on one knee, sword at his side and beset on all sides by fire. Timid opened his eyes, expecting to see the forest floor, but instead gazed upon waves of blackish blue against a starless night sky. His head bobbed up and down as each crest passed, trying to stay above the surface.

Steady thee, Stormwind, and float.

A low rumbling in the distance poked him awake. Growing louder, it plagued the edges of his hearing. Timid stood up, frozen in a cocktail of confusion and fear, unsure of exactly what direction it originated from.

A flurry of thoughts raced through his waking mind. "Was I dreaming? Am I still dreaming? Where's Swait? Is it the monster that made those tracks? What if it can see in the dark better than I can? I can't fight — even with both my arms — we learned that."

The rumbling turned into pounding, approaching seemingly more quickly than Timid could run. So, he did what people like him — that's cowards — typically do: nothing.

Soon, it emerged from whence it came — somewhere deeper into the forest, in the direction Timid was going. The moment Timid laid his eyes on the actual thing, it apparently saw him too. It tried to stop by abruptly jutting its legs out in front of it and sticking a pair of enormous feet into the ground, ripping trenches into the dirt and roots. A cart trailing behind was full of hundreds of something, and dozens spilled out as the cart lurched. The thing sniffed the air, nose up and waving side to side in an effort to figure out exactly what Timid was. Timid, though relatively lacking in olfactory power, was doing the same.

Much to Timid's surprise, it was a rabbit — and yet it was also not a rabbit, for four main reasons.

First, it was about ten feet tall.

Second, it had the posture and body of a human — but with two listening ears perked straight up and the identifiably-rodent face that normally comes attached to rabbits. Its nose quivered and its eyes blinked, staring at him — an obvious threat analysis. Large, human-like hands held the guide bars of the cart — which could just have easily been pulled by a horse. Oversized arms bent at elbows and shoulders, and its legs jointed at normal looking hips, knees, and ankles.

Third, it was made entirely of sticks and twigs. Branches and tree limbs woven together in an organic-looking mass, as if they had grown alongside one another over many years like the strands of a large bush confined to the shape of a gigantic animal. Its feet: thick and robust roots. Its legs: twisted, strong trunks. And its arms: a complex system of vines that crawled down and wrapped around themselves to eventually make fingers. The eyes were not exactly physical eyes, but a series of bends and knots that took the shape of an eye with a dark hole in the center.

And fourth — after Timid had given it a good and rude look-see over — it spoke.

"Hello? Who is it?" it asked, its voice light and loud. "Who's there?" No teeth showed, but its mouth opened and closed with the words — lips flush with life.

Timid kept silent, rightfully confused. This was basically a tree — and it had just talked to him. No amount of calculation could have predicted this would happen to him, so that made his unpreparedness a little easier to swallow. He stepped out from behind the Essai and displayed his hands in what he hoped was a universal sign of peace — forgetting that it had just spoken to him in a language that he understood.

The creature's ears sunk down to the back of its head, and it appeared to relax. It spoke again. "Blast me, I thought you were a wolf. Don't slink around like that, you scared me half to the grave."

"Oh, uh… sorry," Timid said, now realizing that he could talk to it. "I guess I was scared too. I didn't mean to frighten you."

"What are you doing out here?" it asked, sounding bewildered — like there wouldn't ever be a reasonable answer. "Do you need help?"

Thinking on his toes in social situations was really not his favorite hand to play, but here it was dealt to him regardless. But he did remember that, technically speaking, he was an authority figure. "I am deputized by the Boars," he stated firmly, "and… I'm looking for someone."

The creature smiled. "Ah. Well, aren't we all," it said, perhaps in joke, or perhaps because it didn't know who the Boars were. "Just scared me, is all. Never know what's around the corner out here."

They stood in silence until it was obvious that Timid had nothing to say.

"No shrooms in this patch of woods, eh?" it asked.

Caught off guard again, Timid didn't say much for words. Holding a conversation with someone on a different page than you takes a certain energy — which they both lacked. He did notice, however, that the cart behind the creature was full of mushrooms, some of which had rolled towards Timid after falling out during the sudden stop. The creature set the cart's handles down and stepped around delicately to place the stragglers back into the cart.

This would be a good time to talk — breaking the ice is how most people would put it — but the words stuck in Timid's mouth and came out as a pile of garbage. "How are you going are you come from?" he asked.

It didn't acknowledge the oddity. "I'm just on a walk out from the city, you know, kind of a weekly foraging trip."

"Oh, wow, that's amazing…" Timid said, for some reason. "Uh, well, I'm a bit on my own out here, would you mind if I tagged along for a bit?"

The creature shrugged. "Don't see why not," it answered. "I'll need a moment to catch my breath, since it hasn't come back after you scared it into the woods, then we'll be off. You can ride in the cart if you want."

Relief washed over Timid's face; a cresting wave broken broadside by a ship's prow, soaking a young deck-swabber.

"Thank you," Timid said, in his best calm adult voice. "Name's Timid. Timid Stormwind." He extended his hand before he realized that the gesture might not be recognized by other species.

The rabbit took the hand in his own. Timid's arm disappeared nearly up to his elbow in a mass of twisting vines. A smile crested the creature's face.

"Lepori," it said.

CHAPTER 7

The fire pricked at every inch of Timid's exposed skin and soaked his clothes like a warm bath. He wished he were a dragon, so he could lean down and lap up the flames like a dog drinking from a bowl. Lepori mentioned that he usually kept his distance from fire, but that the last vestiges of winter necessitated some dangers.

"How long ago did you leave Goodhaven?" Timid asked through a mouthful of mushroom.

Lepori sounded much the same. "This morning," he answered. "Doesn't take so long on the way back, since I've already been through and stripped out most of the worthy shrooms."

The mushroom tasted like dirt. But it wasn't the worst thing Timid ever tasted, that was for sure. Lots of things go rotten on a boat. And it was the most filling thing he'd had since the inn's stew two days ago. He turned to his pack and dug out his water canteen, washing down a few pesky bits of the mushroom that wanted to stay in his cheeks.

Timid broke the silence. "So, you don't get many people out here?"

"Oh no," Lepori said, shocked that it needed explaining, "finding an outsider is quite strange. We get maybe one or two every year."

Timid should have asked what happens to them. But he didn't.

Bird songs split the silence into fragments lasting a few seconds at their largest. But now Lepori was there to make sound too. Each small movement made his branches creak against each other. He didn't breathe, at least not like a normal animal, but the branches flexed and stressed as his limbs bent. Timid was close enough now to see little green leaves and sprouted buds dotting the sticks, except for on the more root-like portions near the feet. The Essai they leaned against looked almost the right size next to Lepori. That only made Timid feel especially small, and he wasn't the biggest human to start with.

"Lepori," Timid started, "what are you?" The question seemed brash as soon as it left his throat, but he felt comfortable and safe under the Essai. More comfortable than he maybe should have been with a stranger. So he tried to explain himself. "I don't mean to sound too forward, but I've never seen or heard of anything like you before."

"Oh, really?" Lepori said. Strangely, the surprise sounded rehearsed. "We call ourselves Springs."

"We?" Timid repeated, in a very-much real surprise. Lepori was so strange, so foreign, that the idea of there being others like him didn't cross Timid's mind. "There are others like you?"

Lepori let out a soft and gentle laugh. It instantly brought a smile to Timid's face, contagious enough that if the Essai had lips, it probably would have laughed too. "Of course," Lepori said, "hundreds! What do you think Goodhaven is?"

Timid sat back and imagined. "A city full of these things? That's why nobody has come back," he thought, "they're living in a fairy tale."

In his mind, nothing was greater — fairy tales rule Timid. They have everything that the real world doesn't — humble beginnings and happy endings, magic and unexpected death, right and wrong, heroes and villains. And now, finally, he started to see the threads of a storybook peek out from behind a gigantic, walking tree. With hunger and thirst biting at his heels, and a bounty floating somewhere over his head, he needed a fairy tale now more than ever. In fact, if everything had worked out, he would have escaped to a fairy tale a long time ago. That's what the Malachai was supposed to be.

"We should go soon," Lepori said, standing up. "We shouldn't stay in one place for too long. The forest is a dangerous place."

"Even for you?" Timid joked, confused about what could be dangerous for a Spring.

"Yes," Lepori said, not lighthearted at all. "For everyone."

And this is also when Timid noticed Lepori's feet. Not just looked at them, but noticed them. They appeared mostly human, but they had some resemblance of a rabbit's foot. Their knotted, hardened bottoms had been smashed flat by decades of continuous use.

"Lepori," Timid began, "are there other Springs out in the forest?"

"Huh? No, not really," Lepori said. He always seemed a bit surprised by Timid's questions but still willing to answer. "Close to the city, yes. But not this far out here. There's some out by the river, too, but that's on the other side. Why do you ask?"

"Just trying to figure something out. The Boars sent us out here to find someone. A young girl."

"Well I don't remember seeing anyone new in town, and rumors there spread like wildfire." And then, realizing that he didn't want to discourage Timid from looking, he changed his tone to be a bit more optimistic. "But I guess they could have passed through and went out to the river before I'd heard."

"I was hoping you'd say something different," Timid said, "like in the stories. That she went home and lived happily ever after." And at that time, a pleasant thought occurred to him: he had an audience. But Timid knew that a good storyteller is not just one with an audience. A good storyteller considers timing, tone, and the pace of his words. So Timid cleared his throat and waited a proper amount of time.

"Anyway," he began, "I was thinking there were other things like you, or at least something as big as you, out here. You see, my partner and I found something that scared us half to death. Like a large, weird, footprint. And then..."

Lepori interrupted. "What did it look like?" he asked.

"Not entirely sure," Timid answered. "Like a big wolf print I guess."

"We have to go," Lepori barked quickly — as if he knew what Timid was going to say before he said it — and stepped up to the cart. Lepori picked up the handles and wheeled it around on the path, facing the way he came from. "Get in," he urged, "we need to get to Goodhaven. Now."

Timid snatched up his pack and slung it over one shoulder. He stretched barely enough to grab the cart's top railing and haul his feet up onto the bottom plank. He kicked and scraped his way over the edge and brushed some mushrooms off of a plank towards the front, taking a seat.

Timid felt like he was running away from something. A feeling he was familiar with. "Hey," he called out, "why the rush? What's going on?"

The cart jostled into motion. Mushrooms tumbled about. Lepori stared ahead, and answered, "The Beast is back."

CHAPTER 8

Confusion does wonders to fight off boredom. But when you're in need of a little shut eye, boredom can be a drop of milk and honey on a warm spoon. So Timid counted Essai trees to pass time and lull himself into sleep. Though more undoubtedly hid in the dark behind their smaller cousins, he got to seven before sleep took hold.

Not many dreams passed through his head during these short slumbers, his mind too thankful for the rest to think of anything extravagant. This time, though, he was climbing. Up a tree — a tree so big that he could barely feel it curve. The only branches were above him, where they formed a thick, sprawling mass of green that could likely stop an arrow — or a falling person. He looked around him, still climbing, his limbs moving on their own. Mountains with snowy peaks to his back, a sea to his left. And below him, a different sort of sea — ripples of green, with birds swimming from wave to wave and a pit of fire eating its way upwards. It was daylight — the sun pierced Timid's eyelids even as he closed them.

When he opened them again, creaking wagon wheels and thunderous footsteps greeted him. But it was daylight here, too. The end of the longest night of his life — so far.

Over Lepori's shoulders, he saw a clearing ahead of them, where a sharp edge of light emerged from the forest's shadow as the newborn sun dripped its first bit of light onto the ground. It crept closer and closer as the cart approached, until the light burst on him so brightly that he had to shield his eyes.

It wasn't only a clearing, but an open series of fields in a wide circle. Lepori slowed to a brisk walk and the cart rolled more smoothly, no longer shaken about by enormous roots in the path. Timid looked around, not able to tell what was being farmed. Patches of tall grass and small shrubs grew randomly, but the wilderness mostly made way for tilled plots of land. A few buildings stood here and there, wooden and surprisingly large.

Behind them, the forest's edge loomed like a giant wall with distinct layers of color. The bottom remained dark and lined with the vertical trunks. After rising for about forty feet, the canopy began, a thick stripe of pure green that small birds found fit to flutter up, down, and across. On top, many small, bushy mounds — the top of each tree separate enough to make out but still close enough to melt into each other like a green stormfront. And as the lid to it all, the morning sun waved an orange hello, shooing off the last stars that insisted on saying goodbye. Timid thought it was polite of them.

As they wheeled past the houses, maybe two or three hundred feet off the path, Timid spotted other Springs. One was an ox, another was a deer with antlers. One other seemed indecipherable — similar to Lepori, but without the large ears. We can forgive Timid for not recognizing a badger at such a distance.

The buildings arrived more frequently as they approached an enormous wall of trees. They looked like Essai trees, but each had its top cut off and its bottom shoved straight into the dirt like the world's largest fenceposts. Each trunk fit tightly against the one next to it, worked smooth at the seams like giant, unbreachable planks. The flat top of the wall might have done well as a walkway, but Timid couldn't see anyone up there.

They approached a break in the wall and unsurprisingly found a gate. It stood just as high as the rest of the wall, but not made of Essai — wooden still, but the planks were much smaller, likely from normal-sized trees. Here, on both sides of the path, stood two large deer Springs — stags or bucks, to be more precise. Their antlers, green and brown branches wrapped tightly around each other almost like unlit candelabras, stuck up into the air in formidable crowns. The antlers themselves were probably taller than Timid's entire body.

Lepori slowed to a walk and regarded the two guards, who didn't actually seem to pay Timid much mind. But because each guard held a spear with a serrated metal tip like a saw blade, Timid decided that the best course of action might be to keep his mouth shut.

The Springs conducted their conference in hush murmurs, low enough so Timid couldn't hear. The guards obviously knew Lepori, who likely used this gate frequently. "Or," Timid thought to himself, "maybe this place is small enough that they all know each other."

Eventually, the guards gave a call of approval up to an unseen coworker, then worked together to slowly push the gate doors open, inch by inch. The cart moved again — on into Goodhaven, the city where the trees walk and the grass listens.

The city breathed. Grass grew beside the roadways. Vines slithered their way up the sides of houses. Fresh odors of wildflowers wafted through the air, from whatever sprouted up in the space between buildings. Springs walked about, much like people would in any other city. Buildings lined the streets, some apparently open to the public, and the center held a market with about a dozen temporary stalls.

In total, it wasn't very populous, more akin to a town than a true city. Timid could already see the walls on the opposite side as soon as he had entered — something most definitely not possible in Corical or Shrieksport. In those places, fields of buildings clogged your vision and rows of streets intersected at every angle so that no single one led anywhere too far. Goodhaven's buildings might have been larger, to accommodate their larger patrons, but they were a bit more spaced out and few in numbers.

The main streets all intersected at the center square at the marketplace. Lepori turned down a smaller one, into a huddle of houses. Timid felt a bit embarrassed, toting around as cargo in a wagon like a game you'd play with a child. But in a town like this, and with rumors the way they are, maybe this would be less noticeable. Plus, it beat walking.

Lepori's house was modest. For a human, it'd be suitable in total size for a large family in an upper-class neighborhood, like some of the ones Timid had seen in Corical's inner circle. But in Goodhaven, everything seemed enlarged — or that Timid had been shrank, like what sometimes happens in a strange dream. And everything was wooden, no hearth even. That meant no fire — even in winter.

Timid wanted to break the silence but had nothing to say besides a thousand questions. He didn't know the town, where to get food, where to avoid, where to sleep. In the stories, there had always been an inn or a saloon — a place where the adventurer would find help, and eventually more trouble. But Timid wasn't sure how the adventurers knew where the inns were.

And so he decided to ask. "Is there an inn anywhere in town?" he started. "I didn't come with any real plan. I'm a bit tired of the raw ground, too, so I'd like to avoid the dirt if I can help it."

"Hmm," Lepori made the effort of sounding like he was thinking, "I don't believe so, no. There's not too many folks around that need that sort of thing. But I guess maybe the Oxenstone? It's an old saloon-like tavern, they might have something, though I don't go there enough to know." Lepori made obvious thinking noises again for an extra moment. "Oh! I know, you could stay here!"

Lepori trotted around the house, apparently looking for blankets or coverings for Timid to use and assuming that Timid would accept. Though without any furniture made for Timid's kind, and without a fire, it wasn't the most tempting offer. A chance to save on always-limited copper, however, felt incentive enough in Timid's mind — and in his pocket. Being a fisherman was a life lived by surges of money. Timid was always underpaid, as is tradition for young deckhands, leaving him with just enough to scrounge his way to the next push-off. Sometimes he still had to resort to begging or street work, one more reason to elect to stay on and take care of the ship instead. But now the Boars had awarded him a portion of his wage in advance, an added incentive for taking this job. The one nobody else wanted — except for him and Swait.

Lepori's offer was also a harsh portent of where he was — a city with no inns. The thought of being alone in such a place sent a sting into his mind, reminding him what had happened in the forest — and what had made Lepori so scared.

"Lepori," Timid said, "what did we hurry here for? You didn't say anything back there." Timid had to gulp down the spit that fear makes pool under his tongue. "I'm just wondering what's gonna happen to me now."

The rabbit leaned forward and perched its hands on the kitchen counter, staring through the house's only window. Like Timid used to do over the rails of the Malachai. Thinking.

"I'm sorry, Timid, I can't explain very well," Lepori said. "There's a lot about this place that doesn't come across at first sight. I'm sure you heard some of it when you were a child, being told bedtime stories. And you saw more of it, out there when you lost your friend. But there's more you still don't know. I think you caught a glimpse of it, but those that have seen the whole thing either bury it down inside them and never let it out or they don't live to talk about it anyway. That's why they say no tales exist of what lives here."

Lepori's tone suggested he wasn't finished with what he had to say but needed time to think of how to say it.

"I need to go to the Council," he finally said, standing up straight and walking over to Timid, likely unaware of how imposing he was. "The folks who are in charge of things, settle disputes, and the like. They need to be told of what you saw. You can come with me, if you wish, but you don't have to."

Timid thought for a moment. A thousand more questions to ask — what if they blamed him for something? Or what if they didn't let him go?

He decided on a question. "Would it be fine if I went later, maybe tomorrow?" he asked. "I could use some time to decompress and sleep. Especially before subjecting myself to authority."

Lepori nodded, solemnly. "I think it might be wise for you to put off meeting them for as long as you can," he said.

Timid mimicked the expression, trying his best to show that he understood Lepori's implication — though he didn't really. "Well then," Timid said, "I'll probably go check out that tavern anyway."

After all, Timid did have a job to do. As tempting as making a mad scramble to leave the forest as soon as possible was, returning without finding what happened to the missing girl would require him to return the Boars' pouch of copper. And that meant more hungry days and roofless nights — of which he had grown rightfully tired after an entire winter of it.

"Is it easy enough to make my way around town on my own," he asked, "or should I wait for you here?"

"Oh yes," Lepori answered, "feel free to wander. I won't tether you here. You can come and go as you please, no bother to me."

"Thank you, Lepori. That's very kind."

Lepori held the door open for Timid and then followed right behind. They walked together out of the neighborhood, allowing Timid to get directions to the tavern. As they came to the main roadway, they said their goodbyes and walked apart only a few paces before Lepori turned around and called out.

"Oh Timid," he said, "if I don't come back by nightfall, leave the city." Lepori then turned and walked, disappearing among a dozen other Springs on the street.

CHAPTER 9

Two mugs of ale plopped to the counter, spilling foam onto the wood. Set there by a large ox Spring; picked up by a short, bearded, human man who gave the ox a wooden ring in return.

Timid observed from the doorway, realizing that his metallic form of money might not be able to fill his stomach. At least nobody seemed to turn their head and gawk at him like he had expected. Instead, the Springs walking in the wide-open streets and lounging in the tavern's oversized chairs all poignantly ignored him.

But the most worrisome for Timid and his empty stomach was the lack of copper being exchanged. That meant that the small pouch of orange coins that the Boars had given Timid wouldn't officially be worth anything, but maybe they would still work. However, the idea of being a stranger and using a practically-foreign currency brought almost enough anxiety that he nearly turned around and left.

The short man returned to his seat by the hearth — the only fireplace that Timid had seen in Goodhaven. He expected to see it, as the smoke from the chimney gave the tavern away among the otherwise clear sky. The room was almost empty, an understandable situation at this time in the morning with no smells of lunch yet wafting out from the kitchen. The few who felt content with beer for breakfast each added their own unique flavor to the room. The short man sang quietly into his mug. A small, rat-like rodent Spring tried its best to sit at a towering table, where everything was engorged to Spring proportions. And the ox wiped mugs behind the counter with a crude rag, eyeing the newcomer with a silent, watchful brood from eyes that were closer to the ceiling than they were to Timid.

Timid became suddenly aware of the pack strapped to his shoulders. Even if he hadn't been a complete stranger here, the pack gave away that he was a traveler. Whatever that meant to the people of Goodhaven, Timid didn't know — but he hoped it didn't mean pitchforks, life taking, and skeleton stomping.

Approaching the ox, Timid took off his pack and rifled through it for his pouch of coins.

"Excuse me," Timid said as he climbed up onto the smallest stool that lined the bar. Though made for humans and thus a good two feet lower than the other stools, it still had to be tall enough so that its occupant could see over the six-foot high counter. He held up a triangular flake of stamped metal, dirty orange in color and thin as a piece of parchment. "Do you take crown copper here?" he asked.

The ox paused its task and grabbed the coin from Timid with a surprising tenderness. Raising the coin to its eyes, the ox grunted with annoyance.

"Afraid not," it replied, voice deep enough that Timid thought he felt his bones rumble. "Don't know what it's worth."

As if Timid's stomach could understand what that meant, it gurgled and sent him a little sting of pain.

"Would it change your mind if I said I'm a deputy of the Boars guild?" Timid asked, probably not as confidently as it should have been. "Round most parts you can take their word to the bank, I ain't trying to short ya."

"Afraid not," the ox repeated. "Sorry." The large Spring resumed cleaning his ale-horn mugs.

Taking the coin back, Timid swung his feet to the side of the barstool and leapt off. Starting for the door, a voice called out from behind him.

"Crown copper, you say?"

Timid turned to look around the room. The short human man was twisted in his chair and looking at Timid. His red beard, lined with a bit of foam, seemed to glow from the firelight behind it.

"Aye," Timid answered.

"Newcomer, then?" the man replied. "Come over and have a seat. And let's take a look at that pouch." The man turned around to sit normal again and took a long drag from one of his mugs, almost emptying it.

He was, as mentioned, condensed in stature and flush with facial hair. Apparently untrimmed, his beard dripped down and wove among itself as if it wished to compete against the Springs for the title of "Goodhaven's most-tangled mess." Unfashionably, his hair was haphazardly cropped short. His eyes were caught between bushy eyebrows and happily-scrunched cheeks. Most importantly, his clothing — thin, whipcord, and dyed — signaled someone who was not on the road but rather at home and out of the elements.

Timid walked over and sat in the chair next to the man, thankful to be near the hearth. It was a welcome feeling on Timid's flesh and he'd been wanting to take the seat since he walked in, fire always being the fourth thing that everybody needs — after air, water, and food.

The short man held out his hand, using his fingers to beckon for the coinpurse. Timid handed it over.

The man chuckled. "Quick to trust, eh?" he said. "You might want to be more careful."

Timid leaned forward, warming his hands at the fire. "Apparently it's not worth anything here anyway," he said dismissively. "And there's no way that you're faster than me."

"Ah," the man said, smiling, "but you've never seen me run." He opened the pouch and took out a coin, running his thumb over the stamp. "Haven't held one of these since I was a child. Just so you know, Odek there is a bit old fashioned. Some folks here would take these for barter."

Timid leaned back in his chair. His stomach rotated, woken by the possibility of food in the foreseeable future.

The man put the coin back in the pouch and tossed it to Timid. "How much is one of those worth now?" he asked Timid.

"Hard to say, not that much," Timid answered, too deep in an unscripted conversation to come up with a beneficial lie. "It's not the smallest we have, but they're typically how people are paid."

The man picked up the other, full mug of ale. "How many of those for one of these?"

Timid thought for a moment. "Well, changes from place to place. There's a couple towns that have to ship any alcohol in. But in a city it's usually two coppers for one pint."

The man handed the mug to Timid. "How about it, then?" he asked. "Two for one?"

A smile crossed Timid's face for the first time in a while. "Sounds good to me, mate," Timid answered. "I've been eyeing that thing since I walked in." They made their exchange, careful not to donate any precious nectar to the floorboards.

"Happy to help a young lad out," the man said, with a smile large enough to force his eyes shut. He raised his mug and tapped it against Timid's, then put it to his lips and polished off whatever was left in the bottom. "Name's Barend, by the way."

Timid finished his sip, much more normal sized than Barend's. "Pleasure, Barend," he said. "I'm Timid. I guess I should start introducing myself as a deputy of the Boars, but I'm beginning to doubt whether that holds any water in these parts."

"No idea what that is," said Barend, "but it sounds nice."

Guided by simple conversation, Timid finished his beer. When he didn't know what to say next, he'd ask about the tavern's interior features. Lit only by the fireplace and not any torches or lamps, the tavern smelled of clean smoke and dirty occupants — not the telltale odor of whale oil that the rest of the isle plagued itself with. Large wooden beams crossed below the vaulted ceiling, fitted together without any visible iron. Not that the city didn't have iron — a metal grate leaned on the wall next to the hearth, which Barend said was used to block sparks in case a Spring wanted to sit close to the fire for some reason. The tavern's front door seemed about three times as wide as a normal one, which Timid learned was so stag Springs with antlers wouldn't be turned away or forced to walk sideways. Barend also listed places where Timid could likely exchange copper for Goodhaven's wooden rings, or even straight up for food.

Eventually, Timid found a good point in the conversation to exit and did so. He nodded to Odek on the way out, who was still wiping mugs and plates with the same rag or one exactly like it. Odd scratch marks on the doorframe caught his eye as he heaved the giant door open. About ten feet up, they could have been from antlers. "Or from some other crazy creature I haven't discovered yet," he imagined.

Timid found the city easy enough to navigate on one beer. The streets — ballooned in size like everything else — were wide enough that he could usually see where they ended up. The market square at the center of town was simple to find in this manner. In the middle of the square stood a statue about as tall as a Spring, but of a human woman. She bent forward at the waist, as if giving someone a drink of water held in her cupped hands.

Using Barend's incomplete directions, Timid finally spotted one of the places that would barter copper — a bodega named Seeds & Sap. It was an almost human-sized building, with a doorway only about eight feet high. Entering, he found the inside to be filled by tightly-packed rows of shelves — certainly not accommodating for the average Spring — overflowing with tools and miscellaneous things a household could need. A small, circular table sat empty in the center of the entryway. The front counter was unattended, but footsteps echoed out from deep in one of the rows.

Ropes, clothes, and trinkets of all sizes dotted the shelves. Sometimes tipped over, sometimes perfectly aligned — but never organized. The footsteps hurried closer and a Spring emerged from one of the rows. Carrying an overflowing armful of trinkets, it rushed to the empty table and plopped down its armload. Dozens of objects spilled out into a pile, and some onto the ground, as the Spring placed a sign at the front of the pile that read "daily special."

The Spring was a rodent. Not a grotesque one, but rather pleasant. With no tail, it reminded Timid of a mouse rather than a rat or a squirrel. It was only a head taller than him.

The Spring looked up and saw Timid. "Oh hello," it said, "just in time! How are you?"

Timid stuttered. "I… uh… I'm well, thank you."

The Spring walked around to the back of the counter and did its best to impersonate a normal shopkeeper. "Go ahead and take a look around. Let me know if you need anything."

It stood with a statuesque smile and followed him with its eyes. Timid walked among the rows and pretended to be interested in the various things on the shelves for a little while. It was all rather normal stuff, things he'd seen before. Some of it must have been made outside the forest in one of the cities, as they were extremely familiar to him. The ropes seemed to be right out of the Shrieksport harbor, the clay pots from somewhere that wasn't afraid of fire.

Timid returned to the counter, thinking of a way to broach the topic of exchanging his coins. But the proprietor spoke first.

"Haunting, can't it be?" it said. "Each thing once belonged to another, but now it rests here. I've never seen ice clung to a mountain's face, but I have spikes for a man's feet. I have no beard nor can I grow one, but I have a razor that cuts it short. How long did it take for me to get all this, I sometimes wonder. It's hazy even to me. The days melt into one another like candles set too close together."

Timid kept silent, wondering if the strange spiel was over. As Lepori had done a few times now, this Spring spent a moment lost in thought before it spoke again.

"What have you brought me, Timid Stormwind?" it asked. "What can you afford to leave behind?"

With a mouth full of carrot, Timid knocked on Lepori's door and — when no answer came — opened it to find the single room empty. It looked the same as before, with no obvious signs that Lepori had since been home. He set his pack and newly-bartered bundle of vegetables by the door and walked to the kitchen on the hunt for a source of water. His stomach had become so angry at him for not having food that it had apparently put a mask over his thirst. His waterskin had long since run dry, and a mug of Oxenstone ale — which was actually surprisingly pleasant — was the only liquid to grace his gullet since he arrived in Goodhaven.

He broadened his search to include the outside of Lepori's house and along the street, a likely location for a community well, but found nothing. Quite a bit of water escaped from the vegetables, especially the celery, and quenched his thirst for a small while. But time would erase that progress, too.

Timid's forearm still stung at every movement, reminding him that it needed to be rewrapped with something a little sturdier than a shirttail. He took a few minutes to carefully cut a strip of cloth from the bottom of the extra overcloak that he had been using as a blanket. An unsightly pea-soup green and a little overused, it was not as valuable, thick, or rainproof as the blue one that the Boars had outfitted him with.

Eventually he laid out his bedroll and rested on it for what initially he intended to be a moment. When his stomach eventually woke him — apparently unsatisfied with its lunch — he found that the light inside the house was shaded red by sunset. Lepori still hadn't returned, as Timid would have noticed the thunderous stomping that followed Lepori's kind everywhere.

Timid stuffed his belongings back in the pack. Where he was once fascinated by the vegetables' gargantuan size, he now regretted their unwieldy length. The tips of celery stalks stuck out of the top flap, flopping about every time the pack moved.

"If I don't come back by nightfall, leave the city," Lepori had said to him. The unspoken omen inside of that warning made him nauseous again.

He asked himself whether continuing his task was worth it but couldn't find an answer. If he returned without trying any harder to find the girl, the Boars likely wouldn't let him back into their little club — regardless of whether he had seen the city where the trees walk and the grass listens. And that meant they'd take back the rest of their copper, which meant more hungry nights. If they'd actually had given him a badge, they likely would have taken that back too. And if that wasn't enough, something far, far away shook its head. Because abandoning a missing girl would mean that, once again, Timid was running away from what hid in the dark and feasted on his friends.

With Lepori's warning echoing in his ears, Timid walked out the front door and into the street. The Oxenstone was a five-minute walk away, plenty long enough to get into trouble. Walking around a city at night was always dangerous, especially in a city this wary of outsiders. In a city where humans were four feet shorter than the locals. In a city where the trees walk and the grass listens.

CHAPTER 10

The air around the Oxenstone carried a different hum now that it was a more appropriate time of day to visit a tavern. A dull roar of conversation seeped out through the windows, and — in addition to the same smoke trailing out of the chimney — the flicker of firelight made the tavern uniquely visible among all the other dark buildings. Timid put his shoulder against the front door and shoved hard enough to get it open, looking like more of a regular already.

Inside, the bar room had a healthy number of patrons. Springs filled just about every seat. Some stood against the wall or walked between their tables and the bar, ducking under the wooden beams at the ceiling if necessary. Odek was at the same spot, but now was busy serving drinks and taking orders from customers at the counter.

The roar dimmed slightly as Springs turned to look at Timid. Some were more discreet than others, and thankfully some didn't even take a glance or interrupt their conversations. Finally, a familiar voice rose above the others.

"Timid! Over here, lad!" it called out. Barend sat in the same seat as before, but with what looked like a new beer. Looking over his shoulder, he raised the mug in the air, sloshing a bit over the side. Timid walked over, taking the still empty seat beside him. "I'll get our next round!" Barend said, getting up and sauntering over to the counter, loudly ordering two more beers. Judging by the way he walked, he likely hadn't left the tavern all day.

Timid stared at the fire until Barend returned and plopped a beer down on the hearth within Timid's reach. Timid took a swig to be polite before leaning over to talk closely.

"Oy," Timid whispered, "I'm leaving."

Barend, staring deeply into his mug, let out a surprised puff of air that blew foam off the top and into his lap. "Already?" he asked, way louder than Timid had hoped. "What in the hell for?"

Timid didn't answer, instead trying to look stern by taking another swig of beer. In truth, he'd like to sit around a while and get some answers out of this helpfully drunk man. Meanwhile, it was nice to get anything liquid in his throat.

Maybe Barend sensed Timid's seriousness, because he leaned forward and spoke musty breath right to his face. "You think you'll be better off in the forest?" Barend asked. "Listen, lad. Trust your old friend Barend on this, you're safer here than out there. Safer than you know."

"Right," Timid said, remembering why Swait wasn't here with him. "I think I know what you mean, but I don't think what I'm looking for is in Goodhaven."

Barend sat back and shook his head. "No, Timid," he said, "you don't know what I mean. How could you? You just got here. The best thing for you is to stay in Goodhaven till you die. Pay no mind to the passing time, you'll never be late again — 'cause if you never leave here, you'll never have anywhere else to be."

Timid smiled, trying to act like Barend was joking, though he really didn't seem to be. "I don't plan on dying," Timid said, "and I don't plan on staying here, either."

"Better than going out there and having something happen to you," Barend argued. "Eaten by wild dogs — or worse. Look at me, been stuck here for what, twenty years now?" Barend scooted closer so he could poke a finger in Timid's chest. "You should never leave the city. Not while you like having flesh on your bones. And from the look of your arm there, you already found that out."

Timid swatted away the drunk and clairvoyant man's finger. "I'm not supposed to be dawdling around town," he said, trying not to get agitated. "I'm a deputized man. The Boars sent me here to find someone — a girl. A human girl. I don't know much about her. Her name's Cherry, that's about it. I just wanted to ask you if you knew where a good place would be to start."

Barend sat back in his chair again. "I'm sorry," he said, "I know this isn't what you want to hear, but you'd be better off assuming she's dead and sitting here with me, having a drink for all eternity."

"C'mon, mate," Timid said, "you know I can't do that."

Barend took a long drag from his mug, stood up, and scooted his chair closer to Timid's. "Listen, mate," Barend said. "I'm not crazy; I'm stuck. You really want to know what's out there? Why you shouldn't go? You're lucky you came to me, kid, 'cause I'll tell you what they won't. It took me nigh a year to figure this out and I still don't know the whole picture, like these folks got a blindfold on me."

"What do you mean?" Timid asked, looking around. "The Springs?"

Barend nodded.

Finally, Timid had found someone else that felt out of the loop. And that someone was made of the same stuff as he was — flesh and bone. "Go on, Barend," Timid said. "What do you know?"

Barend sat for a few seconds in an obvious attempt to regain his composure before getting up and walking to the bar. He returned with another beer, almost tripping over his untied bootlaces. In a near whisper, barely audible over the rest of the raucous in the room, Barend said, "They call it the Tale of Two Brothers."

Once, there were two brothers who lived in this forest — before anyone knew it as the Living Forest and before anyone had made the city of Goodhaven. They traveled together and were always at each other's side, bringing their own company along everywhere. One day, they decided to rest below the shadowy canopy of an Essai tree.

Fueled by the universal desire to compete against siblings, they argued about who could get to the top of the tree more quickly than the other. The first brother — who was honest and fair — began to climb. Though the bark was smooth and hard to grasp, he slowly clawed his way up. The second brother — who was quick to think — began to tear away at the bark. Though it was tough and rigid, he slowly made his way through.

As the first brother was nearing the top, the second brother picked away the last remaining shred of trunk holding the tree together. The tree teetered and gave way, and the first brother grasped tightly to one of the topmost branches. It all landed to the ground with a crash, and the second brother easily walked to the top end of the tree with a smug grin on his face.

But as the second brother neared the limbs at the tippy top, he saw one that didn't match the others — a bloody arm stretched out, fingers only inches away from the goal. Both life and soul were gone from the first brother, leaked out through all the cracks in the bones and all the broken bits of skin.

The second brother kneeled down to grieve the loss of his brother and curse his own foolishness. Then — from the hewed trunk of the Essai tree — emerged a glowing, green sprite. Now, having grown up in the forest, the brothers had long been told of the Essai and knew that many believed them to harbor portions of the very spirit and soul of nature. Some forest folk — usually the ones untethered to the world around them — told tales of whispers and voices heard with an ear flush to an Essai trunk, deep in the forest's heart on the quietest of nights. But until now, the second brother thought those stories too fantastical, odd, and implausible to believe or take heed of.

The sprite approached, causing a great shame to fall over the second brother, for he realized that he had in truth taken two lives. He pleaded with the sprite to refill his lost brother's body with life, as he believed the sprite could do.

In a low hum, the sprite said to him, "Unfair for you to walk away with toll unpaid and compensate me with a crippled body. However, should you allow me to transfer your life to the other, I shall fill your empty vessel with my own spirit. Thus, harmony will be restored — but both shall live a cursed existence, as do all who have unnatural souls not of their body."

The second brother agreed. He let the sprite drain him of life and transfer his soul to the first brother's fractured corpse. The sprite then fulfilled the bargain, transferring its own soul to the second brother's body.

During the coming years, the brothers drifted apart. The first brother, having known a lonely death, could no longer see any value in life. He angered easily, and began to see death in his dreams. He felt unnatural with his new soul, and his corrupted mind grew to hate anything pristine. So he killed, putting an end to what he saw as tortured lives of misery. Thus began the terror of the Beast.

The second brother, having known a lonely life, could not stand to see others without happiness. He offered help to all that he found, and began to wander in search of those who had lost their way. So he saved, building the city of Goodhaven with all those that he brought out from the darkness. Thus began the light of the Guardian.

"That's only how I know it," said Barend. "I know there are different versions, but they all got the same message."

Confused, Timid tried to clarify. "And what message is that?"

"There's something lurking in those woods," Barend pressed. "Something that's trying to destroy Goodhaven. It doesn't come inside, it stays out there. And it's been gone for a while too, but I stay right here in this tavern in case it comes back. Never left these city walls since I got here."

Timid sipped his ale horn and let the story sink in for a few minutes. It reminded him much of the version of The Wishing Well that he knew — where a family made larger and larger sacrifices in exchange for the fulfillment of their wishes. They, too, eventually wanted their loved ones resurrected. But they had to give up their limbs for it.

Although Barend proved to be a decent storyteller, he obviously hadn't told that particular story before. Some sentences drifted off, others got stuck in the back of his throat. His performance shined in the physical — his forward leans timed with the drama, his hands mimicking the action. Timid noted these habits to himself in the moment, and in the now, as skills to fill his expanding reservoir.

And something still remained unsaid. "How many others are here, Barend?" Timid asked. "People like us."

Barend tilted his head back for a few seconds, trying to get thoughts to run through his drunken mind with the aid of gravity. "Let's see. There's me, Olgar at the church, and... uh... I think that's it. Oh, and you now."

"Three?" Timid asked to clarify. "There's only three humans in the whole city?"

"Aye, think so. No wait, Olgar's gone." He didn't seem mournful, as if he was talking about someone he never had met. "We get a couple new folks every year or so, but they don't last long. Either leave and go back where they came from, or try to go make their way in the forest, I guess. There's probably some who made it out to the river and are still making do, though what a shit life that would be, eh? Scared to go to the privy in case you get grabbed up by something." Barend ended the thought with a chuckle directed into his upturned mug.

Timid remembered all the stories he'd heard of this forest, about why nobody wants to enter it. "Barend," he said, trying to show that he was serious, "nobody ever makes it back. Nobody has ever walked out of this forest."

Barend's eyes narrowed and he leaned forward. "What do you mean?"

"You said that some people leave and go back where they came from," Timid said. "But no one has ever made it back to a town or city from here, except perhaps more than a century ago. I'm being paid an exorbitant amount of money just to try, and they think that I have a chance only because it's usually just farmers and children who go missing."

The thought got stuck in the mud somewhere along the way through Barend's mind, which had been thickened too much by a day — or maybe a few decades — of drinking.

"All the more reason to stay here," Barend cheered. A smile crossed his face as he lifted his mug for the last time and swallowed the rest of its contents. He leaned back in his chair, seemingly exhausted. "I've had enough of an evening, lad," he said. "We'll figure out what to do tomorrow."

The man set his head to the side, resting it on the padded chair back. Only a few breaths passed cleanly before becoming wet and choppy, a sure sign of sleep. After coating his hands in one last wash of firelight, Timid stood up and brought their mugs to the counter. He yanked the door open once more, letting a waft of crisp air float by him and into the tavern.

CHAPTER 11

The evening air wasn't all that chilly, as far as evenings go. The more northern parts of the isle get an earlier and harder summer, and Timid was glad to be on the right side of the mountains to get the benefit of that for once. Winter brings a life of hardship for everyone and adjusting to working in a city like Corical would have been difficult enough, even if it wasn't Timid's first snowy season on land since his childhood. He lacked the connections to be given an apprenticeship with a blacksmith, and didn't know enough about horses to even clean stables. First, it was kitchenwork for Timid. When that fell through — by his own fault — it was a few weeks of hunger. After that, more kitchen work, this time at the Boars' longhouse. When he'd earned enough to keep himself clean and convince the Boars that he could take a job, it was off to the Living Forest.

For the most part, Goodhaven's streets had already said their goodnights, Springs seeming to come and go with the daylight. Timid made his way to the center of town, where the markets were during the day. Passing the statue at the square's core, a nearby sign caught his eye. It displayed a mass of intertwined lines in a ring — the bird's nest symbol of Dekune. The building behind it was evidently a church, but unlike any Timid had ever seen — a round dome made of sticks and trees with two large entrances that could accommodate antlers. For a moment, Timid considered going inside, but he didn't know much about the religion except that it was about the creator of plants. All plants, supposedly — except seaweed.

Timid reached a gate on the western end of the city. Largely similar to the other, this one was also unguarded on the inside. A Spring atop the wall saw him approach and let out a command to the other side, where there were likely other guards. The gate doors slowly opened inward, and two deer Springs appeared from the other side. Deer seemed to be the most common type of Spring and, unlike most others, it was easy to tell the males from the females. The two guards watched Timid as he walked by but gave no resistance and didn't even gaze his way.

"Don't care nearly as much about me leaving," he thought to himself. "I bet they're happy."

The outside of the city on this edge was much different than the other. As soon as he stepped through the gate, he was in the forest again. Branches practically brushed the walls and had obviously been trimmed back. A slim road — merely a footpath — stretched out straight in front of him, but no fields lay to its sides. Instead, more forest. There were houses too, but they lay back in the darkness, silent and still.

After absorbing it for a moment, the forest here gave off a certain comfort. Knowing that people could build homes in the forest took the edge off Timid's fear of being alone. Though maybe these houses only survived because they were so close to Goodhaven. Maybe the city was like a lamp held up against the dark. Night can never be black enough to swallow a flame whole.

Houses stopped popping up after about five minutes of walking — at least for what he could see with the sun fully gone. The darkness brought fatigue with it. With only a couple hours of sleep here and there over the last two days, Timid's feet dragged behind him. His legs turned to knots above the knee and his feet stung as he pressed them into the ground. He could only go for a few miles in this manner before his mind started to wander and look for a place to rest. But if he searched too hard, something poked him in the back. A sharpened stick prodding him on. A cocktail of loneliness and helplessness poisoning his mind. "Not there," it would tell him, "it could see you there. Too dark there, it could sneak up on you." Nothing was good enough or safe enough — until Timid rounded a corner in the footpath and set his eyes on an Essai tree.

Long ago, when Timid was a young boy living in Shrieksport, he used to sit on the rocky shoreline at the harbor's edge. He'd often be within earshot of the captains giving their orders, and he eventually memorized the sequence of commands they used to dock and undock their ships. As the weeks piled on and fishing season bloomed, he learned how to unload a fish hold onto the harbor scales. But one day a seafolk man walked towards him — boots shiny from the black protective slick of whale oil, shirt stained by sweat and fish blood, and a brimmed blue hat with an embroidered yellow squid. He dropped down to a knee and spoke words of wonder to Timid. Words of promise. Words of work and payment. Words of adventure and sea turtles.

As Timid's legs carried him to the base of the Essai, those words rang through his mind again and he let himself forget that they were nothing but empty promises. A familiar chirp and flutter overhead told him that everything was as it should be. "Birds," Timid uttered into the empty forest.

Though he had been outpacing sleep, it now caught up with him. No longer feeling goaded into movement, he crumpled against the Essai's trunk. He brought out his extra cloak and tucked it over his knees. The crunch of celery stalks snapped across the birdsongs like a whip. With a half-chewed mouthful, Timid left the darkness for another world.

Snow-covered mountains, sharp and of sheer rock, rose for thousands and thousands of feet above him. Their peaks spit flames into the sky, clouding the air with black soot that blotted out the light. Timid stood on a paper-thin sheet of ice, extending for miles in all directions until it collided in folded bergs at the mountains' sprawling bases. Below him, more black — not water, just a pit of empty darkness. A figure sat atop one of the alpine peaks, legs hanging over a cliff edge and mindlessly kicking in childlike joy. Faint chuckling came in rhythms as the figure's head playfully tilted side to side. Timid felt its gaze on his skin — that feeling he first met in the forest telling him that something was watching him. He took a step forward and cracks shot out in a web under his feet. He fell.

Morning had not come yet, the world still sleeping under the blanket of its own shade. Though he had been jostled awake, it was not from the sound of birds. A muffled cackling fell on the forest floor, like it had slipped out of his dream behind him through a door left ajar. Timid's eyelids stuck together in an early sign of dehydration. Wherever Timid looked in the space surrounding the Essai tree, motes of dust floated down like snow.

When he gazed up, among the flecks of soft gray he found an oddity — a large, thick branch growing out of the side of the Essai. Timid didn't remember it being there before, as none of the Essai he'd seen had any branches — let alone one this large, low to the ground, and noticeable. But above the branch sat yet another, stranger oddity. The blackness of the night seemed to coalesce into one spot, where he wouldn't have noticed it if his eyes hadn't already been adjusted by a deep sleep. And it moved. Like a child sitting atop a rock watching boats come into port, its legs and tail dangled over the edge of the branch, swinging back and forth in no particular rhythm. And from above the branch came the laughter that leaked out from Timid's dream.

Timid stood up and took a few steps backwards, studying the black shape. It followed him with eyes of pure black — like a chunk of obsidian held up against the night sky. It tilted its head to the side, reminding Timid of a hound's way of patiently waiting.

Timid put his hand on his knife, which sparked a thought from the creature.

"Didn't mean to startle you," it said, in a hollow voice like wind coming out of a small cave. "I was hoping you wouldn't wake. I was surprised when you didn't make a fire. Had to find you another way. But thank you for staying so close to the road, I don't like wandering too far off."

It sniffed the air, pointing its long and extruded jowl upwards. Like a blackened, blighted Spring, it had a wolf's face and a winding mass of branch-like cords for a body. Timid didn't notice the feet before it spoke again.

"I should say that you're not as talkative as I hoped," it said with no humor. "It does get lonely out here, and most passers-by tend to ignore me. Sometimes they act like they don't see me at all, if you can believe that. The rudeness..."

Timid felt much like he did when faced with a Spring for the first time, when he had fallen silent in front of Lepori. But talking there had worked and this thing was very, very much like a Spring — so Timid preferred the idea of talking rather than fighting.

"I'm sorry," Timid said, "I'm quite tired still. What do you want?"

It tilted its head to the other side. "What do you mean?" it asked.

"I mean..." Timid paused for a few seconds to put his thoughts together — which seemed to be an okay way of speaking to Springs since they did it too. "I mean, why have you been trying to find me?"

"I don't know," it shrugged. "Maybe you taste good."

Timid's hand clenched around his knife again and he thought about brandishing it. But that might start something that he didn't want to start. But even though he knew that he needed to talk his way out of this, he got distracted by the creature's feet.

He stared and stared for much too long. They swung like pendulums below the branch and it was hard to see anything in the dark, even things that lay still and let wandering eyes rest upon them. From what little Timid could tell, they were not shaped like human feet. Instead, they had four long toes, with curled claws at the end — like wolf's feet.

"But I doubt it," the wolf said.

"Huh?" Timid muttered, very much lost in imagining what sort of print those feet would make.

"I doubt you taste good," it clarified, sniffing the air again. "You certainly don't smell good. That's just the way things are, I guess. It's the only way I found you and we never want what's easy to find."

"So what do you want with me," Timid started, "now that you've found me?"

"I'm not sure that I want anything from you," the wolf answered, twiddling its long, spindly fingers. "Maybe I want you to leave."

"Well I don't plan on staying very long," Timid responded honestly.

"Not everything goes to plan, does it? Did you plan on meeting me? Did you plan on going home? On finding a little girl?"

"You know about the girl?" Timid asked.

It let out a tired sigh. "Timid, everyone knows about the girl."

Timid bit his lip, thoughts racing too fast to catch one. But he needed to talk. "Everyone knows about me too, then, huh? How is that?"

For the first time, the wolf gave a bit of a smirk. Thankfully, Timid saw that the mouth grew no teeth.

"You're sprouting a bit of bravery up inside you, aren't you?" the wolf said. It pulled its legs up underneath it, getting into a perching position on top of the branch and using an arm to balance itself against the Essai trunk.

"I have a deal for you, Timid," the wolf said.

Timid tried his best to show the correct amount of skepticism. "What's the deal, then?" he finally asked, after the wolf offered nothing else.

The wolf spoke slowly and with an even tone — like it had rehearsed and knew exactly what it was going to say. "Go back to Goodhaven and stay there for the rest of your life. Until you grow old and your hair turns white, until you draw your last breath of air. Don't go to the river. Abandon your quest and give up on your promise." Its voice crawled over his skin, quiet and edgeless like it came from a long distance away. "Do that, and I'll see you back myself."

The offer, without a consequence for denying it, didn't seem like a threat. Timid had learned to spot threats — a useful talent on a ship. Surrounded by a dozen or more men, most from tough backgrounds that taught them violence and greed, you need to know which ones you have to follow unofficial orders from.

"But I don't think that's a very good idea," Timid said, "I don't think I'm safe there."

"Why not?" the wolf quizzed, acting like Timid was paranoid. "What bad things have you seen happen in the great city of Goodhaven?"

"Nothing, but that's not what I mean." Timid took his time to think. "I don't understand how this is a deal, exactly."

"Oh, it is," the wolf said. "Hasn't everyone been telling you that there are dark things in the forest? You've seen some of them, now. I know you're becoming brave, but if there's danger everywhere, why not trust me and take a chance that I'm right?"

"Because I'm not sure I should trust you," Timid answered. "I don't know who you are."

The wolf puffed itself up. "You've finally found someone that you don't trust, then? I feel honored." It turned to the side and put both hands on the Essai, like it was about to climb up the bark. "Maybe I should build some trust with you then. I'd like to amend the deal. I'll let you walk from here in either direction, towards the city or away from it. If you turn around at any point before the river, I'll know that you took the deal.

But I won't protect you as long as you keep walking away from the city. How is that?"

Timid thought of a response, but too many questions were stuck to his palms for him to pick out just one. His brain cycled through them. Could he simply run away from anything, whenever he wanted? But wasn't this the thing that took the girl in the first place? What other things would he want to run away from? Once again, Timid could only see one half of the puzzle.

Before he had made up his mind to say anything, scratching noises came from the Essai. He looked up and saw an empty branch, jutting out of the side of the Essai, against a faintly lit mass of leaves.

The forest floor wasn't as dark as before — light trickled into the canopy from above and caught dust motes in the air, making shiny streaks that cut through the sterile wasteland. Timid patted the Essai to say goodbye, as he thought might be polite, and opted to not rest any more — at least not here.

CHAPTER 12

A lonely soul wandering through a forbidden forest on a winding, night-shaded footpath might have good reason to be scared. However, Timid could simply turn on his heels and secure his safety — if the wolf was to be trusted. And if you can't trust a maniacal, toothless, dream-permeating wolf made of petrified, pitch-black wood, who can you trust? The drunkard asleep at the tavern? Being a fugitive himself, Timid was in no place to pass judgment on anyone. He took people — and not-people — at their word, hopeful that the incongruities were really just wrinkles in the sheet of truth. Eventually, everything would get all straightened out and everyone could live happily ever after.

And since you are familiar with the aura of this particular forest, I shall not repeat myself in too much detail. Strange noises, Essai trees, the feeling of being watched — these are everywhere and yet nowhere in particular. On this leg of Timid's journey to nowhere in particular — in a sleepless, dehydrated exhaustion — he felt like a crab stranded in low tide, becoming crusty under the baking sun. So when the crashing sound of flowing water swarmed him as thick as if he could swim in the noise itself, his body moved towards it with a magnetic attraction.

Not long after, when the sound grew to an overwhelming cascade and night had settled into its full form, he saw a warm glow of orange light prick into existence underneath the forest canopy.

"Springs don't like fire," Timid thought, paying no mind to whether or not he said it out loud to the audience of trees. "And wolves can't make fire. And I can't make fire."

But he stopped after only a few more steps. Now he looked at — and fruitlessly tried to understand — an incomprehensibly large fence that grew out from the ground. Rather than being sawed and sealed like Goodhaven's walls, here Essai trees had arranged themselves in a line, nearly touching in some places and spaced wider in others. It faded into the freshly laid darkness on both sides of Timid. And, more strangely still, another Essai sat alone in front of the others. Dead from about 30 feet up, its top didn't even reach the canopy's underbelly. Instead, it wore a jagged crown like the splintered end of a broken stick — but twenty feet wide. A flickering firelight danced behind partially-curtained windows cut into the tree's side.

Timid saw more as he inched closer. A mailbox in front, at the edge of the road. A small shed in back, covering the remains of a wood pile that had been picked at through a full winter. And a tall, red door carved into the bottom of the trunk.

As the isle-wide symbol of a sanctuary, the red door melted away the last bit of apprehension that stuck in his chest. Though paint offered no true protection, a red door meant a great deal to a traveler. At the most, it could be a free meal and a bed for the night. At the least, a roof to keep the rain off your back for a few hours.

Timid approached and stopped an arm's length away from the door, noticing that its surface wore an etched design. Small lines mixed together in a circle, some poking outwards to make rough edges. Timid had always thought it looked like a bird's nest, but he knew it was probably something else. After all, birds were of the god of sea spirits, Eadron — and Dekune, as the god of tree, plant, and nature spirits, was pitifully tied to the soil.

Taking a weapon of any sort into a sanctuary would ensure a bout of bad luck, so Timid unlatched his knife from his belt and hid it in his pack. He took a deep breath and tried to prepare something to say before tapping his knuckles sharply against the door. A shuffling sounded from the other side, growing into a heavy set of footsteps. Then, a voice.

"Hello?" it called out softly.

"Hello," Timid said in as bright a tone as he could muster, "I'm a traveler from the road. I was hoping you could help me."

The voice didn't return, but a series of clicks and sounds of sliding metal pins came from the door's edge. It cracked open and the occupant obviously still braced itself against the other side. Timid could see in through slivers and between limbs where a Spring's body didn't block the view. The tree's interior, from what he could see, was cleaner and more lavish than Lepori's home had been.

"You walked out here alone?" the voice asked.

"Yes," he answered, "from Goodhaven." It was obvious enough, but Timid didn't want to seem like he was withholding any information. If he could parlay this into a night spent indoors, it'd be the best he'd gotten since the inn at the mountain pass.

The Spring seemed a little flustered, maybe caught off guard by the unexpected and awkward visitor, so Timid tried to fill the silence.

"Uh, I'm just a traveler," he started to explain. "Sort of. I'm not from Goodhaven, originally. I mean, I don't live there."

"Hmm," the Spring sounded rightfully uninterested, "then what can I do for you? You said you needed help?"

"Well, in a way. I'm a deputy of the Boars." Timid paused for a reply, hoping for awe and a respectful amount of starstruckness — but received only a waiting silence. "I'm supposed to be looking for someone," he continued, "but haven't had much luck in that regard. I was just hoping to get out of the night air for a while and see if someone here knew anything that could help. I noticed the red door, you know, and thought that might mean I could come in."

The door swung open the rest of the way. A large, shadowy figure stood in the opening. A Spring, for sure — as its body was just like those of other Springs — but its head caught Timid's attention. It looked very similar to Lepori — about the same height and with the same pointed nose — so it was likely another rabbit. But on top, only one ear stood straight up — and where the other should have been was a jagged cut-out, as if a giant had leaned down and taken a bite out of the rabbit's head.

"Well then," it said, "by all means, do come in." It slowly swung its giant, lumbering body to the side, out of Timid's way.

The Spring closed the door behind Timid, doing up a series of metal latches on the inside door frame. Bronze pins slid sideways into their receptacles, making a bridge across the door's gap. In front of Timid was a decadent interior, much like a real home. The ceiling was high enough for the Spring to walk about, and the walls must have been thinner than they looked from the outside to account for so much space. To Timid's left was a series of bookshelves and a single couch, slightly padded and long enough to allow the Spring to stretch out. Part of the house was dedicated to a semi-private space hidden by a curling wall that intruded out into the rest of the living area. A fire crinkled gently in the far-right corner, made safe by a brick hearth and chimney. The kitchen had a large washbasin, a rack of drying herbs, and a bucket of standing water.

Seeing the bucket stopped him in his tracks. A real drink of water, just a few steps away. He licked his lips absentmindedly, his tongue scraping over cracks, crevasses, and dead skin.

The Spring noticed Timid staring at the bucket. "Are you thirsty?" it asked. "Most... *people*... are when they get here."

Timid swallowed a dry gulp, wondering about the not-people. "Actually, yes," he answered. "Extremely. I haven't had a real drink of water in a couple days."

Timid could now see that the Spring's head hadn't been bitten or torn. Instead, ends of twigs and branches poked out, some farther than others, but all charred and black. The char extended even onto the remaining part of his face where his right eye would have been. An ear and a large chunk of the skull — or whatever Springs called their heads — were lost forever.

The Spring bent down and looked into the bucket. "This is quite dirty," it said unsurprised, like it usually kept a dirty pale of water in the kitchen. "I'm sorry, I'm not sure if it's good to drink, I use it to wash mushrooms."

Timid took a few steps closer so he could see down into the bucket. Bits of dirt floated on top and the inside was murky. His tongue receded back into his mouth and he took a scratchy gulp of air. "Where do you get it from?" Timid asked. He would gladly go refill it.

"The river," the Spring responded, "but I never go out at night."

Timid looked out between the window curtains to see that the light had completely gone. "Oh," Timid said, "why not?"

"Just afraid of the dark, I suppose." The Spring walked away and sat on the couch. "But we can go in the morning. Come, sit. You said you were looking for someone?"

Timid eyed the bucket again. He had likely drank worse on the Malachai, with so many ignoring the cup and dipping their hands in directly. Timid cupped his hands and dipped them into the water, melting the caked dirt and bits of blood off his skin. He raised a handful of water to his lips and filled his mouth. It tasted like copper coins, but even a single mouthful made his mind and skin feel plump again. He drank to his heart's content.

"Yes, I am," he finally answered. "A young girl. All I know is that she might be in the forest, I'm not sure if she's even alive."

"Interesting. And she's not in Goodhaven?" the Spring asked.

Timid shrugged, trying to avoid admitting that he didn't do a very thorough investigation. "I don't reckon so, no."

The Spring shook its head. "I'm sorry," it started, "but I haven't seen anyone here in quite some time."

Timid's pack grew heavy on his shoulders, as a reminder that he didn't need to carry it any longer. He sat himself in an empty chair and set his pack down beside it, a single stalk of celery still sticking out of the top flap. He realized only after sitting that the chair was obviously made for a human.

"Perfect fit," Timid said.

The Spring looked at him with its lone eye. "Yes, perfect."

With a quarter of its face missing Timid could hardly interpret its expressions. He felt an uncomfortable silence settle in. It needed breaking. "Nobody's been here for a while, you said?"

The Spring reached one hand up to stroke its chin like a pondering human might do. "Maybe two winters?" it answered. "Since I've seen a stranger, I mean. I see other Springs sometimes."

"Oh, do others live around here?" Timid asked, recalling that Barend and Lepori seemed to think that there was a small community here.

"No, not really," the Spring answered. "Most just come to see the river or to forage. The mushrooms get better the nearer you get to the river."

Timid perked up at this. "I met someone gathering mushrooms," he said, "named Lepori. He helped me actually, on my way into Goodhaven." The thought came organically to Timid, but now he realized that many Springs probably did such a thing.

"Huh, interesting." The Spring again twiddled its thumbs. "And who are you looking for? A loved one?"

"No, no relation. I was hired to find her. Her name is Cherry. She's a young human, maybe ten years old."

"Wow, that is young. Do humans usually go out on their own at that age?"

"No," Timid huffed, "they don't. Not girls, definitely. Still just a child, would have been in school for another few years typically." Timid had learned to read and write at Shrieksport's Church of Stridelong, but they only did that for children younger than fifteen. At twenty, after no longer being kicked out of bars, Timid had just now stopped feeling like a child. Then Swait had reminded him that, as far as true experience went, Timid was not yet what the land-locked folk would consider a man.

Timid continued his thought. "I'm not sure that she's still alive, actually. I just have to check all corners before I can get paid."

"I'm sorry to hear that," the Spring said. "I hope she's okay."

In the ensuing silence, Timid's mind went towards the fire. It gripped some part of his human spirit and tried to reel him in. Air, water, food, fire — the four things that a human's soul must be fed — and he now possessed them all.

"You want to sit by the fire." The Spring's voice tapped him on the shoulder in a gentle way as to not startle him. "I can tell."

Timid looked at the Spring with a noticeable plea. "Do you mind?"

"No, not at all," it responded. "In fact, why don't you stay here for the night? I can stoke the fire and there's enough space on the ground in front of it. I wouldn't send you out into the night even if you were an unpleasant guest, which you aren't." A smile crept across its face, stretching up into the charred section on one side. "And in the morning I can take you to the river."

"That would be wonderful," Timid said. "Thank you, truly." Timid stood up and bent down to grab his pack.

"You're welcome, Ti..." The Spring interrupted itself. "I'm sorry, I never got your name."

Timid lifted his pack off the ground and held it at his side. His eyes went past the Spring and landed on the multiple, complex locks on the door. The silence joined only by the crinkles in the fireplace and a new, steady rustling from outside, as rain began to gently drip down and mist the forest.

"Timid," he said softly.

The Spring smiled again. "You can call me Rute."

CHAPTER 13

Timid awoke to stomping feet. Not that they were stomping on purpose, but by their nature. His cloaks appreciated being out of the wet forest for a night, caked-on dirt now crumbling off as it dried. The fire lasted most of the night but was out by morning. Some coals still gave off a bit of smoke or a speck of red, and a trickle of light peeked in through the open curtains.

Rute walked around the kitchen, pulling about a half dozen different types of vegetables out of cupboards or off the drying rack. He washed some in the bucket of water and peeled others. He began loudly chopping them into chunks with a knife. It was large, like everything else, and obviously not very sharp.

Apparently, Rute noticed that Timid was awake. "I was thinking of making a soup," Rute said, "but I do need fresh water for the broth. How about we go to the river? Is that fine by you?"

"Of course," Timid said, "that sounds perfect. Thank you." Though this morning wasn't as bad as the last, he did feel a penetrating dryness throughout his body. His face must have expressed his delight at the idea, as Rute smiled in response and picked up the bucket of dirty water. Rute trudged over and unlatched the several locks on the door. As Rute swung it open to reveal the red side and Dekune's insignia, Timid felt a wet draft that tickled at his skin and beckoned him closer. The cold air pinged a shiver down his spine, prompting him to walk back and grab his thick, blue Boars cloak before returning and putting on his boots at the door.

Outside, Rute poured the bucket's outdated contents onto the ground. As Timid followed behind, the roaring of water became suddenly obvious — as if he had gotten used to hearing it muffled inside the house, like the years he had spent ignoring waves against the Malachai's hull.

The path to the river snaked through the row of giant Essai and over a small embankment where the ground rose up to house the trees like a row of crop seedlings. Essai didn't normally grow this closely together, at least from what Timid could tell, so the limbs high above him appeared to fuse into each other.

Only a few steps later, the river sprawled out before him until the far shore was almost just a line on the horizon. The water — crystal clear and smooth at the edges — was slowed at the edge by a shallow section that extended for a few feet. Distinct white dots peppered the middle of the river, rocks turning swoops of swift current into permanently crashing waves. On this side was a small beach, rocky in some places and sandy in others. The other side didn't have its own line of Essai — or any of them for that matter. So here he was, the far reaches of the Living Forest.

The sky above was a darkened blue, the trailing edge of night. Birds flew among the treetops and over the water, their squawks and songs delivering memories of a pleasant life to Timid's ears. And birds, he remembered, are of God.

Following Rute, Timid stepped down onto a sandy section of the riverbank. Rute waded gingerly into the water, betraying its icy temperature. He rinsed the bucket a few times before filling it up and hauling it back to the shore. Timid walked near and dropped to his knees at the edge of the water, forcing a bit of mud onto his pants. Leaning forward to the river's surface, he sucked a bit of water up through his pursed lips.

His mind cleared as if it had been told it would never go thirsty again. He sat back up and took a deep breath with his eyes closed. It was like coming back to the Malachai after a hungry shore leave — like coming home.

He leaned down again, this time not simply to enjoy the freshness of water on his lips but to quench his deep thirst. He sank his hands into the water so he could lean out farther. It stung the backs of his hands as it glided over his skin, and likewise cooled his throat as it went down. Obviously, it had been ice not long before this and hadn't had any restful, sunny days to warm it up.

Heavy footsteps approached him from the side, sloshing through the shallows. He expected a voice to tell him that it was time to go — to try to pry him off of the river's surface. Instead, a grip as hard as iron and rough like weathered bark clamped onto his neck, forcing his face into the riverbed. His legs gave out from under him and the front of his body fell into the water, bringing an instant of cold that made his breath gasp in shock. Water drew into his lungs, choking him and causing a fit of coughing that only gathered more liquid in his airpipe. He thrashed his feet and tried to push himself up with his arms, but the clamp pressed him too firmly to the river bottom. It dragged him farther in, submerging his whole body as his face scraped over the edge of the shallows and dropped down into deeper, colder water.

Timid opened his eyes to see the riverbed once more before he slammed into it again. The grip retained its vice-like tightness, pinching his skin where fingers came together around his neck. His spine tweaked awkwardly in a sting that warned him of damage to a nerve or disk. He reached his hands up behind his head to pull at the clamp, but his fingers found no holds and weren't strong enough to pry it off anyway. Light from the rising sun filled the water with a delightfully greenish blue. He forced his coughing to stop and tried to keep his throat clear of water by retching it up, but afterwards desired a breath so badly that he swallowed another lungful of blood-filled water. As he thrashed against the rocks, a black ring crept towards the center of his vision. Slowly, all light faded to a speck and his mind bobbed up and down weightlessly. His jaws fell open as his chest instinctively gasped one last time, allowing a final rush of water into his lungs. The back of his eyelids turned a blackness so pervasive that it seemed to truly be a dark blue. At the center of it, a shadow spiraled out in a circle, forming a wisp of flowing strands at one side.

Steady thee, Stormwind, and float.

PART TWO

OUT OF THE PAN

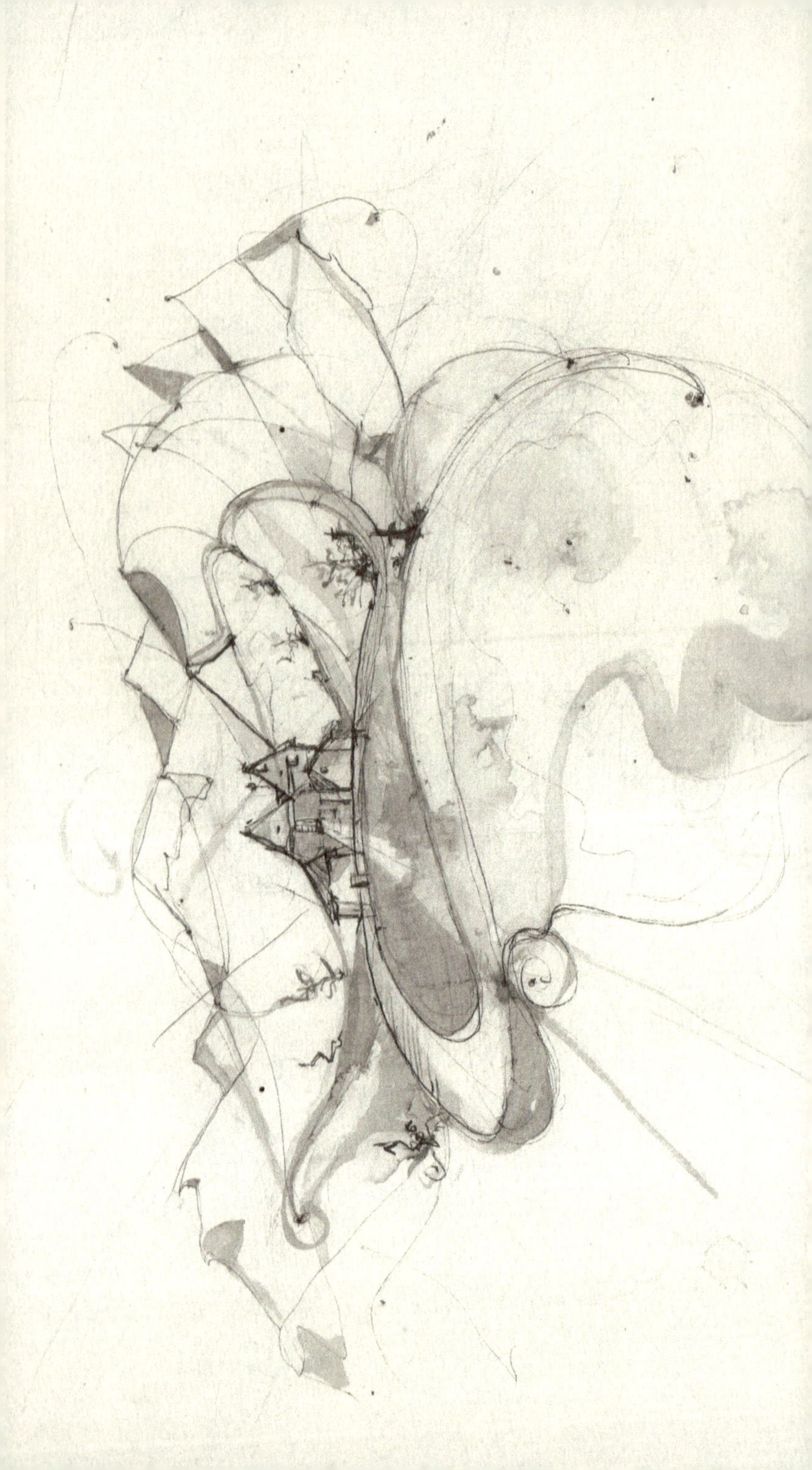

Seabreeze wafted through the basement's open doorway to greet Burgush. Even at the bottom of the stairwell, pressed tight between exposed dirt and the jail's stone walls, he could still smell the ocean. He scrunched his mask into a ball in his clenched fist. He hated it. Not only because it scratched his face every time he moved or because it blocked most of his vision and breath — but mostly because people who hide their faces are usually ashamed of what they're doing.

Burgush devoted many restless nights to figuring out why he should feel ashamed. "Why should I hide my face if I'm not doing anything wrong?" he often asked himself. At a late hour he usually decided that all killings are — on some fundamental level — wrong. Even sanctioned ones.

When he took this job, he didn't think killing criminals would get under his skin. They had, after all, done something to deserve it. But even they didn't have to wear masks. In fact, they sometimes asked if they could wear something over their head. One time a man handed Burgush a soiled, sodden potato sack — with no holes for eyes or anything — and asked him to put it over the man's head. Burgush gave him the same answer that he gave to everyone else — no.

The stairs creaked as he climbed them, passing the pit where the bodies would drop out of sight after he cut them free. Another part of the job that he despised, moving them through the dungeon and up to the death cart. Ten-stone sacks of lifeless jelly. Not to mention that they stank of unwashed wounds and crusted excrement, even when they were alive.

The mask pricked his face as he pulled it on, and it too smelled of sweat and blood. Through the frayed eyeholes, he saw a crowd — again larger than the last one. Burgush gave them a hidden smile. "They love me," he said to himself.

But another voice answered him. One that came with no teeth and no tongue — one he was fairly certain nobody else could hear, no matter how nearby they were. "No, they love what you give them," it said. "They hate you. But the tides will soon turn. This is the slackwater."

The rumbling faded as the crowd spotted Burgush. Seabird caws floated overhead, an inextricably linked portion of the Shrieksport symphony. Rain drizzled down in bursts from the outstretched fingers of a new spring storm. The breeze had cleared the coastal fog and from the gallows platform Burgush saw the entire harbor, out past the Spit, and even over the barrier island that shielded the port. Dark clouds had silently crept over the horizon, pooling their rage just offshore until they were ready to let it drop and punish whoever had been foolish enough to trust an early spring calmness.

Burgush walked to the other side of the gallows to inspect the trap mechanism. That was the half of the job that needed skill instead of only brawn and even keel towards death. This batch was typical — all human, and all male, which made it easier for him to stomach. Tripping the dropfloor for a woman or an Oruk was the type of thing that followed him home, haunting him into fitful bouts of sleep. But he still always unlocked the gear and let them fall. The crowds were half this size the last time Burgush killed an Oruk — when that voice had first come to him.

Two human guards, poised stiff with spears at their front, manned the back corners of the platform. Loops of rope hung down from the beam overhead and dangled near each prisoner's ankles. Burgush worked across the line, taking the loops and slipping them over the four slouched heads. These were not brave men. Murder and piracy required no strength in the soul. It only required a sickness — one that most humans were born with, as the voice had said.

The guards flinched as a series of cracks whipped through the air. The ropes — their slack now pulled tight — creaked and groaned as the weight at their ends swayed and twisted. But all sound, even the seabirds, was drowned underneath a raucous wave that peaked high and crashed against the gallows.

Normally, Burgush would wait a few minutes for the squirming to stop and then cut the ropes from up on the platform. However, these last few weeks had been different. He followed his new routine — the one that the crowd gathered for — and walked halfway down the stairs before stepping out onto the courtyard lawn. Under the shadow of the platform, between the wooden support pillars, he made his way to the ropes and what dangled at their ends.

Two more guards escorted four more people up to Burgush from behind. Their coughs and sickly groans — and the cutting cry of an infant — came close enough that he heard them over the crowd's roar. Burgush took a knife from his belt and pulled a body towards him. He pressed the knife against the skin on its forearm and drew down in a straight line — parting the flesh into a long, red chasm. He stepped to the side and commanded the first person in line to approach. She produced a small wooden bowl and repeated a hushed thanks as Burgush took it and held it under the arm's limp fingertips.

He did this for all of them. One bowl for each body. Lines of overcast daylight escaped through the imperfect gallows platform, striping the ground. Bits of rain fell through the cracks, too, but not enough to wash off the blood that had now coated Burgush up the elbows. More guards held the rest of the crowd back as the guests emptied their bowls down their throats. The mother held the baby's head as another helped pour the blood into its screaming mouth.

The voice returned. "This is what they cheer for, not you. Not yet."

Burgush didn't need to stay for the rest, so he didn't. He worked across the line of bodies again and cut their ropes. Crumpled heaps — streaked in red — lay in the pit as he walked down the staircase to the dungeon's open door.

"So much more blood, so much more life, gone to waste."

He ducked through the doorway, hating that it had not been designed for Oruks — though Oruks had undoubtedly hauled the large stones and beams that had built it.

"Think of all the people you'll be able to save, once they're ready. Once they love you."

He pulled the mask off his head and held it in his hands, marking the fabric with prints of blood. "But will they still love me when they know what I am?" Burgush asked.

"Yes," the voice answered, "they will have to."

He put his thumbs through the mask's eyeholes and pulled. Stitching ripped and the burlap tore apart into two pieces.

CHAPTER 15

Stinging pain streaked across Timid's face. Rocks planted into his skin like seedlings where his forehead had ground into the riverbottom. Blood ran out of his nose like it was supposed to come out of there, bringing a metallic tinge that brought memories of splintered planks and drawn knives. But nothing pressed against him anymore. He moved his neck freely as far as the pain would let him and he kicked his legs in circles. His hands drifted weightlessly with the motion of the water.

A voice called out from seemingly nowhere. "Right yourself. In my waves find lasting breath."

Timid's mouth filled with salt and the sickly feeling that comes with it. But he was done choking. The water came and went out of his throat as his lungs willed it. His nose, too, sensed saltwater and the things that smell like it.

Above him, the water's surface flowed sideways in ridges, some catching moonlight for a slight moment in time and then melding back before being replaced by an identical brother or sister, younger by mere seconds. Black picked at his toes like feeder fish did when he'd dangle his feet over the end of a dock and let them clean up the ragged edges of his calluses. A spiral shape in the water drifted nearer and nearer, inching out of the darkness. Wedges of white and wine red colored its shell like spokes on a wheel. Long, flat tendrils floated behind — or maybe in front — of its shell, some coming out of sheaths and others flowing freely along their entire length. A flat, triangular hood covered the dense mass where the tendrils came together at the shell's mouth. And at the center of it all, a rudimentary eye — more akin to a hole than a lens — watched Timid.

He had seen things like it before, only smaller — about a handspan wide. They sometimes came up in fishing nets, where they'd be chucked overboard or kept for bait. Some seafolk considered it bad luck to kill one, but the pearly lining on the inside of their shell fetched good prices for jewelry. Many ships, too, were named Nautilus. But it was most familiar to Timid and all of the Shrieking Isle as the mark of the Church of Eadron — a backwards "e" with three wavy lines streaking out to its left.

Timid wasn't sure if he could talk. His instincts didn't want him to try, but his instincts also had told him to not breathe water. After a few silent moments, words suddenly rang in his head.

"Can you see it?" the nautilus asked.

Timid looked around. The moon shone above too obviously to go unnoticed. The nautilus in front of him was just out of arm's reach, so of course he could see it. He didn't know what else he was supposed to see.

"What I took from you," the nautilus answered before he had asked.

The floating shell tilted sideways, pointing its eye downward into the darkness.

"You have floated. Now sink."

His brain told him not to. Without air, a person should swim up — not down. But the voice carried a certain confidence. Like it already knew that Timid would do it.

Timid waved his arms around and thrusted them upwards to push against the water. He didn't move. He contorted his body to point down, and then kicked his legs and pulled with his hands. He still didn't move. His hands cut through the water like it was air. Like the water moved out of the way for him. Like he wasn't really there.

The nautilus melted into the darkness below. Bringing his hands back to his side, Timid stopped kicking his feet against the water. As he stilled, his instincts crawled back and told him to fight against death. The human in him still pushed upward like a buoy held under the surface. But now there was something else, too. It tugged at his ankles, pulling downward and beckoning him to the frigid depths with a promise that he would find belonging.

And he did. He was no longer alone. Just past the reach of his fingertips, a pole jutted up out of the black. It seemed to emit a pulse of patient glee, as if it were pacing at a doorway anticipating a welcome guest. He soon found that the pole was attached to crossbars and held metal pulleys. Not much farther, and it became tangled in a web of ropes and torn cloth.

Timid's feet came to a gentle rest on a flat and hard surface. Though his vision only extended a few feet in any direction, he knew where he was. He crouched and placed his hand against a familiar surface, the same planks of wood that he'd scrubbed clean hundreds of times. They wore multiple coats of red stains, first on the outside and then again on the inside after they had splintered and tore through the flesh of his crewmates. But the deck was intact now, as if someone had picked the shreds up and put them back together.

"A man can be redeemed," the voice said, "even if men cannot be."

He didn't need to peer off the deck's edge and see the mangled corpses to know that they were there. After all, he knew where he was.

He was home.

CHAPTER 16

White sheets rolled against each other, folding into creases where the winds drove them together. Timid's eyes squinted in the brightness and he raised a hand to shield himself. His mouth spewed extra water as he breathed, devoid of the sickly salt flavor that it had held moments before.

Wet grass pressed against his back, cold and uncomfortably bumpy. Green flanked him on each side, wafting rhythmically in waves as if pushed by an invisible force. But Timid felt no breeze on his damp skin.

A sound pulsed through the forest, incessant and dull. Timid sat up on his elbows. His neck panged sharply and protested when he moved his head or shoulders too much. The grass was a bit of an oddity in the forest, though it sometimes popped up in patches where the light managed to hit the ground. But he had seen nothing like this place, a meadow under a hole in the canopy. On all sides, about a hundred feet away, stood a ring of trees — all Essai.

The sound, a familiar hum to all dockworkers and log-haulers, came from one end of the meadow. A dark shape hunched over near one of the Essai and moved its arms back and forth spastically. Its wooden hands wrapped around the handle of a giant saw, which it yanked and pushed with a grunting effort.

Timid wanted to run away from the creature while its back was still turned. Though he couldn't see its face, he knew that it was half-burnt. He could almost smell it. Just about everything smelled of fire and melting flesh the last few days. His nose didn't let him forget something so stomach-wrenching.

His spine complained as he rolled over onto his front and got his feet under him, now realizing that he wore only his shirt, trousers, and boots. His overcloak must have been lost to the rushing water or the deliberate fingers meaning to leave him helpless. And his bag remained where he left it — in a stranger's home.

Crouching low enough, he could almost hide among the grass. He scurried away from the sawing sound, squishing water out of his soaked boots. After only a few steps, he came upon a large circular chunk of wood stuck into the ground. The grain on top was flat but patterned with a rough texture. On the opposite edge, splinters stuck up like a miniature forest of their own where they had been torn away by an enormous force. He laid his hand on the surface and felt nothing but dead wood — a sawed Essai stump.

He walked around its edge, stepping over the most exposed of the roots. He tried to dash into the dark edge of the forest but again he ran into another stump. And again, he found another — this one long since grayed from being out in the elements longer, like a tombstone with its etchings eroded away.

Timid snaked his way through the rest of the meadow to the nearest Essai. It reached out to him and placed a dark cloak over his shoulders.

"Running away, are we?" a voice said from above him. It was calm, quiet, and familiar, but it startled Timid enough to make him look up sharply, sending a wash of pain down his neck again.

A large, bare branch stuck out from the side of the Essai far over Timid's head, but still much lower than any other branches. A pair of legs dangled down and kicked in a slow cadence. Above the branch sat a tangled mass of wooden sticks that looked like a person with a wolf's head. Every part of it was black as pitch, especially with the day-lit sky as a backdrop. Long arms and spindly fingers wrapped around the branch to hold itself steady as it leaned forward and looked down on Timid and spoke to him again.

"These weren't our terms, remember? I don't have to let you go. The deal's off."

Timid stared up at the wolf, taking a moment to catch his breath. But he didn't feel compelled to speak. It looked at him like Timid looked at caterpillars. They would climb all the way to the edge of a leaf, seemingly unaware of the drop beyond it. But before it would fall, Timid would stick his finger down for the caterpillar to walk onto. Sometimes he'd hold it up to his eyes and look at it, twisting his hand so it never fell off. They never spoke and never said thanks, not even after he set it down again facing away from peril.

The wolf continued. "I am a bit surprised to see you. I always try to watch as he drags the corpses into the brush. Rarely does one come back out."

"I need your help," Timid said quickly, still catching his breath.

"Yes," the wolf said, "yes, you do. But tell me, Timid, what exactly do you want?"

"I want to leave," Timid said, "I need to get out of the forest." The sawing sound still reached them here, not letting Timid forget that eventually there would be a creak and a crash and someone would come looking for him.

"Oh, is that all?" the wolf quizzed. "You'd be happy if you ran all the way out and collapsed and never woke up again? I can give you that, but I don't think that's really what you mean."

Anxiety pooled at Timid's ankles like a thick fog hugging the ground. He wanted to not be bothered, to not have his every move examined by these monsters, and to be back where he belonged — back home.

"Right now, that is what I want," Timid finally said. "I need to get away from here. Away from that thing." He looked past the tree, back to the meadow.

The wolf didn't look. "Don't worry," it said, "he hasn't noticed. And you need a better answer. All this way and you only think about yourself. I'll help you. Let's start with why you came here. Don't you have something to do?"

Timid shook his head, trying not to break under pressure. "I never found her," he said. "And nobody knows anything."

"So you choose to run, then?" the wolf pressed. "Letting others do bad things, while you save only yourself? Is that how you think of it?"

"She's probably dead," Timid barked, trying not to yell. "Like I should be. Even if she was alive, I probably couldn't save her anyway. I know nothing, I can't fight, I have a bum arm, I have no food, and I can't even start a fire."

The wolf took a moment to think, in the way that all Springs seemed to. Like it was running through options of what to say, picking out only the little pieces of information that it wanted Timid to know. Which was probably one reason why they all seemed to be hiding something. When the wolf did speak again, it said, "You're right. You can't save her."

Timid furrowed his brow, interpreting the remark as an insult. "What do you mean? You know what happened to her?"

"There is no girl," the wolf answered. "There's never been a girl here."

"What? I was sent here to find a missing girl."

The wolf sighed. "That's what many of them say. There is no girl."

Timid stammered, trying to explain himself in case the wolf was confused. "But we found her cart."

The wolf nodded. "Yes. They're getting better."

Timid swam through the memories of all the times he'd thought he was on her trail in the past few days.

The wolf interrupted, repeating itself. "What do you want, Timid?"

Emotions welled up from too many places to hold back. Death had surrounded him for months. Now that it was inside him — again — it was an infection that leaked out through any crack it could find. His hands brushed wetness off of his cheeks. "I want everything back," he stammered. "Everyone back. I see them when I close my eyes. I saw them when I died. I want them back."

"You can't have that," the wolf stated blankly. "No amount of pitch or twine can stitch a soul back together. Unless you're him." Now the wolf looked back, over its shoulder.

Timid wiped his eyes again. "What do you know about him?" he asked.

"Everything."

Timid didn't want to prod too much and overstay his welcome, but the wolf seemed willing to give answers, if only cryptically. "Is he your brother?" Timid finally asked.

"In a way," the wolf answered.

"Is the story true, then?"

"No stories are entirely true," it said. "They all get trimmed. The bad parts get cleaned up. The frightening parts get left out."

"Then why do they call you the Beast?" Timid asked. "If they already left something out, why aren't you as evil as the story makes you out to be?"

The wolf dropped down and landed softly on the forest floor, using the branch to hold some of its weight. Although the branch was over twice as high as Timid could reach, the wolf could stand upright on the ground and still hold onto it. Timid kept forgetting how big Springs could be. It walked towards him on all four limbs. Timid thought it looked more like a human imitating a wolf than a wolf itself — just enough wrong to be really, really wrong.

The wolf paused to think again, changing its expression repeatedly from curiosity to skepticism and back again.

"The Beast... I do not like that name," it said in Timid's face, oozing out a stench of decomposing mulch.

Timid backed away but eventually pressed up against another Essai. "I'm sorry," he said.

"They gave it to me," the wolf said. The odor hit Timid again and he wasn't any closer to getting used to it. "My name is Lupei."

It backed off of Timid, giving him a bit of fresh air.

"Okay. Lupei," Timid repeated. "I can call you that, if you'd like."

An odd and extended bit of silence lay between them — cut only by the grinding of metal teeth, chewing on bits of thousand-year-old wood. But Timid remembered how scared he was of that sound and what made it, and how much he wanted to be anywhere else.

"Lupei," Timid said, "what is it that you want?"

The wolf smiled, enjoying the first time that someone had asked that question in a very, very long time. "I want the same thing that you want," Lupei answered. "I want to have enough courage to do more than just watch."

"Then what should we do?" Timid asked.

"I do not know," Lupei said, "but someone will die today if we do nothing."

Timid gulped. "Me?"

"Maybe," Lupei said, "but there are others."

Timid thought of who else there might be. He hadn't seen any other humans out here by the river — and there was only one other human in Goodhaven. "What about people in Goodhaven? Are they safe?"

Lupei shook his head. "Not anymore." Lupei looked back again, towards the meadow. "They will want it to go somewhere now that they're going to let it out."

"Going to let what out?" Timid asked.

"The tree."

Timid now realized what he was talking to, and what had been walking around Goodhaven all this time. Things that belonged nowhere because they weren't a whole anything. But somewhere near the center of this wolf — and likely the others too — was someone a lot like Timid himself.

The grass in the meadow stopped its waving. The saw slowed and came to a gentle halt, but the grinding was soon replaced by a crackling sound — like a thousand bones breaking between two giant hands. Like planks snapping in the night when a mast crashes down into the water.

"You must go," Lupei whispered. "Those in the city will soon know that you lived."

"How?" Timid asked, mirroring Lupei's hushed tone.

"The grass will betray us."

When the tree fell to the ground with a booming thunder, so did the grass. One blade at a time, a final wave moved through the meadow and then through the bits of duff and leaf litter at Timid's feet.

"Timid," Lupei said, "listen to me. You must go. I will meet you there if I can."

"What are you going to do?" Timid asked.

"I don't know," Lupei answered. "Not nothing."

Timid turned and ran. Though he didn't know where he was, he knew that the river was close. He tasted invisible drops of water in the air like it was his own saliva running out from between his gums. And he ran away from it.

Timid stopped for a second to look back at Lupei. Hundreds of silhouettes stuck up against the meadow's bright burst of green, like oddly spaced posts in an abandoned shipyard. But one was different from the others. It was in the shape of a wolf — but it was not actually a wolf. With its snout raised into the air, it opened its jaws slightly and filled the forest with a winding howl. One that would greet an old, lost friend — or a brother.

CHAPTER 17

Selah stepped partially through the doorway into her women's house and pulled the door towards her body, closing her date off from the inside.

"It's not that I didn't have a good time, Grenbo, it's that I have to work in the morning."

"I believe you," Grenbo pleaded, "but I'm just getting to the good part." He hated leaving a story unfinished, especially one that had actually happened to him.

Selah shook her head. "Not my fault that you didn't talk fast enough," she said. "And you took ten minutes to set it up."

That much was true. "A story is a piece of art," Grenbo argued, "and all great art needs a frame." He pointed his finger in the air to emphasize his point, as if it was some profound sentiment.

Selah sighed and glanced over her shoulder in an effort to make her impatience obvious. A woman's life on the Isle is much different than a man's, and most men didn't understand that. Or care.

Grenbo put his hands up in front of him, palms out. "Okay, okay. Will I still see you tomorrow?"

Maybe this man wasn't so bad. "That depends, will you buy my drink again?" She flashed a smile to make it seem like a joke, though it wasn't.

Grenbo relaxed a bit. He'd been making his way well since getting a bonus for that escort assignment. "I'd be happy to," he answered. "Same time, same place?"

"Actually," Selah said, biting her lip and doing her best to seem agreeable, "can we go somewhere calmer? Not that I don't like the Cheering Giant, but they have the same drinks other places."

"Fine by me," Grenbo responded, just happy that he had done well enough to be granted a second date. "Meet here at sixth bell? I get the hint, and I'll think of somewhere that's a bit more... better."

"Sure. Goodnight." Selah closed the door slowly, with a hint of a smirk on her face.

Grenbo stood still for a moment, resting his hands on his hips. His most successful date in months. Not that he had many, but he did try. Maybe it was the new shirt.

He began the walk back to his district, absentmindedly kicking small stones and pebbles as he came across them. The street wasn't paved stone, but also wasn't entirely unmaintained like some others. An early spring storm had pelted the city in the morning, settling the dust down for the time being. The folks who studied the weather said that the storm would hit hard for a couple days then go up to the pass and freeze, delaying the boom of trade from Riverport for another week or so. The Isle's transitions between seasons could be volatile — just yesterday it was hot enough to justify the purchase of a new summer shirt. But even if the true spring hadn't arrived yet, at least he met a cute seamstress who was willing to get a drink with him.

The sunset always seemed to fall quicker on Black Tide. It caught them by surprise at the Cheering Giant, only noticing because the crowd left in a hurried mass. By the time they got to the women's house where Selah lived, it had already been dark for an hour. He was glad to not be on patrol for a Black Tide, thinking that he must have caught favor from doing the escort job. But regardless, his luck was bad enough to find himself out at night during one anyway. In addition to the universal fear of the dark that all people find heightened on a Black Tide, city folk fear the night with no moon for an extra reason — there are people, too, who use the black air as a cloak.

He kept his head down as he meandered through the streets, partly because it felt heavy from the puppy love bouncing around inside it — and partly from the Seafoam. Selah was right when she said that other places served the same drinks, but something about the Cheering Giant's taps made his favorite beer just a tiny bit better.

Ninth bell rang out in the distance, signaling a formal end to the evening and an end to the bells until sunrise. His district didn't have a belltower, so along with the abrupt change in road texture to something akin to hog slop, the weak sound of the bells told him that he neared home. His neighborhood was lower on the city's list of priorities than Selah's was, and the road showed it. Maybe they'd pull a gravel cart through next week — after they fixed the storm's damage in the nicer districts.

Small alleys etched their way between the buildings. They typically reeked of excrement, from a common understanding that it was better there than in the mainways. Because the buildings weren't arranged in a grid and varied in size and shape, it was easy to get lost in the scribbling patterns. But going through alleys was just something you had to do if you spent enough time in a shoddy district. And Grenbo patrolled them. And lived in one.

It was from an alley he was passing that he heard a thumping noise and low chatter. The city was always full of sounds of people out and about or shuffling around in their homes behind thin, uninsulated walls, but this noise was close enough so that when he glanced towards it, he could see what it came from.

Three men stood close to each other, looming over another figure slumped to the ground against the alley wall. One noticed Grenbo and patted the others on the shoulders to get their attentions. Grenbo looked past them to the shape on the ground. Its skin was unlike the others. Pale green instead of a shade of cream, with flecks of brown and black instead of one smooth tone. Its clothes had been torn in patches, and shreds hung from threads at the sleeves and collar. Blood ran from its flattened nose and several wide gashes in its lips that traced its protruding lower canines.

The three standing men stared at Grenbo. One of them turned to face the end of the alley and took a step in front of the others. Grenbo didn't move, but his mind raced and his heart pounded against the inside of his ribs.

It was none of his business. He turned his body and readied himself to leave, putting his balled fists back in his pockets. The men in the alley chuckled lightly and turned back towards the grounded Oruk.

A voice struck him suddenly, pinging against the interior of his skull.

"They'll kill him."

It wriggled out of his brainstem like a worm escaping the soil during a rainstorm.

"Think of the pain," it said.

Another sound echoed out of the alley, the slap of something hard hitting a slab of meat. Grenbo looked back to see a bloodied club and the Oruk sinking farther down against the ground. If there was one thing that Grenbo hated in this world, it was that pain — the pain of an unforgiving tool against the soft parts of the face.

He turned around and approached the end of the alley again. He wasn't even being paid to be a guard tonight. He didn't have his mailshirt on, his badge, or even his boots. His day-off shoes had been already soaked through by the piles of filth that dotted the alley's floor. Some sort of excrement squished between his toes as he took another step onward. He wasn't being paid to be a guard tonight — but nobody said he couldn't do it for free.

Grenbo walked forward so that he was halfway towards the group of men. Grenbo was about the same size as two of them, but the other loomed almost a head over him. And each weighed more than he did. He had always been skinny in school and other city guards still teased him for it.

"I think it's best you take off now," Grenbo yelled, voice stern and booming with confidence — his guard voice. "Looks like he's had enough."

The taller man, the only one with a smile, spoke first and with a slumdog accent. "Yeah? I ain't think so. Boy's gotta learn."

The shape wasn't a boy. Someone wasn't a boy just because he lost a fight three-against-one. Or because of his race.

"Just get on out of here and I won't report you. Leave it at this." Grenbo used this line often, but it rarely worked. There was no way to report someone and make it stick, it just put the guards on notice that a crime had happened.

It didn't work this time either. They weren't big talkers, apparently. One of the underlings had a club, the other just put his fists up. Fighting two on one wasn't all that bad. People are usually scared of getting hit, if not the first time then definitely the second. Hit first, move back, then take on the one that you hadn't hit yet while the other put his hand to his face. If someone had a blunt weapon like a club, get as close as possible so they can't use it. Usually it was the hit you didn't see coming that put you out. Grenbo had seen a man die from an unseen punch to the side of the head, or really from the smack on the ground that came right afterwards.

He led with a kick this time, just trying to push the club-wielding man back out of range for a moment while he jabbed at the other. The thug was a bit heavier than he'd hoped and the kick didn't move him much, so Grenbo didn't have a lot of space before he was rushed again. But things broke down predictably. He fought two-against-one several times a month in training, sometimes on one side, sometimes on the other. City guards were basically professional fist-fighters.

People never expected elbows. They hit hard and suddenly, and worked well with no room to move, like when your back is against a wall and your hands are covering your head. He landed one on the man with the club, but the other man took the opportunity to grab Grenbo by the shirt and throw him towards the middle of the alley, near the tall man.

They all stopped moving. The man he'd elbowed nursed a broken lip. Then, light began to fill the alley. Starting off dim, a red glow bounced between the alley walls — bathing all five men in a deep firelight.

Now that the moonlight wasn't alone, Grenbo could see the Oruk on the ground more clearly. Patterns of brown and black on his skin — arranged roughly like handprints — peeled back to ooze pus and blood. The stench of burnt flesh floated its way into Grenbo's nose. It wasn't the same color as man flesh, but apparently it burned the same.

He turned to look down at the source of light, a budding fire resting in the tall man's palm. Flaming sludge dripped down off the man's fingertips and fell to the ground, splashing and fizzling against the wet alley floor.

Footsteps approached Grenbo from behind, squishing into the muck.

The voice returned. "I'm sorry," it said. "I should have chosen you."

CHAPTER 18

A whisper crawled throughout the city this afternoon like a wildfire. Children ran home to their parents, or to their friends' parents, and spread the news like little firebugs. It consumed everyone within an hour.

And so everyone started to prepare. Some Springs gathered green branches and bright flowers to weave into wreaths and headdresses, others crafted torches to light the streets in the evening — something only to be done on special occasion.

For Lepori, this meant a hectic day. Mushrooms to bring to the gate, buckets of water to fill. But it was a happy day, too. A day to celebrate that everybody in Goodhaven would get a new friend.

He pulled his cart over to his stall at the square. People crisscrossed the streets everywhere, making travel sporadic and slow. Groups of rebellious and contrarian children caused even more disruption — throwing bird seed into crowds, stealing food off of carts, or just avoiding the ceremony altogether and causing their parents to worry. But their chaos brought a certain charm, and Lepori had been like that once, too.

"Did you hear?!" a high-pitched voice called out right behind him.

He turned to see a small rodent with eager eyes looking over the front of his stall.

"There's someone coming," she said, mouth open and out of breath. She had certainly been running around telling everyone she knew, regardless of how obvious it already was.

Lepori smiled back. "Yes, Cherry. It's very exciting."

Many Springs came home early from the fields to be with their families and friends on these days. Lepori wanted to beat the rush and set up in a spot where he could see the action, not just the backs of people's heads.

"Cherry," he said, "would you like to help me?"

"Oh yes, yes!" she answered, literally jumping at any opportunity to take part.

"Can you grab that pale," he pointed, "fill it with water, and meet me at the gate?"

She took it and darted off, into the shuffling crowd. "I wonder if she knows how much water weighs?" Lepori joked to himself. But keeping one like Cherry busy was a good thing, whether or not the task was possible. Boredom eats discipline from the inside out.

The sun bled orange into the sky by the time Lepori found a prime location for his cart. Lighted torches popped up in hands of adults and in doorways to homes, lining the streets and alleys, letting the sun know that it could fall all the way down — that this Black Tide wouldn't be completely dark. The sun took the hint, and went over the edge of the world.

He saw Cherry working through the crowd towards him — without the bucket. It would have been a good time, too. His water was dirty and he didn't want to leave things unattended to get more. Customers parted as Cherry appeared at the cart, bug-eyed and obviously full to bursting with some type of news.

"They want me to be the flower girl!" she yelled. "The flower girl! I was talking to Mrs. Jenni and she said they hadn't found one yet and said I could do it! Isn't that amazing?" She talked fast enough that if Lepori hadn't known her, he wouldn't have understood a word.

"Wow," he said, playing up his excitement, "that's something, Cherry. Congratulations, you're a very important person now."

"They said that I go out first and everything. And I'll be right at the front when they open the gate."

Lepori smiled earnestly at her. "That's wonderful. What kind of flowers?"

"I don't know," she was confused at why it would matter, "big ones!"

Then she was off again, into the dark figures that crowded the gate. And sure enough, when the guards eventually pushed people back to make room, Cherry stood there alone with a basket overflowing with pink and red petals. Roses.

"Where do we go from here, Timid?" he said to himself. Once again, he questioned how heroes always knew where to go, and what that implied about him.

His breath fogged the air as he rested his hands down on his knees and panted. Early spring days could be warm and pleasant, especially in the sun. But the nights could still grip you with an icy chill — so tightly that the unsheltered might never wake up the next morning.

Goodhaven's walls loomed over him. He had used the footpath for most of the way, once he had found it — which was only possible in the daylight. But now that was gone. In the new sheet of fallen darkness, a dim fireglow bouncing off the clouds was the only thing he could see by. The stars hid behind their blanket, and the moon didn't even have to hide — it wasn't there.

He wondered to himself, "Is Black Tide better or worse behind those walls?"

The guards outside of the gate could probably see him if they knew where to look. But they were distracted — the gate opened, shedding a bright patch of firelight onto the road.

And the guards weren't alone. Behind them, a gathering crowd murmured and held lit torches. One Spring gripped a large green headdress, another hugged a basket of apples. A rodent Spring — this one small, young, and straight out of a fairy tale — emerged from the crowd and walked forward. She carried a basket of flower petals and began sprinkling them gently over the ground, working her way back and forth to give it an even coat.

When she finally retreated, nothing else happened. Everyone stood unmoving in the rain, with a patience that gave no tell of when it might break.

Timid cut wide around the gate to avoid the little cluster of homes that lay around the city's edge and the Springs that might see him from inside. Eventually, the forest came to a halt as it met the open fields that surrounded the city on every other side. He used a low-hanging tree as an umbrella while he studied Goodhaven's walls. They appeared black against the orange-tinted air and thankfully the ramparts on top showed no pacing shadows. But their bark felt slippery to the touch.

Even if he had full use of his injured arm, he couldn't have climbed it. Though the cut on his left forearm wasn't festering —

a gift of luck — it hadn't been getting much better over the last two days. An intense stinging still prevented him from closing his left hand into a full fist. But sometimes the pain distracted him from his stomach's incessant rolling. The few mushrooms he had foraged didn't do much to soften the next wave of hunger.

He stared up towards the top of the wall for some time — letting rain hit his face and even drip into his mouth — until he felt a sudden fear. Like a noose slipped over his head, fear tightened sharply and choked the breath out of his throat.

Behind him, a soft crunching sound inched its way closer. Footsteps and a tall lanky shadow moved among the trees and the falling water. It, too, was a tree — and it was also a wolf. But just as much so, it was neither of those things.

The rain fell off of Lupei's body from all the overhanging bumps and grooves that covered his surface. Timid wiped the water from his brow and greeted his newest friend. "I'm happy that it's you, Lupei."

Lupei smiled. "I am too, Stormwind."

Lupei walked on all fours, gently stepping over and around the wet obstacles on the forest floor. He didn't look at Timid any longer than he looked at other things. His eyes tracked the city walls up to the top, where he too checked for guards.

"What happened?" Timid asked.

"A lot," Lupei answered. Timid knew by now that Springs usually talked at a glacial pace, but Lupei didn't indicate that he would say more.

So Timid summarized the results of his brainstorm so far. "I'm afraid that if I try the other gate, they'll recognize me."

"They will," Lupei answered. "But you should get moving, the grass will tell on us soon. Do you know where he is?"

"Barend? No," Timid said, not giving himself enough credit. "Not for sure, but I have an idea. Bloody seawitch, he better not be passed out. I'll need time to find him. And to get out."

"I can't make time," Lupei quipped. "But I can make them forget about you, for a moment." His voice strained with every sentence, and when he sat on the ground next to Timid, he looked to truly need the rest — even more so than Timid.

"That'll be just fine," Timid said, "but I have no idea how I'm going to get over this wall."

Lupei tilted his head and looked sideways at Timid. "Over?"

CHAPTER 19

Waiting in the open night air is one thing, and waiting in the rain is another. Just a few weeks earlier, it might have frozen where it landed. Or even before it landed. Even being on the warmer, northern side of the mountains wasn't enough to escape winter on the Shrieking Isle.

This storm didn't deliver lightning and fire — too cold and early for that. Those were the storms to fear for a Spring, not the ones that brought frost. Luckily, the forest floor was bare enough to snuff out any flame that tried to shatter the darkness. But sometimes treetops do catch flame and leave behind leafless patches of death — like woodpeckers do to some older, slower Springs.

The crowd stared outward at the fan of light that escaped beyond the gate. The rose petals caught the light well, making a glowing walkway for their guest. Any minute now, and a Spring should appear out of the shadows and be showered in gifts of décor, food, and friendship.

Raindrops fizzled on the tops of torches, which had burnt down to a low flame in the hour since they'd been dipped in oil and set alight. The children grew anxious. Some asked to go inside and a few parents had already given in. The same thing happened on starfalls, with most children not staying long enough to catch a glimpse of even one of Celesta's tears. He first met Cherry during one such starfall. With no folks of her own, she picked a spot next to Lepori and talked his ear off for several hours.

"Why is she sad?" Cherry had asked.

"I don't know," Lepori had honestly answered. "Some think it means that she's lost someone."

For a moment, Cherry sat silently — finally — and then said, "I hope she finds them."

That memory was pleasant. Unlike so many others. Ones about loneliness, about being scared. Or about death, about laying traps and lies. If Lepori thought about it too hard, he'd turn tonight into one of those memories. So he didn't think, and made tonight about life — about a new start for someone who'd learn to appreciate it.

He heard the murmur roll through the crowd before he saw anything. People nudged others and pointed out into the night. And then a scream. And then more screams and other sounds of panic. A wall of bodies pushed against him and attempted to scatter, but ran up against the ones at the back who didn't yet know what was going on. Guards shouted orders at each other, apparently trying to get the gate closed. The chaos parted around Lepori's cart, letting him peek through moving bodies at what they ran from. It was large and walked on all fours, but its body was like a human's. It most certainly was a Spring, and it also most certainly wasn't. Its surface seemed to be covered in a shiny layer of pitch or tar. It had the head of a wolf, and a foamy spit dripped from its jowls onto the ground — where pink and red blossoms were trampled by black hands, claws, and feet.

"The feet," Lepori thought to himself. Not long ago, Timid had told him about a set of peculiar footprints. But the excitement of today — the belief that everything had actually gone right — had pushed that concern to the back of everyone's mind. They thought they were rid of it, that it was just a scare — until now. They all knew who it was as soon as they saw it, even before the first person screamed out, "The Beast!"

Odek tapped his fingers on the Oxenstone's counter in an impatient tick. This evening was bound to bring him a wheelbarrow's worth of tree rings, some even passing through his door for the first time. But nay, the Oxenstone had only one customer — who was fast asleep.

The ruckus usually broke around this time, releasing a horde of ale-thirsty partygoers to the surrounding businesses and — most importantly — Goodhaven's most comfortably-curated pub. Tonight, however, the new Spring was running late.

A shout sounded from outside and Odek turned to see a wasp Spring shove the door open and stumble inside.

"Ay," Odek yelled, "what's the rush?"

The wasp slammed the door shut and leaned on it as if to seal out a strong wind. "The fest broke," the wasp yelled back, "you've got to lock up."

Odek vaguely recognized the wasp — as Goodhaven had only a few — but it wasn't one of his regulars. Which made it odd that he came to the Oxenstone, of all places, in such a rush.

"And you'll be the first locked out," Odek said. He flung his washrag over his shoulder and strode out from behind the bar.

The wasp stayed put. "I'm serious," it said. "They're saying it's the Beast!"

"*The Beast?*" Odek mocked. He stuck his arms out and regarded his surroundings. "Last I checked, my tavern's behind the walls, not outside of them." He grabbed the door handle. "Now you either get out, or get away from the door and show me enough rings for a drink."

"I'm serious, Odek," it said.

So the wasp did know him. "I'm serious too," Odek said. "I need either paying customers or no customers."

The wasp looked across the room to the occupied chair by the hearth. "What about him?" it asked. "You throwing him out too?"

"That chair's as much his as it is mine by this point," Odek said calmly.

The wasp took his shoulder off of the door. "If you're not locking up, I don't want to be here anyhow. But you should be careful, brother." It pointed at Barend. "The Beast might be after him."

Before the door closed behind the wasp, Odek saw a few torches darting around in the dark. It was still sprinkling, but the rainstorm was apparently short and mostly over with.

Odek looked at Barend. Small, defenseless, human. Surely an object of desire — or at least of interest — for the Beast. And for Odek, a friend. What was the price of friendship nowadays? A few rings' worth of ale a day? Keeping the only woodstack in the city? Brooding stares from other oxen who walked only with their own? Or was it more, a price repaid in only blood or sap?

He tapped the bearded man's shoulder and found it spongy to the touch. A forgotten feeling by now, only ever refreshed by the small chance that they would accidentally brush fingers when trading currency at the bar. When Barend didn't stir, Odek shook the chair. Life stoked up out of Barend, as if Odek had instead blown breath onto a bed of hot, ashy coals.

Barend's arms stretched upwards and he looked blinkingly at Odek.

"Mornin'," Barend mumbled.

Odek mumbled back. "Good morning, Barend."

Barend looked into his empty cup. "About time then, eh?" he asked.

"Actually, no." Odek crouched down to his heels and put his arm on the back of Barend's chair. "There's something wrong with the fest. You might want to go home."

Barend's eyes turned quizzical — no doubt helped by the daily three pints. "Home? You're just making up excuses, O. Just ask me like a man." Barend leaned down to put his boots on. "Or, I guess, like an ox."

"You don't have to go," Odek said. "Just makin' you awares, as you'd say." Odek moseyed across the room to the back door and exited through it.

Barend sat in silence. Head swimming, eyes heavy. It didn't seem that late, and the sitting room wasn't chocked full of other — more paying — patrons. Or any other patrons, for that matter.

Odek soon returned, as always, with a few split pieces of log. He stacked them half-gently in the fireplace, then picked up the metal grate laying next to it and set it in front of the opening. The chair next to Barend groaned in a familiar way as it accepted Odek's heavy burden.

Barend leaned forward to rest his cheek on his fist. "Can you even remember how long it's been?" Barend asked.

"Been since what?" the ox tried to clarify.

138

"Since we've been here," Barend said.

Odek shook his head. "I don't remember much."

"That boy the other day, he had these coins," Barend said. "Remember them?" He took one of the triangular coppers out of his pocket and thumbed its corners. "You and I would work all morning at the vineyard — on those hot days — just to get paid one each. We'd buy a sweet cream and go down to the river and nurse it with our feet in the water."

"Mmm," Odek grunted, "and talk about girls."

Barend sighed. "I miss girls," he said quietly.

"Me too."

After a while, the fire put itself into a fitful sleep. And so did Barend. The rain stopped and the outside chatter faded into calmness. The chair beside him stirred him awake, with the sound of someone leaving it. Then a door opening, the one that led to the firewood. Then a voice, soft at first but growing urgent.

"Barend," it said. Probably a dream, something that would eventually reveal itself if he ignored it.

But it continued, and cursed at him. "Hey, Barend… God damnit… Barend!"

He nudged his eyes open and looked at the window. There was a face, too. A familiar one, that he had just been thinking about. The face that gave him the coins. Barend waved.

Timid beckoned Barend over, but the urgency was lost in translation. Barend stayed put and only shouted in response. "Ay, what in hell's name are you doing out there?" he yelled. "C'mon in, door's open."

Timid shushed him, which failed just the same.

Barend put on a quizzical look. "What's got a hold of you, eh?" He rose from his chair and approached the window.

"We need to go," Timid whispered. "Please, I came to get you out of here."

"Lad, it's not that late," Barend said. "Come have a pint, eh?" Barend reached the window and looked like he might try to pull Timid through it. "O's in a good mood t'night, might let you put your head under the tap."

"No, Barend," Timid said sharply. "I'm serious. We have to go, we're in danger."

Now that Barend was right up close, he could see that between words and after sentences, Timid's teeth chattered against each other.

"You're frigid, mate," Barend said aloud as he realized it. "Get in, O's gonna stoke the fire back up."

"No, nobody can see me," Timid spouted.

"Huh?" Barend didn't follow. "I can see you right now."

Timid couldn't tell if he was joking and didn't appreciate the stubbornness either way. "No, mate, I'm not supposed to be here. They can't find me."

Something in that managed to seep its way into Barend's skull. Odek had said that something went wrong with the fest, and here was a strange man trying to get him to crawl out of a window.

"Lad, don't worry about O," Barend said calmly. "Come in, before someone else sees you out there. We'll take care of these things."

And something in that sounded right to Timid, too. The way Barend talked about the ox Spring, calling him O. Like the time in his life when he let someone — just one person — call him Tim.

Timid planted his hands on the sill and hopped up until he teetered over the edge, face first. Barend did little to soften the fall, mostly for a lack of trying. At the same time, the back door opened and a load of chopped firewood clattered against the floor.

"Ay! Who's that?" Odek yelled, half surprised and half out of frustration that yet another person was hastily making their way into his tavern.

Barend turned and pointed at the front door. "Put the bar up, O."

Odek stepped forward with a dismissive wave of his hands. "No, no, no," Odek said, "not in here. He's got to get out."

"Look, O," Barend barked, "he's freezin' his tackle off."

Odek flustered for a moment then huffed and did as Barend said, placing a large plank of wood through two latches across the doorframe. Barend led Timid over to the raised hearth and pushed him to sit. Warmth spread over Timid's backside, as if he had been dipped into a hot bath. His wet clothes clung to his skin with perseverance, but the hearth carried enough heat to pierce them. Returning with some of the dropped firewood, Barend moved the grate out of the way and stoked a flame back to life.

Barend and Odek exchanged glances. They looked ashamed, Timid thought. Obviously they hadn't expected him, but there was something else, too. Something — as of yet — unspoken.

"Did you lie to me?" Timid asked, still with his head pointed at the ground, watching water drip from his hair into a messy pool on the floorboards.

"No," said Barend.

"Yes," said Odek.

Barend glared over his shoulder. "Well, in a way. Nothing I said to you was false, though."

"But you knew what would happen," Timid stated.

"We didn't know for sure," Barend said, shaking his head. "Not everybody even comes back at all. And I told you not to go, I remember that."

"I'm not angry, Barend," Timid interjected. "You couldn't have told me everything."

They were silent for a moment, until a deeper voice cut in. "What happened?" Odek asked.

Timid started talking. And talking. Telling them the truth about the Beast — about Lupei — and Rute. And the drowning. Eventually Odek had another question. "How did you get into the city? The gates were closed, weren't they?"

"Yes," said Timid. "Well, sort of. But Lupei went to distract everyone and I swam under through the creek."

The other two heads both recoiled slightly. Barend tried to clarify. "The creek?"

"The one that goes under the wall," Timid said. "There's metal bars to keep stuff out, but I fit through them."

"Oh, that's not a creek, mate," Barend said flatly. "That's the poop trench."

"Uh…" Timid stammered, "excuse me? There's a river of water going under the wall and there's a little cutout for it."

Barend stifled a fit of laughter. Odek kept it together better, but only slightly.

"Aye," Barend said, "that just fills up with water when it rains, it'll dry out by summer." Timid still looked lost, so Barend explained more. "The farmers who have animals put the extra poop in there."

"It's where I throw my rotten food," Odek said.

"Aye, and it's where I throw my poop," Barend followed.

Timid remained confused, as he didn't notice anything strange about the water — and because it was just weird enough to be hard to understand. "But why have it go through the wall?" he asked.

"So the farmers can take what we put in," Odek answered. Barend nodded.

Timid tried to put it past him and reroute the conversation back on track. It wasn't that big of a deal after all, he hadn't swallowed any. But Barend and Odek began jibbing at each other. Joking, pointing at Timid. Plugging their noses, waving their hands. They really broke when they remembered that Timid wanted to leave the city and would have to go back through it.

"And you know what they say," Barend made a pointing gesture, "what goes in, must come out."

Timid, too, finally smiled. He let them go for a bit, and then finally interrupted. "Barend, I don't know why you're laughing."

"Hehe, why's that, mate?" Barend asked. "It's funny."

Timid spread his arms out. "Because you're coming with me."

CHAPTER 20

When you really need to convince someone of something — when there's an emergency — you can take a certain tone. It means that there isn't any extra time, that action needs to be taken now and the details can be explained when calmness comes again.

Unfortunately, people are reluctant to appreciate an emergency after an evening of beer and a conversation about sewage diving. So that's partly why Barend took a little longer to understand that he, too, had to leave.

Something else wasn't spoken of, however, because of who was in the room with them. The same fate that they ran from sat in a well-worn wooden chair, leaning forward and staring into a small bed of orange firebrands as if it were a painting of a homely seascape or a lost loved one. If you watch this thing for time enough, you'll notice that its leaves, buds, and branches flex and compress in a slow rhythm. And much like a mountain to a mouse — it will remain long after Timid and Barend are gone from this world.

The only thing left to be had was a goodbye between the two old companions. They embraced — for the first time in ages. If Odek needed any extra convincing that letting Barend go live a mortal life was the right choice, feeling his friend's soft flesh against his own hard, scratchy limbs was the final ingredient.

As they set off, Timid asked how they might sneak about the city safely.

"There's a few back alleyways," Barend said. "I know my way around them in the dark well enough by now. We oughta be fine."

"Okay," Timid nodded. "Have you got the coals?" he asked Odek.

The ox retrieved a small kettle full of smoldering left-over fire and handed it to Timid. "As long as it doesn't get soaked or snuffed," Odek directed, "it should stay hot enough to puff back up."

"Thanks, mate," Timid said. The warm kettle against his hands reminded him of the hot bowl of stew that Odek had just fed him. It had been Timid's first real meal in over a day and the warmth had seeped through the clay bowl to make his fingers tingle their way out of stiffness. And just as kindly — without being asked — Odek scrounged together a couple sacks to sling over their shoulders, full of bread and plump waterskins. Timid gave the giant, lumbering ox a friendly nod. "Thanks for everything."

Odek returned the gesture. "Just take good care of him. He's like a dog, more than anything." They looked at Barend, who was fiddling with something on the ground. "If there's ever another time or another place," Odek said, "I'd like to meet you again, Stormwind."

"I'd like that too," Timid said.

"You think that's what I'd be?" Barend asked suddenly, in an uncharacteristically pensive tone. "A dog?"

"Maybe," Odek answered. "Or a pig. Better than an ornery ol' ox, anyhow."

Timid turned and stepped off into the black night behind the Oxenstone, giving Barend and Odek a final, small shred of privacy. The last moment in a friendship can be tender — and Timid had a fire to start.

Lepori took longer than normal to slug his way back to his house, pulling the cart through muddy, rutted roads.

A wheezing breath came from somewhere in the shadows, and then a Spring who looked almost exactly like him stepped into the alley. The shape of its face — much like its voice — was ragged, unwelcome, and unmistakable.

"Where is he?" Rute asked, out of breath as if he had just finished a sprint, which he likely had.

"I don't know," Lepori said sharply. "There's a lot going on. But I'm sure you had something to do with that."

Rute nearly shouted back. "Then where is the other one?"

Lepori stepped down the stairs to close the distance and allow smaller voices. "The other human?" Lepori clarified. "I have no idea, I don't watch him. He might be at the saloon. Or at home."

"Take me there," Rute said, "his home. Now"

"I can, sure. It's not far." Lepori turned away. "Let me put my cart in back."

"Now!" Rute shouted.

Lepori whipped his head around. "You're not in charge of me, you know. I don't owe you anything."

Rute lunged at Lepori and grabbed at his neck, yelling, "You owe me everything!"

They fell to the ground in a tangled mass, but Lepori landed on top. He pried the fingers from his throat and pinned Rute's arms to the ground.

"You think I asked for this?" Lepori spit the words out of his mouth. "I begged for my life!" Lepori stood up, surprised at how weak of a fight Rute had put up. "Not everyone remembers. But I do. Clean up your own mistakes. I'm done."

Lepori climbed the short steps to his house, leaving his cart and the half-faced rabbit on the ground.

"Your house is this close?" Timid asked. "Why not just live with Odek at the tavern?"

Barend shook his head. "O doesn't live there. He has his own place."

While that might have been true enough, Timid also sensed a social pressure. Timid couldn't guess why Springs created norms about where humans should live if they had only one.

"You're sure you're okay with this?" he asked again.

Barend laughed. "Why not? I'm not going to need it anymore. I'll get my things out first."

The kettle still puffed a little bit of heat and smoke out its top, which Timid left ajar so the flame wouldn't snuff itself to sleep.

They came around a final corner, Barend first and Timid on his heels, to find the tiniest little hut that Timid had ever seen. Only one wall was upright and the other slanted to the ground like the canvas on a lean-to. Both ends were open, and Barend could only stand up straight if he kept his head poking up into the top of the triangular space inside. A mess of blankets and bundles marked where Barend slept, tucked down into the small corner where the slant met the ground. Barend stuck his hand into one of few makeshift trunks and crates that held some belongings at the hut's far end. Barend produced a shiny object, put it to his mouth, and puffed his cheeks to make a perky cascade of sound.

"A harmonica?" Timid asked, more out of shock than actual confusion.

"Aye," Barend said, "the neighbors hate it! But I'll bet we won't have that problem in a short bit, eh?"

Timid smiled. "No, I guess not."

Barend shook some dirt and dust off of a pair of blankets and stuffed them over the top of their sacks. Sleep would be hard to come by for plenty of reasons, but they'd want the warmth whenever they tried for it. Winter was holding on much longer than it should have, and that meant unpleasant nights until it was truly gone.

They set to figuring out how best to start the fire. But they found dampness in every crack and crevice.

"If we manage to light the bottom corner here," Timid said, "it should crawl up. The logs aren't quite soaked through."

"Aye," Barend answered, toiling his beard and appearing deep in calculation. "But it's damn muddy. Rain just runs straight down in there. Maybe we could put something underneath?"

"Like a board or something," Timid said, and looked at the crates holding Barend's things. "How about something off one of those?"

"Hmm?" Barend looked confused.

"It's wood, Barend. Wood burns."

"Ooh, good eye." Barend walked over and emptied one of the crates on the ground. The sides were crisscrossed with small boards, almost the perfect size for kindling. Though it was glued and nailed together, a few minutes of stomping and pulling sufficed to rip the planks apart under Barend's bootheel.

"We just need a bit of tinder now, eh?" Barend said.

They could gorge the blankets, but then nights would be cold — maybe even too cold. Barend had no paper or books, and travel clothes were firehardy wool.

"Nothing around is dry," Timid pointed out.

"Blow on some moss or something?" suggested Barend. "Air it out?" He walked away for a moment, presumably to a neighbor's house, and came back with strips of bark and a tiny bit of tree moss called old man's beard — both soaked.

"Moss is almost always wet," Timid said. "I don't think people use it too much for fires."

"I think they use this stuff. It hangs up off the ground." Barend displayed the old man's beard — which was practically a small, green version of his own facial hair situation.

Whatever the difference might have been, the rain had erased it. It was all too wet, even after they rung it out and blew air over it. The only thing they succeeded at was turning their own hands frigid. And Timid's left hand could barely close anyway, the wound had taken bad. He had been ignoring it and hoping infection wouldn't come, but the sewage diving rejuvenated his fears.

Timid tried to put some of the old man's beard — the moss kind — inside the kettle to see if it would catch, but it fizzed and melted with almost no flame. They sat for a moment and tried to scrounge up some dead, dry grass and twigs from inside Barend's hut, but it was mostly bare earth. Barend fashioned a pyramid of the crate kindling on top of the leftover crate bottom, leaving a little hole where they could reach in and dump the coals.

"I've never been much of a firestarter," Barend admitted, "but that looks like how they do it."

Timid agreed. He'd never been the one to start his fires. Swait or the guards started them on the way in, and Lepori started the one when they first met.

"That man I told you about," Timid said, "the one I came here with, that died. He could start fire out of nothing." Timid snapped his fingers. "Like that."

"Some just have the touch for it," Barend said, missing the imagery.

Timid shook his head, "No, Barend. I mean it. He did it without any tinder. Out of thin air. It's how I escaped the wolves."

"You mean like magic?" Barend's eyes and tone were skeptical.

"Yes, like magic." Timid held the tinder in his hands and stared at it.

Barend sat still for a few seconds, then snorted and got to his feet.. "Well I reckon if he were here, we'd be in a different boat altogether. No use wondering about what ain't be. We're surrounded by magic anyway, aren't we? That's what's hunting us."

Timid largely ignored him, lost in his thoughts. As far as he knew, there were no rules for magic. Sometimes fairy tales liked to put their own spin on it, but no two were ever the same. You just had it or you didn't. Men could make fire, Oruks could mend their wounds. A few stories here and there spoke of other things, but right now Timid needed fire. Unfortunately, it usually came to Stridelong's most pious — kings, priests, and holy warriors. And Swait for some reason.

Growing up as a seafolk, Timid never went to the Church of Stridelong more than he had to for school and the occasional free meal from the soup kitchen. Though Stridelong is the god of all human spirits, seafolk have long attached themselves to Eadron instead — viewing the sea as their lifeblood and to whom they gift their destinies. Timid cursed himself for that now. What good had Eadron ever done for him, Timid thought. Let his friends drown? But then again, Timid was still here — and something had made sure of that. Twice.

Barend stopped moving — Timid noticed that much. But Timid didn't notice that Barend was staring right at the bundle of moss and tinder in Timid's hands.

"Tim … how did you do that?" Barend asked.

Timid looked up, snapped out of his wandering thoughts. "Do what?"

Barend crouched down and touched the bundle in Timid's palms. "It's dry," Barend said. He was right. The moss had curled in on itself, the bark and twigs were dry and crispy. "What did you do to it?" he asked quickly.

"I don't know … nothing." Timid looked down at his hands. They were vaguely wet, as if he had just gotten out of a bath or a swim but had already toweled off.

Barend picked at the sticks. "You sucked the water out!"

"Uh, I didn't suck anything," Timid insisted.

"Yeah, you did," Barend said, "you sucked it bone dry."

Timid stood up. "Oi, let's not put it that way," he said. "I don't know what happened."

Barend motioned at the kettle. "Hurry, pour the coals in."

Timid grabbed the container and poured them into the center of their little pyramid. Barend came over and piled the dry tinder in the middle of it all, then puffed his cheeks and blew a strong harmonica-player-breath over them and made orange out of black and white.

Light filled the hut and long shadows filled the clearing surrounding it. Heat licked the larger pieces of wood and carried a black corrosion up to the underside of the roof. The warmth tempted Timid's fingers and toes and tried to drive the wetness out of them. He wanted nothing more than to pull up a seat and bake the parts of him that had been cold all day, but that would defeat the urgency of all other things.

"What now?" Barend asked, his face covered in a flickering wash of yellow.

Timid smiled again. "We go swimming."

CHAPTER 21

Something caught Rute's eye as he slinked from shadow to shadow — a flicker of movement and a speck of light. He snuck down the alleys towards it and found something more akin to a beacon than a torch. Flamelight filled the ground between the buildings and turned the walls anything but black.

Others had noticed now, too. Shouts rang out one after another, causing a cascade of awareness and movement. He arrived too late to see who had set it, but the loose ends were easy to put together. It was only a few minutes old and the fire had much more to burn before it put itself out. A distraction, no doubt. But a threat would only work on those who had something here to lose, not strangers.

The way out of here was obvious — the wall wasn't far and Rute could see its silhouette towering over the houses. It hadn't stopped him on the way in and wouldn't stop him on the way out, not even with a body slung over his shoulder.

"You know, you'd think we could smell it," Barend said. "I sure can smell you."

Timid didn't respond — the jokes were incessant and if you responded to one, it just meant more would be fair game. He kept his eyes to the Black Tide's smothering darkness, trying to figure out where exactly the trench might be. Firelight had left them by now, the alleys only visible by stray torchlight and dark contrasts. Once, they had come up to one of the main streets — a sign that they were lost and close to being caught. But they were near the wall again, and getting so close to freedom that Timid thought he could taste it — though here that might not be a good taste.

Now with the sun gone for an hour or so, the air fully let go of its heat. Timid pulled the blanket tight over his shoulders, dreading the thought of disrobing and wading through the water again.

"I just want to get out of here," Timid said. "Let's keep moving."

"Wait, Timid," Barend said as he grabbed Timid's shoulder. "We're going the wrong way."

Smoke filled the air as the wind turned on them, and the smell of char whispered that the fire was only around the corner. If they looked down the right alleyway, a tiny bit of light still flickered on the walls — but with no giant flashes of bright yellow.

"Damn it!" Barend let his voice get loud.

Timid shushed him, and Barend's eyes grew wide in embarrassment as they heard boards creak on a rooftop behind them.

A great thud shook the ground behind them, and the two men spun to see something that was definitely not a man — or a woman or an Oruk. It uncurled itself and stood up straight, bringing its one-eared head up as a shadow against the night sky.

It didn't pause to speak, it only lunged at them. They pushed off each other and split down two opposite alleys. For some reason, Timid expected it to go after him. But it followed Barend, who must have also expected it to go after Timid — because Barend wasn't running.

"Run!" Timid yelled, hoping to prod Barend's brain out of surprise and into action.

Barend turned in a rush and slipped on the ground, his legs kicking faster than the ground would give him traction. Rute almost reached him before he got solid footing and took off.

Around the corner, the hut lay crumbled and dotted in small flames. It had collapsed in on itself, snuffing out most of the fire. Barend ran around it and up against a dead end at his neighbor's wall. The Spring stopped with the fire between them — and now in the light, Barend saw that it was a rabbit, and that half its face was burned black. Timid appeared behind it and stopped too, huffing for breath.

To Timid, the firelight lit only Barend and left Rute as a silhouette flanked by waves of heat and flame. Rute took a step toward Barend that sent a burst of panic through Timid.

"No! Me!" Timid screamed. "Remember me?!"

Rute did nothing but take another step.

So Timid ran — he planted his feet into the soft, wet ground and dashed forward. And if you were there, you could tell that this was not the Timid of old — the one that had drowned. Or the one that had lied his way back to the mainland to escape the noose. Or the one that had left his guide to die in the dark. Because this time, he ran towards his friend.

Rute turned and swung an arm behind him, brushing Timid away like a fly. But Timid felt like he fell off a cliff, and his next feeling was hitting a wall. The next memory, him stumbling to his feet. But time had passed, and Rute now cornered Barend and reached out a hand to take him.

Timid tried to yell but only coughed up smoke and blood. The fire still lay in its bed, almost to sleep. It was night, after all — they should all be sleeping. But it is when we defy the things we should be doing that stories are made.

Timid crawled to his feet and limped around the fire. Rute looked over his shoulder and seemed disappointed.

"You should be dead," Rute said — and it was unclear to Timid whether that meant just now or when his head had been held underwater.

If Timid had something heroic to say, it is lost — because Barend broke the rhythm by jumping onto Rute's face and screaming.

They tumbled to the ground and Rute tried to pry the small man off of him. But Timid was there too, and he stepped over and grabbed a fistful of the Spring's branches. Rute's hands wrapped around Barend's throat, and Timid saw Barend's eyes bulge at each squeeze. So Timid squeezed too.

A web of crackling wood spread out across Rute's body, out from where Timid's hands held on. The giant hands let go of Barend and tried to swipe at Timid, but they had no force behind them. The animated mass of wood was no longer green — but gray, stiff, and dry.

Timid stepped away and Barend crawled out from underneath the thing. It was almost not a Spring anymore. When you look at a Spring, you are reminded of a forest — of life and all the things that call the trees home. Though this thing moved, it did not resemble life.

Barend's face and neck wore thick scratches and his fingers bled at their tips. Grass and mud filled his beard, and altogether he looked like a different man than had left the saloon a half-hour before.

"What now?" Barend said.

Timid looked back at the gray husk kneeling on the ground in front of them. Its attempts at crawling away only caused bits and pieces to crack and break off.

"It's wood, Barend. Wood burns."

CHAPTER 22

If Lepori had lived closer, he might have heard the commotion. But he didn't, so he didn't.

Instead, he sat on the edge of his bed — a long, flat piece of wood raised off of the ground with a small bit of straw for padding. Nights still brought shivers without a blanket, so he kept one folded away to the side. Another lay tucked under the bed, crammed against the wall. But that one was old and much too small.

He reached under the bed, his arms very much long enough to do so, and grabbed the old blanket. It was thin, but of good wool — a gift from someone who had loved him. He did not remember exactly who, that much was too far away for him, but he remembered the feeling it provided. Something more than warmth.

Maybe he would sleep with it tonight.

Water — and whatever else was in it — rose up to Barend's chin, even with his head tilted back. Timid's shoulders were cleanly above the surface and, as people tend to do, he hadn't thought of the problems faced by those who didn't look like him.

One perk of having almost nothing is that you can hold it all above your head as you wade through water that you really, really don't want it to touch. They had stripped down to their skivvies, too, in hopes to keep their shirts and pants moderately dry for the night.

For Timid, the second trip in the trench was much different than the first. It didn't smell particularly bad, but sometimes the imagination is worse than reality.

Luckily, the small gap in the wall was made to keep larger, more misunderstood creatures out — not humans. On the other side, suddenly in the midst of farmlands, they climbed out over the steep, muddy bank and put their clothes back on. Barend's beard was soaked through and dripped water onto anything he got near or tried to put on.

"You know," Timid said, "I just thought of this. But you don't really have to leave anymore, do you? Since the trouble is gone."

Barend huffed. "The thought occurred to me as well, about two steps into the poop trench."

"Do you still want to go?" Timid asked. Though he didn't want to walk through the forest alone again, that's not enough reason to make someone uproot themselves.

"I made my peace already," Barend answered. His voice lacked the little ting of jolly that it normally carried.

Timid bit his lip. He felt sorry for his new companion. Trading everything you have is not an easy thing to do at the drop of a hat, especially when the only thing you get in exchange is the promise of adventure. Timid knew how prickly that needle could be if things didn't turn out as expected. But this somber side of Barend was still new to Timid. Maybe Barend had more going on inside his mind than just jokes and joy.

"Plus," Barend continued with an exaggerated frown, "you burned my house down." There it was.

"We, Barend," Timid corrected. "We burned your house down."

Barend huffed again, but smiled. "Whatever makes yourself feel better."

They cut wide around the gate when they got near, trampling through the farmlands but close enough to the road so as to not lose it. And soon Timid noticed something he hadn't been close enough to see before. Large, cleanly sawed stumps dotted the fields every now and then, making holes where only crop lines should be. He looked back towards Goodhaven and realized that the whole city was a graveyard of sorts. The walls, too, were a fence of bones and skeletons. The thought remained in his mind and out of his mouth.

When Timid returned to look towards the forest again, a friendly sight greeted him. An obsidian Spring sat patiently on a stump at the forest's edge. Its canine face bore an expressionless and steady gaze that pointed down at the two men.

"It's good to see you again, Stormwind," Lupei said from his perch.

Timid smiled. Barend did not.

"It's good to see you, too, Lupei," Timid said. "I was worried."

Lupei tilted his head, confused. "Worried? What for?"

Timid glanced at Barend, who had been standing wide-eyed and didn't look to be changing that. "Oh, well, inside the city, we ran into Rute."

Lupei understood now. "Ah, I'm sorry. A grumpy fellow."

"But I don't understand," Timid said. "I thought you… uh… took care of him at the river?"

"Mmm," Lupei hummed. "You thought I'd kill my own brother. Do you think every disagreement need end in death?"

Timid looked down, in equal parts guilt and something else — confusion maybe, or something close to it. He didn't know what to say, so he looked at Barend.

Barend wasn't totally lost, because of what Timid had caught him up on at the tavern, but he felt and looked the odd man out.

"Excuse me," Timid said. "This is my friend Barend."

"Howdy," Barend said in a friendly, genuine way that rolled off the tongue, proving that he'd said this many a thousand times before.

But a macabre smile spread across the wolf's face. "Howdy," Lupei mimicked. It didn't quite have the same charm that time.

Timid cleared his throat. "What should we do?" he asked. "I mean, are you coming with us?"

Lupei shook his head slowly. "There's no other place for me. I'm as much this place as I am anything else."

Barend, who until now had been uncharacteristically quiet, spoke up. "You helped Timid. Helped me," Barend said. "Why are they so scared of you?"

"Stories have power," Lupei said. "Different people remember different amounts, different things. If they're told that they were once saved by someone else and that I might destroy them, they might choose that story. Maybe not every day, but most."

"But they know now," Barend said, "don't they? That they're wrong."

Lupei stayed solemn. "Are they?"

"So this is goodbye?" Timid asked.

Lupei nodded.

"So long," Timid said.

"So long," Lupei replied as he turned to look straight ahead at the city — where if you had watched closely enough, you could have noticed that a slight orange glow had faded back down into nothing.

At the forest's edge, the Black Tide's full darkness hung in front of them like a curtain. Timid imagined himself reaching out and finding that it had no seam. Perhaps Barend felt the same, as he had stopped before the first line of trees.

Timid turned and nodded his head towards the way they had to go, into the thick of the woods. "C'mon," he whispered.

Barend stood still. "Perhaps," he said, "this is a bad time to tell you that I'm afraid of the dark."

Timid leaned his head back and set his jaw in frustration. "Barend, you just led me through the city in the middle of the night." He returned his gaze to the shorter, frozen man. "Don't you go out late all the time?"

"Not really," Barend said with a shrug. "Sometimes I sleep in my chair. Or I have enough swill to make me not bothered."

Timid walked over and placed a hand on Barend's shoulder. "It's okay," Timid said. "You don't have to get over it. You can be afraid. I am too."

And on his own time, after a few more shaky breaths and skittish turns of the head, Barend stepped forward through the black veil.

CHAPTER 23

"How many more people can squeeze into this city before they start falling off into the water?" Burgush said, under his breath but not to himself — Zacharai could always hear him.

"Not many," Zacharai answered. It was the name and face to go along with the voice in Burgush's head.

They brushed shoulders with a crowd flowing in the opposite direction. Market hour, the only reason that Shrieksport even existed, was the most important of the day. The end of slow season was in tow, with the pass set to let trade through at the first touch of summer. You could sense it if you had your finger to the city's pulse. People surged and ebbed through the streets as the harbor bells rang out the important marks. Fish was the city's blood and the ports were its heart and lungs.

That much held true even here at the river port that dealt with trade towards Corical. Burgush liked this port more than the fishing port on the bay. He felt more at home among those that looked like him and looked him in the eye. Plus, fishing proved to be more of a human occupation, at least on the Shrieking Isle.

"How many of them are criminals?" Burgush asked, gesturing towards a group of the majority.

"Just about all, after a certain age." Zacharai's voice wavered on some words, growing soft and harder to pick out — but Burgush didn't expect more from someone who wasn't really there. "You are, too."

"My crimes are petty," Burgush snapped back.

"So are most of theirs."

"How petty is willful blindness?" Burgush grew agitated, partially because he hated the sight of Oruks hauling sacks, barrels, and stones from dock to dock while their human employers did not — and partially because he could tell that Zacharai only advocated the other side to annoy him.

"There are several hundred thousand humans on this hunk of rock," Zacharai said, "not all of them are murderers."

A crew of gulls flew overhead and landed on the lines that spanned above the street. He looked up at the gulls. They perched there for only a handful of seconds before a stall owner turned his back on his wares and — after a few quick flaps and dives — lost a sardine.

"What about thieves, pirates, drunks, and crooks?" Burgush said.

"Now we're getting somewhere." Zacharai smiled, flashing his pointy lower canines. Unlike Burgush's, they didn't always show. Zacharai also wore his hair much different than Burgush and other Oruks, loose and straight down the back of his head — instead of the socially acceptable bald or tied up. Burgush had kept his head shaved for most of his life. When he worked his first job as a stone hauler, long hair got in the way more often than not. And now at this job, a bald head and close-shaven face made for less places for mess to cling to.

They turned a corner onto an avenue wide enough for carts and carriages. This street, like the others that went anywhere inland from the harbor, went uphill. Guarded walls lined the edges of the city at its highest points, forming a bowl of sorts. Everything ran downhill to the sea.

Burgush looked at City Hall, which could be seen from most places in town. It sat near the center of Shrieksport on a patch of flat ground and stood taller than any other building. At its front he saw a wooden platform.

"You can see the gallows from here?" Burgush thought out loud.

Zacharai nodded. "Of course. If you know where to look."

He could see almost every slum in the city when he looked out from the gallows — except for the worst one which was conveniently out beyond the city gates — but he had never thought about whether that meant they could see him back. He imagined himself too small, insignificant with the towering City Hall as a backdrop.

"Do you think they watch?" Burgush asked.

"If they don't now, they will. Just give them time," Zacharai said. "You are doing everything right."

Beyond City Hall, however, lay a grid of houses. Entire neighborhoods where every house rose two stories high and surrounded itself with personal fences, lawns, and gardens. Though City Hall was taller than any one of them, together they rose up behind it like a wave waiting to wash over a sandcastle.

"I don't know that I've ever hung a person who lived in a house with stairs," Burgush said.

"Sometimes," Zacharai said, placing his hand on Burgush's shoulder and looking up with him, "to catch the big fish, you have to catch the little ones first."

CHAPTER 24

Becoming lost in time is easy in the dark. And when you're following a single trail, time is also a place. The seconds drag on for miles it seems, and they only pass when you aren't thinking about how tired you are — which is difficult because you are so very, very tired. This is why daybreak hits you so hard; it reminds you of a night that you should have spent sleeping. The rising sun gives color to the sky like a yolk spilling upwards out of a cracked eggshell — and when you've been walking all night, this does nothing but make you wish the night was longer, warmer, and equipped with a cotton bed.

That is why Timid and Barend chose dawn as the time and place to make their camp. They laid out their packs and blankets under a tree big enough to create a dry circle on the ground. Sleep came in fits — as the waking birds and critters paid no mind and carried on with their mornings — and didn't last near long enough. Even during day, with actual bits of sunlight poking through the web of leaves overhead, something in the forest told them to move on. A fire would have helped — but with no way to start one, they sat cold and damp and exposed.

For what it's worth, their remaining time in the Living Forest was rather uneventful. And there was nothing that could have made Timid happier, except perhaps seeing Lupei again and being told that he was being watched over — which was true but hidden to him. However, there are two things worth mentioning, each a conversation between the two men. Let us deal with them in order.

"So, I've been wondering," Timid said, "how did you end up here in the first place?"

Barend cleared his throat. "Oh, no real story," he answered, slightly out of breath. The hills — though short by themselves — wore Barend's lungs down with their endless repetition. "I'm just a runaway, simple as that. I grew up in a little village outside Riverport. Just small enough that you know everyone, just big enough that not everyone is your cousin."

"Why'd you do it?" Timid prodded. "Why leave, I mean."

Barend stopped walking, partially to catch his breath and partially to think — thinking and walking is a dangerous game for a man like Barend. He crouched down to offload his sack and dig around in the bottom for some bread. "Well, that there is a good question. I don't recall the exact reason. I was mad at the family for something, at my mother I think. You know how kids are, how they think. I thought I'd teach her a lesson. What a lesson that was, ay?"

Timid nodded. "I know the feeling, sort of. When my mother wasn't working, we were usually arguing. Just me being a stinker, mostly. I regret a lot of it now."

"I think most everyone does," Barend said. "We were all kids at one time or another. Even our parents."

"What about Odek?" Timid asked. "You sound like you've known each other for a while. From back then?"

Barend plopped down to the ground and tore at his bread. "Aye," Barend answered. "Wherever I went, he went. His father worked on my family's vineyard. We spent every day together."

"Oooh, vineyard," Timid mocked. "You just gonna drop that little nugget in there?"

"Well, don't get me wrong," Barend said quickly, "it's not like we were rich. It was pretty modest, from what I can remember. But aye, we had help. Mostly Oruks, though. All we could afford."

Timid cocked his head sideways. "Wait, if you come from money..."

Barend objected. "Not that much money, mind you."

Timid continued, "Why do you talk like an old deckhand?"

Barend rolled his eyes. "So not everyone can dream of being a sailor, ay?" he said, talking more like a seafolk than normal. "Did you only recruit yer scallywags from squalor?"

"No one says scallywags," Timid said.

"I was stuck in that forest for a couple decades, you know," Barend continued, "pushing three maybe. All that land around me for so long, I started to dream of the ocean. I saw waves in every street at one point or another. That's just something about this isle — we're all seafolk in part. Give it enough time, you'll see it too."

Timid nodded absentmindedly. "I already do," he said.

"So," Barend piped up again, "your turn."

"I told you most of it," Timid answered as he propped himself up against a tree. "Our guild, the Boars, sent us to find a missing girl."

Barend shook his head. "No, not that. You're more seafolk than you let on."

"Can't fool you, can I?" Timid said with a smile.

Barend crossed his arms. "Nope. Nobody can."

Another chance to tell a story for a young man who had yet to tell one. If Timid was waiting for an opportunity to wade into the water slowly, this wasn't the worst spot to dip his toes. "Well," Timid began, "the short of it is that I was shipwrecked."

"Ohhh," Barend let out. "So you'd figure you'd trade in for some land legs for a while?"

"Maybe forever," Timid said, chewing on his own hunk of bread.

Barend huffed. "That's what they always say. I assume. But you'll go back to it, they always do. I assume."

Timid picked at the dirt with his hands. "I don't know," he said. "I don't dream of being back out there, scrubbing decks and hauling nets on someone else's ship. I'd want my own, you know?"

"Is that the plan, then?" Barend asked. "Stockpile finder's fees until it's enough to buy you some sails?"

"I don't know," Timid answered. To him, this was all hypothetical — years down the line when people forgot his face or his name, if they ever did. Sailors have a knack for remembering the things you don't want them to and yet, all in the same day, forgetting where they set their nets. "I don't know all that much, anyway," Timid said, "I wouldn't be that great. Doubt I would ever be. It takes a certain something — a toughness, a spark. Something you're born with, or at least something you have to work really hard for. I don't have it. And I don't think I have the wind in me to get it."

Abruptly, Barend jumped to his feet and hovered over Timid — which was only possible with Timid sitting on the ground. "Why make music if you'll never be the Bard of Saint Elm?" he asked in a whimsical flourish that meant he was being rhetorical. "Why cook if you'll never serve the king, eh? Why sail if you'll never hit the wind as hard as the legendary Gelvin Whard? Is that what you're saying, my boy?"

"No," Timid stammered, "I don't know. I don't want to be famous. I just want to be able to do what I want to do. Not feel tied down." And that reminded Timid of the anchor he felt wrapped around his feet but couldn't see.

Barend interrupted. "What was your captain's name?"

Timid wanted to answer, but even thinking about saying the name made his teeth clench up and his throat swell up in the way it does before we cry. But he's seen Barend cry already, so it'd only be fair. "Ezira," he answered.

Barend pointed a finger down at Timid's face. "You think you'll never be as good as Ezira?"

Timid shrugged. "He wasn't that good."

A toothy grin spread across Barend's face. And he laughed. And Timid laughed. And for a moment, the forest laughed.

"So what's standing in your way?" Barend asked.

"Nothing," Timid said, "it's just that... I feel like I'm not in control. Like I've been chosen for something that I didn't ask for and now everything good that happens to me isn't because I'm strong, or skilled, or smart. I'm not those things. It's because this thing picked me and it's causing all these lucky breaks." Timid felt the anchor pull on his ankle.

Barend put his hands on his hips and stood up straight-backed against the bright-green canopy. "Maybe," he said, "it picked you *because* you're lucky."

"Sails or feet?" Barend asked, his arms folded in front of his chest, slightly below his beard.

The options were clear, mostly because the road went only two directions from the junction at the forest's exit. On the left, they could walk the North Road towards Riverport — away from Corical — for who knows how long, perhaps hitch a ride to Riverport with a gullible villager, then sail for about a day to Shrieksport, and finally hitch another ride up to Corical. On the right, however, they could head towards the pass on foot for a day, make it over the next day, and then perhaps hitch a ride to Corical on the third.

About three days either way, one requiring a lot more walking and a steep climb into alpine air. However, the pass did have the fish-packing plant near the top and an inn just on the other side.

And sailing came with its own price for Timid. One that the kingdom — and all the honest sailors in it — wanted paid in blood. Unfortunately for Timid, both Riverport and Shrieksport were havens for seafolk — and they all knew each other's names. So, for Timid, it was anything but sails.

"Are wings an option?" Timid said from one knee.

Barend shook his head and acknowledged the joke. "Nay, I reckon."

"Well then, I think sails might be out — we don't have money to pay anyone to go anywhere." Timid's coin pouch sat far, far away in a place he had just escaped from.

"Aye. Unless we go stowaway," Barend said.

Timid fed Barend a sharp glare. Barend backed away with a grin to show that he wasn't serious. When Barend smiled, his teeth betrayed him. They were mighty yellowed, sure, but nearly all there. Wouldn't pass for a sailor anywhere, even if he talked like one.

"So," Barend said, "we only have those two coppers you gave me. Which, unless my mathematics have gone dull, isn't enough money for a meal or bed in either direction. But Riverport's got that summer sunshine year-round." He rocked back and forth from his heels to his toes.

He was right. Logic favored the warm side of the mountains. Even if they didn't have enough coin for passage, they wouldn't freeze. However, for Timid, getting recognized by someone who knew him was worse than a few cold, hungry nights.

So he confessed. "Honestly, I'd rather not sail."

Without taking two seconds to think, Barend snorted. "I suspected as much."

Timid looked away, down at Barend's boots. Old, cracked leather. Maybe the same ones he had worn on his way into the forest all those years ago.

Barend uncrossed his arms, turned away as if to give Timid privacy, and continued, "The open ocean is a scary enough place as it is. I don't like to imagine what it would be like after the kind of thing you've been through."

Now here, we've reached an important moment for Timid. His newest and — for the time being — only friend didn't yet know why Timid wanted to avoid the sea. And Barend handed Timid a perfect avenue for keeping that way. So if this was no longer the old Timid — the one who earned his name all those years ago at the beginning of things — he'd show it here. Timid would have to unstick his feet from the mud this time and many more like it if he was going to avoid being swept away by the oncoming tide.

"Barend…" Timid began, "it's exactly that."

And so, as the two men marched towards the mountains, the tide came.

CHAPTER 25

It is uncommon to wander any path in the world and not meet another traveler. Thus, the two men were less alone than they believed. After emerging out of the forest where Timid had once entered, they walked south towards the mountains for only a short while before they happened upon a somewhat lively scene.

Fresh tracks left the first clue that others had recently come over the pass. And next was the rising smoke of a traveler's fire, stretching up into the dusking sky like a dancing snake. The bottom of its tail rested at a small crossroad, the kind that usually led to nowhere. But people knew that if you connect enough of them, two nowheres can lead to somewhere. With the spring melt almost at its end, more and more folks tried their luck at that.

Two separate caravans looked like they were settling down for the night in the elbows of the tiny junction. One hosting an entire family propped up its campstuff on the far side, ready to harness its twin horses and shoot off northward in the morning. Another, smaller caravan lay in a nest of clotheslines, storage trunks, and general clutter. This peculiar mess told Timid that it was no typical traveler's trolley — but a witch's wagon.

There are few things safer to travel with than a witch's wagon. But that's only because the consequences of harming a witch are both unknown and deserving of fear. And for that reason, bandits and thieves kept their distance. Timid made sure that he and Barend steered clear of it, too.

They soon made their own camp. Now the junction was rounded by three fires — one at each corner. Except their fire was dark and sounded like two rocks clanging against each other.

Timid drew the short string to ask the family caravan for a bit of fire help — though he made Barend come with. He approached and caught the eye of the head of house, a man maybe Barend's age but a foot taller and the same weight. But it soon became clear that the man was not willing to bargain.

"Just a hot coal or a lit stick, is all," Timid tried to explain.

"Consult the witch," the man replied, unmoving.

Timid leaned in a little to get a better chance and hear clearly. "Sorry?"

"Consult the witch," the man repeated.

Timid and Barend looked at each other and at the children and the wife, who poked their heads around their carriage. "Consult the witch," the youngest said.

"Consult the witch," said the older of the boys.

"Consult the witch," said the wife through a toothless underbite.

So Timid and Barend returned to their dark corner and made a tactical assessment of whether to consult the witch. And keep in mind, this was Barend's first taste of complex human interaction in some decades.

"Most people aren't like that," Timid said.

"I thought the littlest was gonna stick a fork in me," Barend whispered, peering over his shoulder.

"Positives of consulting the witch?" Timid asked.

"We get fire and a warm night of rest," Barend answered.

"Negatives of consulting the witch?"

"I know nothing about witches," Barend stated.

Timid sighed, "Well then that's one-to-nothing consult the witch."

It was Barend's turn this time, and he had his own way of doing things. Arms outstretched, holding a tuft of freshly plucked sourgrass, Barend tiptoed towards the colorful nest and called out. At first, the only thing that regarded him was the wagon's horse, which looked up from its grazing with an untrusting eye.

Approaching the Witch's Wagon required a deft set of feet and good eyes that could spot tethers against the dark ground — neither of which Barend had. When he got close enough — or maybe shook the wagon enough by tripping on its lines — a crackling voice answered him. "Yeees?"

No movement or sign of the witch followed.

"'Allo, madame," Barend cleared his throat. "I come to ye in a time of need. For we are without light or heat, and wish to borrow some of your oh-so-magnificent flame — which you undoubtedly toiled long and hard to stoke with your good hand and good heart. As payment, we offer this bundle of fresh sourgrass."

A head popped out from the carriage's rear curtains. Her face — though lit brightly by the fire — was a dark gray etched with even darker wrinkles. Wispy black hair surrounded her head in all directions and her eyes sank into her skull like two stones in a mound of whipped cream.

"I have no need for sourgrass!" The voice matched the face. "But I am amenable to some sort of terms."

She climbed out of the wagon down a short set of portable, rickety stairs. Nearly as thin as a flagpole, Timid wondered if she'd fly away in the next passing gust. She turned and opened up a side flap on her wagon. "I will give you what you ask," she said, "some of my fire and wood. But you must take something else, too. My load is too heavy for my old Jezebel to pull much farther — surely you can carry away some of my burden." The horse — who looked like a Jezebel — chewed on a dirty clump of roots.

Barend, eager to pounce on the two-for-one deal, strode up and perused the wares. The witch had divided the wagon's side into small, square compartments. With the sheet open, it looked like a grid of boxes full of junk and trinkets.

"What's this here?" Barend asked, holding up a metal necklace with a clasp at the bottom that looked like two arms shaking hands with each other.

"Ooh, a ghastly curse that one brought," said the witch. "The lightning chain, I call it. Haven't been able to rid myself of it for some time."

Barend gingerly set it back down and moved farther down the cart. Timid grew restless, and cold, and prodded the witch in hopes of concluding the visit.

"Have you got anything in mind?" Timid asked. "Something small, we only have sacks to carry things in."

"Well, you could take that necklace," the witch said cheerfully.

"Uh, we'd rather something more ordinary. Like without a curse."

"Ah, well then, nothing here is ordinary." The witch grinned, showing a surprisingly white set of chompers.

Barend had apparently found something. "What's this little critter?" He pointed to a small, wooden cage with bars on each side and a handle on top. The cage fit snugly into one of the wagon's boxes and — though it could have escaped with almost no effort — the creature inside remained calm and looked at Barend with a steady bead.

"Ah, behold," the witch proclaimed, "the snake of a thousand burns."

"Ssssss," said the snake.

"What does it do?" Timid asked, while Barend outstretched a finger towards the wooden bars.

"It gives you gonorrhea," the witch answered.

"Uh… sorry," Timid said, "I don't think that's quite what we're looking for." Barend retracted his hand and rejoined the group.

"I'll tell you, though," the witch said, "the worse the curse, the better the fire."

The two men sat in front of their bonfire. Nearly as tall as they were, it gave off constant licks of heat and — with free access to the witch's woodpile — showed no signs of slowing down. The snake nestled against the cage bars and reflected a warm orange glow over the flame-like pattern on its scales. And just as the friendly pattern of birdsongs settled down for its nightly rest, an exorbitant barrage of croaks began to emanate from seemingly every patch of grass. At long last, Timid was right back in toad country. He wasn't home, but it was a start.

Barend, sad that Timid didn't want him to play the harmonica to drown out their amphibious foes, was the next off to sleep. Timid stayed up for a short while to reposition the clothes and boots they had left out to bask in front of the fire. For the first time since he took the involuntary swim under Rute's supervision, he considered himself dry. But he stayed up for another reason, too. His left forearm had made little or no progress healing its gash, and in fact seemed to hurt worse each of the last two days. Even under his makeshift bandages it grew red and irritable, leaving his left hand stiffer and stiffer. So he set on an arduous task of cleaning bits of off-colored grime and lint out of the exposed flesh.

CHAPTER 26

When Timid finally got to his feet in the morning, he was glad to see the snake still in its cage — though Barend had rolled a couple lengths towards it in the night.

At some point after their visit last night, the Witch's Wagon grew another peculiarity. A wooden sign had been planted at the edge of the road. It had a white, painted arrow pointing south down the road which the two men were about to travel — and in bright, fresh letters it read the word "Stormwind."

Prodded by the sign, and wishing to converse with the crossroad's other occupants as little as possible, the two men got an early start on the road. After an hour or so, when they were surely outside the eye and ear of last night's strange woman, they found a patch of grassy meadow suitable for a reptilian way of life. If the snake had meant to say goodbye, it must have forgotten.

The road tilted upwards at the toes of the mountains, though it slithered back and forth to stay as low as it could. When gentle hilltops turned to rocky outcrops, Timid began to recognize some of the more extravagant features — peaks that looked like speartips, and glacial fingers of ice that clung to anywhere they could.

Using the pass wasn't necessary to get to Corical from the northern plains, and in fact this whole adventure was the first time Timid had done it. Sea shipments went year-round from Riverport to Shrieksport, and a fairly sophisticated road and canal system made extremely easy work of the remaining trip to Corical. But the King didn't like to put all his fish eggs in one basket, so he encouraged trade over the pass whenever it was doable. And the summertime supply of ice was the cherry on top.

They spent the entire day putting one foot in front of the other — with a bit of help from the seafolk remedy for mundane tasks. Unfortunately for Timid's eardrums, Barend's harmonica took too much breath — which was already in short supply — so Barend tried to sing along too.

Gristle and wire, stale bread and cheese,

I'd swear I was eating my old granny's knees.

Give me some comfort, give me a bed,

One more night below deck and I swear I'll be dead.

Wither away, wither me to nothin',

Just find us a doctor, 'cause old Johnny's coughin'.

Wither away, wither me to nothin',

Just take us to port, 'cause the waves are a frothin'.

Eventually, the ground wore an old, white coat of snow. And when they got near the top, they found a surprise. Snow wasn't a surprise because it was there when Timid came through the same place a week ago. The wind wasn't a surprise either, because it had been blowing directly in their faces all day. The surprise — when they managed to reach the ice-packing camp just before the top of the pass — was that nobody else was there.

"Hello?" Timid shouted, but he almost couldn't hear himself. The howling wind and falling snow worked together to hide the sound and drown it. He pounded on the wooden front door to the larger of the two buildings, which Timid remembered was a mess hall. Several flat, wide boards haphazardly covered each window — and there were a lot of windows, one every five feet or so down the length of the hall meant to house and feed a crew of ice haulers.

"They were unboarding these last week," Timid said, "I watched them do it."

"I can't feel my toesies," Barend said. Snow stuck to his beard in bits and pieces and he shivered in the quickly falling darkness.

"We need to get inside," Timid grunted, throwing his shoulder against the door.

"Aye," Barend agreed, "or we'll look like that." He pointed to a patch of large icicles dangling off the edge of the steeply slanted roof.

"Nobody is here, they'd all be inside," Timid said. "And I don't see any fires in there."

Barend looked around, still shivering. "Then where in tarnation did they go?"

Apart from two buildings that the two men were attempting to do an old fashioned breaking-and-entering into, the camp had nothing but a skinny, mile-long hauling path that led up to the harvesting glacier.

After digging around on the mess hall's wind-sheltered side where less snow accumulated, they landed their hands on a pig-iron pry bar. But the thing might literally have been the coldest object either of them had ever touched.

The nails pinning the door shut came off one-by-one as the two men took shifts at the mercy of their fingers. During one particularly gusty moment, the blizzard enveloped them enough so that Timid couldn't see anything beyond his outstretched arm. An all-white everything swallowed him up and stole away his place in the world. His body shed its weight and the ground disappeared from under his feet. And, worse, something moved out there in all the wind and icy spit — just far enough where he couldn't see it. But he knew it could see him. He felt the daggers it stared into him while it wondered if it had made a mistake.

When the blast of snow sharply faded, Timid found himself again near the top of a mountain pass, watching a short, stout, bearded man try to commit trespass. But if anybody happened to give them trouble about it, he'd try the deputy line again — since they were back in a relatively civilized part of the world.

Finally, after a good ten more minutes, they made a final pull and the door swept snow out from in front of it.

They locked the door shut with a plank from the inside, and it seemed to want to hold. A high-pitched howl leapt over the roof with an impressive persistence, and every so often decided to let a low grumble rattle across the mess hall's aching wood. Barend set his course on stumbling about in the dark, and did so until he bumped into a wood-burning stove.

"Mother of pearl," Barend shrieked, "this is a miracle!"

Timid wandered over, rubbing his hands together and noticing that the temperature wasn't any higher inside.

"This thing has been off for hours," Timid said. "All day, at least."

"So let's light 'er up!" Barend looked around him, but only saw darkness and a few empty bunks. "Where do you reckon they leave the woodpile?"

"No idea," Timid said. "We didn't really stop here last time through."

"Maybe it's in the back, or in the other barn." Barend got to his feet. "Let's hope it's not outside."

"Aye," Timid thought out loud, "let's hope they left one at all."

Cold brings about a unique desperation. Heat has its characteristic manias, too, but kills in a slow drawl. Polar expeditions and mountain ascents come with a certain urgency. Find shelter now or die, make camp now or die, find food now or die. Timid and Barend found shelter, thankfully, though remained plagued by a shivering hunger that wouldn't simply diminish with time. Timid recalled the four needs of man: air, water, food, fire.

If only he could make fire.

Seafolk had their own god, sure, but they didn't completely shirk the human spirit. Oruks did that and look where that got them. Humans seemed to get the best of both worlds. Timid remembered the sight of Ezira — the ideal man of the sea — casting Stridelong's sanctioned flames over the merchant vessel and everyone on it. So maybe Timid simply wasn't worthy of Stridelong. And maybe, Timid thought, that was a good thing.

He sat in front of the mess hall's wood stove and held a piece of kindling in his hand. They did find firewood after all — out behind the building, covered in a foot of wet snow.

He didn't need the blessing of two gods — either one would do. And if fire wouldn't appear from his fingertips, maybe he could ask a favor of water.

"Would you come out, please?" Timid asked it.

It didn't respond.

He thought back to that night outside Barend's hut in Goodhaven, trying to remember if he had said anything special. He even mimicked his previous self and tried to provoke it.

"I blame you for the death of my brothers!" Timid thought in a fierce frown.

Eadron didn't take the bait. The water remained steadfast and locked in place, suffocating the firewood's deep reservoirs of heat.

So yes, right now Timid wasn't worthy of a miracle. Fortunately, unlike many others, his fate was in his own hands — or more precisely, in the confession that needed to come out of his mouth.

CHAPTER 27

There's an old adage in the Shrieking Isle that goes something like: "Men bring value to the family, but women keep it there." The men who say those things mean them as compliments, though they are not. It's not entirely accurate either. Home and service work involve a lot of things that men don't realize existed, or at least don't appreciate. What they mean is something closer to: "Give women the work you don't want to do, and say something to make them feel good about doing it."

But Selah didn't feel good about doing it. And to make her feelings sharper, the man she'd been on a first date with most recently hadn't shown up to their second. She hoped it was some unexpected city guard business and not because he found something better to do with his evening. The three other women she shared the room with — Maria, Delilah, and Simi — promised to take Selah out on another night to make her feel better. And that night looked like tonight.

Corical didn't have many options for a group of middle-class women wishing to go out and enjoy an evening for themselves. Daytime coffeeshops and lunch counters were mostly closed by afternoon with an assumption that unescorted women would eat dinner wherever they lived. For Selah and the gals, that meant the same table shared with a random assortment of the three dozen other women that lived in their women's home. About half would be on shift somewhere each night — usually including at least one of Selah and her three bunkmates. So for them to all have tonight off mandated a little bit of adventure.

The obvious venue of choice: Mollybeck's — a grimy little pub especially popular with and tailored for Corical's young, single women. A classic example of purposeful norm-subversion. As the city's premier venue for purposeful norm-subversion, it'd be packed to the brim on a pleasant pre-summer night like tonight — even with the rule barring unaccompanied men.

Of course, nothing could make it completely safe. Getting there required trekking through open city streets, the favored territory for the native anti-social species of man. But by operating on a trained sense of risk-assessment, women could thwart those foul creatures with the learned tactic of traveling in numbers.

Another, more adapted predator posed the real danger. Friendly, persuasive, manipulative; you only found out that his idea of willing participation was different than yours after it was too late.

But Selah, her friends, and all single women in the Isle had royally-proclaimed equal rights — which included the right to go out and drink and have fun. So they did. And they looked out for each other as much as they could, since most men couldn't be trusted to do it for them. Often, their idea of intervening in a predator's business meant chewing their cud and muttering "That's not right" under their breath.

At Mollybeck's, their booth sat four. Sometimes, a passing server would brush Selah's arm on accident. Maybe her elbow wouldn't stick out so far if she wasn't sharing a bench with Simi. Maria, seated next to the very-much-thinner Delilah, didn't get nearly as many bumps.

"I think I'm gonna throw up," Maria said. Her mug of Seafoam — the evening's first — was not nearly empty enough to induce vomiting even for the lightest of stomachs.

"I think, therefore I am," Simi said. She pulled her own mug to her lips and let a little bit of the ale's trademark foam accumulate on her upper lip. She smiled, which meant that she didn't see what Maria was looking at — a man across the pub.

A few weeks ago, a woman living at their women's home had come back late at night crying. The reason had been her first date with the man who Maria recognized. Now, he had his arm slung over a young, blonde woman's shoulder and was obviously partway through a story meant to hype up something about himself.

"Well, gals," Deliah said, "we gonna trade in our night for someone else's?"

The other three sat silent for a moment. Selah took a long pull of Seafoam even though she didn't really feel like drinking beer tonight. But it was part of the fun of Mollybeck's and she'd bought into that a while ago. The part that wasn't supposed to be at Mollybeck's was sitting there at the bar finishing up his story.

So she was relieved when Maria said, "Yes."

Luckily there were four of them, because their strategy probably would not have worked with just one or two. And they were also lucky that the last woman had come home and spilled the beans. The four of them formulated a plan — a pact really — then and there in their bunk room after none of them could fall asleep. Selah remembered lying awake on her lower bunk, staring up at the underside of the mattress above her and wondering what sort of thing that other woman had been forced to look up at.

Maria, the self-appointed leader of the moment, cut through the crowd with her hard shoulders and a soft "excuse me." Selah brought up the rear, glad to not be in the spotlight or expected to talk — she just had to look tough.

The girl, who was maybe 18, looked barely old enough to drink and likely had needed someone to vouch for her legality to get through the door. Obviously confused, she looked up at Maria and then back at her date — who hadn't yet noticed the four women pouring out of the crowd and forming a half-circle around him.

"Excuse me, miss," Maria said, "but his night is now over." Just as rehearsed, without giving her the option to stop them. The most dangerous part about these men was their ability to convince women that the problem didn't exist, so in the moment a woman's own belief that she could take care of herself might be her worst enemy.

Maria displaced the man's arm with her own, Delilah got the barkeep's attention, and Simi and Selah crossed their arms like bodyguards. Clockwork.

"Mollybeck," Delilah said to the woman behind the bar, who was wringing out a wet towel, "this man is unaccompanied."

Mollybeck — with her typical business-like efficiency — reached under the counter, took out a notepad, and recited the man's total. "Four copper," she said, and held out her hand, distracting the man for a moment by putting his mind on his coinpurse.

Maria and Simi pulled the girl off her barstool with a gentle half-hug. But this final hint allowed the man to finally catch on to what was happening to him. "Wait, what the fuck do you think you're doing?" he yelled. His speaking pattern — designed to command attention — somehow put emphasis on every word.

But none of the women answered him. Selah, again, was the last through the crowd. Their booth now sat five.

CHAPTER 28

Between the folds in his ball of blankets, Barend's nose stuck out the bare minimum amount that allowed him to breathe.

"I'd take out my harmonica and try to cheer myself up," Barend said through chattering teeth, "but I'm afraid me lips'll freeze to it."

Fireless, the mess hall lay cold and dark, but not quiet — furious wind drove against its sides violently enough to prevent sleep from accumulating for much of the night.

They sat on two bunks next to each other as the morning sunlight — dulled by the thick overcast and continuing snowfall — crept through the cracks in the boarded windows. Barend shuffled his blanket-covered self around the room to get a better look at things in the light.

"Think we can round up some grub?" Barend asked. He made a desperate ruckus as he searched the kitchen cupboards. But he found nothing, and because their bread hadn't lasted the night, they ate what they found.

Timid's thoughts raced to keep his attention somewhere other than his stomach. Last night's prolonged state of half-sleep had dredged up a swarm of stray threads that hung loose at his mind's edge. Now awake and able to separate the real from the surreal, he ran his fingers across their ends — tugging at each one-by-one, letting them unravel as they pleased. Why was nobody here? Why had a winter storm shown up this late? How had the witch known his name? Why didn't Stridelong give him the same power over fire that Swait had? Why, after everything, couldn't he tell Barend the truth?

Timid stewed for a bit longer, until Barend returned foodless. "Whelp," Barend said, "we're gonna stay cold *and* hungry."

"I lied to you, Barend," Timid said, his eyes staring a hole in the floorboards.

"What do you mean, ol' chum?" Even on this topic, Barend's flame never dimmed.

"I'm not scared of the ocean," Timid said softly, as if he was admitting it to himself instead of the short, red-bearded man in front of him. "Or at least, that's not why I didn't want to sail back."

Barend didn't respond, but did start stroking the end of his beard — which had grown rather frayed throughout the journey so far.

Timid gulped, somewhat surprised that it went down over the frog in his throat. "I didn't want to sail because I likely have a bounty on my head."

"Mmm," Barend grunted, "for what?" There was less judgment than curiosity in his graveled voice.

"Piracy, most likely."

"Woof..." Barend said, opening his eyes wide.

"Yeah. Woof."

"Well, what's the story?" Barend asked. "You ain't stabbed me and took me holdings yet, so you're not the 'stick first, ask questions never' sort of pirate."

"It's not that crazy," Timid started. "We hadn't found any fish in days, some notorious shed of bad luck. So we held a vote, and the hunger won out. And then we found a ship that looked like easy pickings."

Timid had practiced this speech over and over in his head for weeks, and now that a little bit had fallen out — like an anchor pulling on a chain — the rest ran out with it.

"I didn't do anything, I swear. I just… watched. They offered everything they had in exchange for their lives. But we hadn't taken the nameplate off the ship, and one of our men — Brawlin — caught someone looking at it. So… things devolved." Timid paused for a few seconds to wipe his face dry.

"That was the first time I ever saw magic. Ezira snapped his fingers and up went the flames. I just hid. I had my knife and everything. But I couldn't do it. I couldn't do anything. I couldn't stop them."

Barend interjected, "Do you believe that?" His eyes were firm and unblinking.

Timid wiped his face again. "No."

"How did you get away?" Barend asked.

"We actually did get wrecked," Timid answered, "that part is true. But I think I'm the only one that survived. I got picked up by a small fishing trolley. I just said I was shipwrecked."

"But how would they have you pinned for a crime?"

Timid shrugged. "I had to buy passage back to the mainland, and I saw some familiar faces on the way. Plus, seafolk have a saying, 'nameplates always float.' Always."

"That's a tough bid," Barend said. "But you're not a killer yourself."

"Doesn't matter," Timid said bluntly. "They hang for any sort of piracy in Shrieksport."

"Aren't you worried you'll be found in the capital even?" Barend asked.

"Not as much. I'm not sure how the bounties work or if they'd make it up to Corical at all. And less people know me there, just the Boars. Who I only met a few months ago and, as far as I can tell, don't have a reason to suspect me."

"And those are the ones that hired you for this?"

"Yep, that's where I'm headed," Timid answered. "To pick up a gold purse."

Barend's eyes squinted with intrigue. "Worth how much?"

"I don't know," Timid said. "Depends on how much they believe our story."

A blinding sunlight bounced around the mountain pass a million times before it hit Barend right in the eyes.

"Up to my knees!" Barend shouted from the open doorway. "Worse in some places. So tie your boots shut."

The snow had slowed to a dead stop and the wind returned to a normal mountain breeze. Now the loudest things in the mess hall were their growling stomachs and chattering teeth. So, knowing that it might take a couple days for the packing crew to return, they decided to foot it.

Without any heat source, their boots still wore ice from the previous day. Timid tied cut strips of blanket around his pants so less snow would fall down his boot tops — hypothetically. Meanwhile, Barend cut holes in two more blankets so they could fit them over their heads as a first defense against the driving cold.

They stomped their way beyond the threshold of the door and Timid found himself cursing for a lack of gloves. For most of the night, his forearm had oozed a greasy fluid that soaked through his shoddy bandage. Now his left hand was seized in equal parts pain and cold, and his fingers curled only at the bottom knuckles.

In perhaps a half-hour, they summited the last upward bit of road. This terminus provided a bit of visibility — but exposed them to a blast of wind that they had previously been somewhat protected from. In front of them, an etching of switchbacked roads wound tightly against itself and descended sharply into a white void. The road — though as colorless as everything else — could be found by its borders, where it dropped down a hundred feet at each coiled turn.

Timid took point position and tried to put on a mask of confidence. He thought a bit of self-deception was going to be necessary to make it all the way to the bottom in one still-breathing piece. Ezira had once told him that the will to survive was the greatest forecast of a life that extends past the present moment. Maybe — through the eyes of his mask — Timid would find that will again.

The men benefited from the lightness of their packs. Trudging their feet through near-two-feet of snow was hard enough, even downhill, that any extra weight of food or gear might have been too much.

"No wonder they didn't have firewood," Barend said at one point. "Imagine getting a woodcart up through this."

Timid had already thought about that. "But they could have brought up extra stores when the roads were clear," he said.

"Aye," Barend laughed, "but how smart are ice packers?"

"They know this place well," Timid said, dodging an attempt to disparage the people who had unknowingly kept them alive last night. "This type of storm must be really unusual. For them to not have extra wood and food — and to pack up and haul tail down — means this doesn't typically happen."

"So what are we being punished for?" Barend yelled over the wind, trying to make light of the situation as normal.

"I don't know," Timid answered, "but I'm glad it's letting up."

Barend, wanting to lead on the next stretch of road, pulled his blanket poncho tight against his shoulders and took another step in the snow — and sunk up to his knees and then his waist and then his chest and then his neck as he fell off the road's hidden edge.

CHAPTER 29

"How do you not come to me before you do this?" Mayor Percy asked. "Huh?"

Burgush leaned back in the comfortable cloth-lined chair in the mayor's office and didn't respond. He'd found that if you don't have a great answer, it was better to just keep your mouth shut and let the other person keep talking. Silence can hurt people who don't expect it.

"I come back after a week — just one week, hangman." Mayor Percy jabbed his finger out, pausing his pacing for a moment and punctuated each of his words with a stab towards Burgush. "And all hell breaks loose."

Despite the delightful chair, Burgush found it quite difficult to get comfortable. These were certainly the nicest clothes he'd ever been dressed in — selected and put on him by an unfamiliar woman downstairs. Short in both stature and temper, she finally found a wool jacket wide enough for his shoulders that didn't hang too loose over the rest of his torso. He wasn't too bothered by her demeanor, though — all Oruks got used to it long before adulthood.

But he hated being called "hangman." An insult specifically tailored to the person often hurts more than a general one. And as there is no community in the profession of death, no general ones even existed. To his fellow citizens, he had more in common with a pirate —after all, they both killed for money.

The Mayor resumed his pacing. "You have certainly overstepped the bounds of your authority."

"Mayor Percy," Burgush said calmly and with his fingers woven together in his lap, "I was under the impression that we were here to discuss our next steps, not to criticize the ones already taken."

"Nobody's been hung in this city for theft in fifty years!" This time, the Mayor pounded his plump fist on the table to emphasize his point. Little silver trinkets and fountain pens hopped and jangled with the quake.

Burgush acted like he didn't notice. "Your father did it," he said. "I checked the records."

Mayor Percy flared his nostrils at the mention of his predecessor. Though Shrieksport was free to elect its own mayor, the monarchy in Corical chose the candidates. And King Hallond, like most other royals, did respect a dynasty.

The Mayor put his hand on his hip and brushed aside his jacket — a strange, frilly, purple thing that was more monarch than it was elected official. He revealed a rolled parchment from his inside pocket.

"Regardless, if you're going to bleed those folks — dead or not — you need my permission." The Mayor set the parchment on the desk. A wax seal held the page in a coil, which told Burgush that it was already signed and he planned to hand it over.

"Why call me here for this, then?" Burgush tried to speed things along so he'd make it to the noon hanging on time. "You could have sent this down. Or just let it go."

"You've become quite popular…" the Mayor began, not exactly answering the question, "wrongfully. This is my town and these are my people. I set the charges; you just do your job. How you do it, when you do it, who you do it to — that's all up to me. So far, the selection process for the blood drinkers seems quite random. Without purpose, some have been saying. You'll now heal who I select, starting today."

"And if I refuse?" Burgush knew that he couldn't be replaced. Because he wasn't just a hangman anymore.

Mayor Percy smiled. "Then you'll find yourself at the bottom of that pit."

A bluff, most likely. The people of Shrieksport were happier now than at any time they could remember. The sick climb out of bed; the old stand upright. But the Mayor's point wasn't worth pushing on, because it didn't conflict with Burgush's plan.

"Fine," Burgush said. "I have no quarrels over that. I do, however, request permission to expand my repertoire."

The Mayor looked skeptical but sounded curious. "What do you mean?"

"I mean that the hangman's noose is a reliable method, but may soon grow tired. You said it yourself, how I do my job is up to you. But to keep the people interested in our little shows here, we might need to introduce some variability. A little change here and there to keep the audience guessing. And maybe even — to stimulate compliance — allow some of the more gruesome techniques used by the executioners of old."

The Mayor nodded and stroked the small goatee that he — for some reason — felt necessary to keep. He paced to the window that overlooked the city hall's front lawn. The gallows sat practically under his balcony — a relationship that he had rarely taken advantage of before now. "What did you have in mind?"

CHAPTER 30

Acting more like claws than anything else, Timid's hands ripped trenches through the snow. Luckily, they had been close to the end of a switchback, and so Barend hadn't fallen far. And it was really more of a tumble than a fall.

Still, the snowdrift here was thrice as deep as the rest of the road — and it had a hole in its top in the shape of a short, stout man. From what Timid could tell, Barend hadn't quite landed on his head — so he was likely intact.

Timid hadn't thought enough to wrap his hands in his cloak or blanket. They were pink as the flesh of a salmon — and felt as numb and foreign to him as if they *were* salmon — and now when he finally struck an upside-down boot, he knew only by the pain that jolted through his wound.

Freed from its icy prison, the booted foot wiggled back and forth — much like a beached salmon. Unexpectedly, the next thing Timid uncovered was a bearded face. He thought for a moment that perhaps Barend had been split in half, with the previous movement spurred by a postmortem twitch in the nervous system. But Barend's face sported a cheery grin and he let out a bellowing laugh.

"Timid! Thank the sun, I thought you might have been a frost troll come to gobble me up."

"You okay?" Timid asked, out of breath and blowing warm air onto his frigid fingers.

"Aye, but me arse is full of snow." Barend's arms struggled free and tried to press against the snow to lift the rest of him up, but they sank with each push. Timid extended some help but couldn't do much with his left hand except make a rudimentary hook.

Barend soon crawled out and slid down the snowdrift, writhing around to release the acquired snow from his pants. Timid put his hands in his own pants, but on a different mission — to warm them up. The tips of his fingers stung when they absorbed his crotch's heat, and though he was able to work some dexterity back into his right hand, his left stayed numb and stiff.

"We need to go," Timid said, gingerly putting his sack and poncho blanket back on.

"Aye, I've had enough of laying around." Barend looked fairly normal, a smile on his face and a beard full of ice. "And I think it's still my turn to lead. A couple more hours, eh?"

"Aye," Timid answered, his mind on something else.

Barend took off, as slowly as to be expected in two feet of snow. The wind had since picked back up, so Timid bundled his covering closer to his face. And as he did so, he looked at the fingers on his left hand — pale, blue, and unmoving. Much unlike a salmon.

A few thousand feet downward is no trial for falling water. Whether flowing over a sharp edge or wafting gently through frigid air, it will — in the fullness of time — meet the dirt. That is the great gift of a planet. Not only the dirt, but the desire for all things to come to rest upon it.

And so is the luck of the men and women who trod upon all inclined ways. For if one who walks an earthward path thirsts for the end of it, a great feat of speed may be performed. And on this day, these two men craved the comfort of shelter with a hunger known only to those burdened with frosted skin and frozen bones. And so the nature of the earthbound road bestowed upon them its boon of great haste.

No longer was the road beset on each shoulder by sheer rock and crag with slope too formidable for anything — snow or shrub alike — to grow tired and rest. And so the black arms of dormant bushes and trees dotted the snowfields like gravestones in a great necropolis. From the cornice of an exposed turn in the road, they caught sight of an inn's sharply-crested roof. Soft, yellow light escaped from its windows and lay a patch of warmth across the fallen snow like a sheepskin rug. Thus the brown-sided inn furnished the lone patchwork of color before the world once again lost its edges to the snowstorm's all-white everything. Shuttered dormers gave the inn's skyline the ears of a cat, and its smaller neighbors — stables and storage barns — nestled up against its belly for warmth and fare as kits do against their mothers.

The next providence was that the road wore only a thin layer of packed snow easily trodden by frigid toes. A sign above the inn's grand entrance read "The Saddled Salmon" and showed a cartoonish fish behind stall doors meant for a horse. Timid was here once before — not long ago but under entirely different circumstances — but hardly recognized it under its new, white coat. The two men spent little time knocking the ice off their boots — as would be polite — and instead clambered up the porch's wooden steps to treat themselves to the blast of warm, smoky air that they knew lay quietly past the inn's sturdy, red, front door.

As unusual as unexpected guests — by definition — are unusual, the two men shuffling through the Saddled Salmon's doors were on the more unusual end. They themselves did not appear too odd; it was the when, where, and how about them that the inn's other patrons thought bizarre.

The door's clang brought enough attention, and Barend's decision to gallop up to the fireplace brought the rest of it. Furloughed fish packers filled the saloon's chairs and stools, which set Timid to wonder whether they'd recognize him from their brief meeting last week — and he hoped their memories were as bad as the stereotype suggested. Timid walked gingerly to the hearth and joined Barend, careful not to catch the examining eye of anyone sitting alongside his path.

They set their frozen sacks and snow-covered blankets to the side for a moment and focused on themselves. Barend's nose and ears wore a red shared only with plump tomatoes, and Timid's were not far off from that. But Timid's left hand — the one so stiff, fraught with pain, and useless that he kept it by his side until now — shied away from the heat like a ghoul hiding from a torch's light. His numb fingertips were not colorless, but the beginning shades of black that you'd find at a shadow's edge.

Seeing Barend cheer up immediately at the sight of fire, and seeing him now rub his toes in its orange glow, caused another wave of guilt to crest over Timid. He felt responsible in some unexplainable way for condemning them to the terrible last day they had. Not because he convinced Barend to leave Goodhaven or because he wanted to go over the pass, but because of the lie. He couldn't shake the folktales that seafolk told, where Eadron punished ne'er-do-wells with belligerent storms. And so another lie — even one not yet told and holding its harm in secrecy — would weigh Timid down so fully that he feared he'd never get up again.

"Barend," Timid called over. "Look." He revealed the rigid hand, pulling it out from under his shirt.

Barend's eyes showed surprise, as did the shape of his mouth. "Oi, Tim," he said, "that's got frost rot."

"Aye, yeah." Timid turned it over to show that the white tinge ran down the back of the hand past the base of his wrist.

"How does it feel?" Barend asked.

"Hot, if anything at all." Timid thought it ached even more in the inn's dry heat.

As the two men huddled against the fire, a heavy thud of footsteps sounded behind them. A large, well-built woman with a bar towel slung over her shoulder — equal parts cook, barkeep, and proprietor — appeared from almost nowhere and bore down on them. Her demeanor was an instruction to not waste her time.

Barend looked in love. "Howdy," he said with bulging doe-eyes.

"Howdy," she said, "what can I do you for?"

Barend obviously had not thought about this moment before it had been upon him, and his jaw was thus left agape. So Timid replied, "We're short on shrift at the moment, and that means near flat out, but we'd like to take advantage of this here fire for a small while. If you don't mind."

"That's fine, lads," she said in a tone that told Timid it wasn't actually fine. "Just come up to the bar when you know what you're after." She caught sight of their snow-covered belongings. "Where you in from?"

"Uhh, over the pass," Timid said.

"No shit? Then you did what these fellas wouldn't." She ticked her head back to acknowledge the fish-packers. They all watched the conversation, some through the side of their eyes and some straight as an arrow.

"Well, I'd say they were in the right," Timid said, hoping some of them overheard. "How are the roads downhill from here?"

"Don't know," she answered, "but it's seen traffic today. Some went down that way this morning, and we got someone stuck here on their way on up." She gave them another top to bottom look. "Are you looking to stay the night? We're not full."

Timid and Barend exchanged glances, both wanting the other to speak. After a few confused grunts, Timid put some words together. "We don't have enough, I don't think. Actually, I was in here about a week ago — I'm one of the Boar deputies — and you charged two coppers per cot. And we only have two coppers between us now."

The woman huffed. "Not that big of a problem. That rate still stands."

"Oh. Well then we don't have enough, right?" Timid clarified. "That'd be four coppers."

"No," the woman shook her head like she was explaining something to a child. Her long braid swung into view from one side to the other. "It's two per cot — not per person."

Timid and Barend looked at each other again.

"I'll let you sort that out," the proprietor said. "Holler if you need me, name's Bertha. Enjoy the fire for now."

CHAPTER 31

"One cot, please." Barend placed the two triangular pieces of copper on the Saddled Salmon's hefty oak bar. Though the ice and snow had long ago melted from his beard, his boots still sat drying on the hearth — leaving him barefoot. In fact, most of his clothes were still drying, and thankfully his remaining underlayers covered most of his body.

"Sure thing, sweety," Bertha said. She handed over a wooden token that was simply a slice of tree with a number 7 fire-branded into the rings. She pointed at a set of saloon-style doors that led to a short hallway and said, "Go through the double-doors, and it's the room with no door, just a curtain. Washroom and bath is across the hall, that one has a door. Two-holer's out the back door, and it's a bit frozen so no promises out there."

Barend cocked his head sideways. "That's a lot to do with doors," he said, "but did you say bath?"

"Aye," Bertha said. "First come, first serve."

Barend wandered back to Timid, who had also mostly stripped himself once they decided to stay. "They have a bath, Tim."

Timid didn't look up, just spoke. "It's getting worse," he said. He kept his left arm hidden under his cloak of blankets and hoped nobody else would see the blood dripping onto the floorboards.

"Let me see," Barend commanded. "Have the fingers gone yet?"

"Just about," Timid answered. He revealed his hand to the firelight, which didn't sting like he expected it would. Actually, it didn't even feel warm — like his hand wasn't even there. And it partly wasn't. The fingertips were gone, and the rest of the fingers were nothing but whittled, thin spires. Cracks spread down his wrist as it, too, began to melt.

After carrying their stuff into the long room with two rows of cots and stowing it under number 7, they hurried to the washroom. Nobody answered their knocks at the door, so they entered and found a moderately-sized metal water trough sitting in the middle of the floor. More akin to something you'd find a cow drinking from than a man bathing in. Timid was a little disappointed, rightfully so — but Barend's eyes bounced with excitement.

"Whoa! I used one just like this all the time as a wee lad." He ran over to it, slipping and nearly falling on the wet stones.

It was only halfway full and the water was a dull gray, as if clouded by silt. No pump or drain was attached in any way, but an empty bucket sat by the door, begging to be used. And without a stove or fireplace in the room, the water would obviously be quite cold.

Timid, however, had an idea. Yes, he smelled like the poop trench. Yes, he might have touched the snake of a thousand burns. But most importantly, his arm dripped flesh and blood onto the ground. He wondered to what extent he could really take advantage of this small, man-made pool of water — and whether it was deep enough to get his head under.

There is nothing as disappointing as a cold bath when you desire a hot one — especially when you are quite literally thawing.

"Do I really have to be here for this?" Barend asked, holding his now empty bucket.

"Yes," Timid asked, frustrated because Barend already knew the answer, "stop whining and bar the door."

The biggest hole in their plan was the washroom's come-and-go nature. The door leading outdoor had a bar to lock it shut against the alpine wind, but the interior door wasn't meant to be held closed for a private session. So Barend would have to hold the door shut if he heard anyone coming.

Timid left his pants on, sparing them both the grim fate of being forced to look at his genitals. The water was as cold as the ground surrounding the outdoor pump, and Timid's feet seemed to fight back as they were lowered in — and so did his genitals. Some of the old, grimy water was too difficult to bail out beforehand, so Timid wasn't entirely thrilled about the prospect of swallowing any of it. He also pulled his hair out of its bun, figuring he might as well make this into as much of a real bath as he could.

"Are you sure this is gonna work?" Barend interrogated. He'd been uncharacteristically uneasy ever since Timid had told him the plan.

"Nope. But it happened the last two times, and I can't think of a meaningful difference here." Timid's rear sat on the bottom of the tub now, tense against the frigid metal. "And if there's a chance I can get answers to what the hell is going on with me, then it's worth a shot."

"Timid, it's not worth a shot if one of the consequences is death."

Timid laughed. "That's unusually calculating of you, buddy."

"Not when my friend is trying to drown himself." Barend crossed his arms.

Timid had learned that crossed arms meant Barend was trying to make a point. "I'm not drowning myself, Barend. You are drowning me."

Barend's nostrils flared and he exhaled a large sigh through his nose. "I am so nervous already, and saying that doesn't help."

"And you're making me nervous," Timid spat back, "so quit it."

The water came to a slow rest at Timid's stomach. He thought that if he bent his knees, he could slide down and put his head under. His body shook with nerves at the possibility of this plan turning suicidal, but slowly stilled with the quieting waves. Saliva dripped from his mouth so heavily that he couldn't wipe it all away, and his body's aches drifted out of sight. His right hand's knuckles turned white from squeezing the trough's rim, while his left hand — now missing — stung at its jagged stump as it dropped into the water and clouded it red.

"Ready?" Barend asked, stepping away from the door, where he was listening to the rest of the inn's bustle.

"Aye," Timid answered. "I don't want to get too comfortable. Should we have a signal?"

Barend looked down at him seriously. "If you start thrashing, I'll interpret that as a signal."

Timid was concentrating too hard to smile. One more breath of air and he was ready. He pulled his head back and slid his spine down against the tub's bottom. His hair floated around his submerged head and — pressing his eyes closed against the cold shock — he held his breath. Then, remembering what he was supposed to be doing, he opened his mouth and let the silty, metallic bathwater replace the air in his throat. Mercifully, he didn't choke. He forced water in and out of his lungs and felt it slide against his breathing tubes.

He waited — toes curled, eyes closed, chest expanding and compressing. He heard Barend's feet shuffle against the washroom's wooden floorboards, likely going back and forth from the door to the tub. But the sound slowly drifted away from him like a small raft under a gentle breeze. His limbs floated where they pleased, for he was now upright and totally submerged — a loose piece of seaweed floating in the calm surf. He took another long, deep breath of water and noticed that it tasted not of silt or blood, but of salt. He opened his eyes to see nothing — nothing but a cold, deepening void with no seabottom or sunken ship below him, no light above him, and no shape swimming around in the dark.

PART THREE

THE MAN WITH THE AXE
IN HIS NECK

CHAPTER 32

Burgush stood on the gallows platform, feet planted firmly against the smooth, sanded wood. The long handle of a silver-headed axe rested in his hand. With a cutting edge far too fanned and slender for industrial use, it was obviously for show — for the near-thousand people spread across the lawn and street corners surrounding the Shrieksport City Hall.

Late evening provided the proper dramatic lighting for Burgush's tastes. Torches caked the courtyard in a dull yellow and if it was raining — which in Shrieksport was nearly always — the fizz of raindrops against the many small fires peppered the tense silences. His new axe, too, caught the torchlight and therefore the onlooker's gazes.

The new improvements provided by Mayor Percy also masqueraded this ordeal as something other than the depravity it was. New platform planks, a new axe, a mysterious new contraption — all were fresh cogs in this machine with Burgush as the helmsman.

And, for the second time, no canvas masked his face. Although they previously suspected the truth, the crowd now looked in the eyes of the uncomfortable fact that they had been cheering for something with skin unlike theirs. Something they thought many untruths about. Something who couldn't control its own slobber from falling out between its protruding lower teeth, and who could barely understand a language beyond violence, and who should be utterly thankful for all the modern comforts it's been allowed to enjoy. And standing on their own two feet, they turned their chins up to this thing and prayed to receive its salvation.

Burgush followed the murmurs and turning heads to see two guards pulling a chained man in their wake. Even though Burgush stood alone on the platform, Zacharai's voice pecked its way into his brain.

"Can you feel yourself stepping over the threshold?" Zacharai asked.

"Yes," Burgush answered in his own head.

"This is going well," Zacharai said, "unlike other things in other places. I feel that they are beginning to act."

"What will you do about it?" Burgush asked.

"Nothing, for now. They will come to us. Stridelong is a hobbling corpse compared to what once was. And I don't fear the others."

The chorus of shouts and cheers met no challengers, the previously squeaky steps having been silenced by repair and investment. The chained man was shoeless, unwashed, and matted to an artificial level. Bareskinned except for a short cloth wrapped around his waist, he instead wore scrapes, bruises, and bedrash across his ribs and back. As the trio arrived at center stage, the guards kicked the prisoner in the back of his knees to drop him down. They bent him forward until his chest rested on a raised block and shoved his hands through two holes in the platform. The guards locked a steel plate over the man's chain with a sharp clang, then marched to their arranged places on the platform's rear corners behind the vacant and recently redesigned gallows stanchions.

The crowd hushed. They knew the ritual. Even in a different form, they remembered the timings and the feel. But this time, the unmasked executioner walked to the platform's cornice and cleared his throat.

"By order of law," Burgush boomed, "this man — who shall go nameless to all that do not recognize him — has been convicted of the crimes of fraud against the crown, civil disobedience, mischief, and resisting arrest. With the powers vested in me by the presiding official of the Shrieksport township, I — Burgush the Hangman — have judged his sentence to be death by the rapid severing of the spine and the essential arteries."

His jade knuckles wrapped around the axe handle, and he lifted the great thing so it rested horizontally across his waist. Without further drama, and with an unceremonious tempo, he stepped back two strides and raised the axe. Silent excitement fell over the crowd like a blanket of wet snow. The man on the block quivered. His chains rattled.

An arc of torchlight glinted off the steel blade. It buried itself in an inaugural mark in the sanded wood. A long, shallow tray attached to the front of the block overflowed with red. Burgush lifted the head by its hair and — though he didn't hide it from the crowd — stuffed it in a sack so it would do less repulsing. The axe remained where it was.

Burgush said no more things, only gestured to another guard waiting on the ground. Six townsfolk were led up the steps and over to the scene. Burgush dropped to a knee and retrieved the crimson tray. He turned to the first person in line, then the next, and so on — pouring a bit of the liquid into the bowls that each of them carried. They raised the bowls to their lips for a moment and wiped the spillage off their chins with their sleeves.

CHAPTER 33

Although Timid could breathe, he could barely see. For the moment, it made no difference to him if he floated in an endless ocean or that deep, dark void that hides itself from the sun. It felt, too, as though a void surrounded him. If his skin hadn't plumped with moisture and his throat hadn't been coated with salt, he might have thought himself lost in the numbness of true death.

He suddenly appreciated his isolation. Barend and the inn's other patrons were more than worlds away. And that scared him. Alone again, after all his effort to avoid this feeling — befriending the wolf in the forest, convincing Barend to come with him, digging Barend out of the snowdrift. Alone without even a hint of a tentacled monster lurking just out of sight.

Strands of black hair floated in front of his eyes, as uniquely dark as the rare strips of night sky that held no stars. If the bottom wasn't near, he wasn't sure how much darker things could possibly get. His airless breath made no bubbles to tell him which way was up, but he thought about sinking and it happened

— the water parting for his feet like a soft breeze around a sail-less mast.

With nothing to do but wait, high on the priority list was seeking some clarity on his melting arm. No bone hung out of the exposed stump, as if his flesh had been clamped by the jaws of a great steel beast. Once, he saw a man get his leg tangled in a mess of ropes thrown over the ship's railing — the meat slid off his calf like you would do to a well-cooked chicken bone. This was not like that.

For now, the blood streaming through the saltwater contained no chunks of red meat, so maybe the melting would not creep up his arm and eat into his chest. Prodded by instinct, he reached over with his remaining hand and grasped at his stub — and felt a soft resistance as his real fingers meshed with liquid phantoms. He pressed his right palm against where his left would have been, feeling the water push back. Real water, too — not the empty, anesthetized feeling of this place.

Silt pounded against his bare feet and squeezed out between his blistered toes. The soft seabottom emitted a cloud of swirling dust and Timid gladly waited for it to settle before trekking forward. He couldn't see it, but he knew where to go. In the same way as recognizing an old friend's voice or the footsteps of a loved one, he knew the creaks and groans of familiar deckboards.

Barend sobbed into his hands. A meaty, callused set of fingers rested on his shoulder and partially propped him up. All eyes in the inn stared into either the cavernous recesses in the fire's coalbed or somewhere else a thousand yards away. Nobody inspected the dead body on the floor of the Saddled Salmon's saloon

"I don't know what to do," Barend spit out between his shaky breaths. Snot ran across his lips and audibly fought against the air coming up his nose. "I might have to go back."

The inn's walls mostly concerned themselves with anything other than winter. Gold pans, fishing rods, taxidermized trophies, and landscape paintings showing sunny days where the breeze might smell of sweet, nectar-filled wildflowers and feel like the warm breath of a close embrace. The single pair of snowshoes that hung by the door were more a result of necessity than lavish decoration.

And Barend found the expectations he held about these people — reinforced by their stoic disapproval of his and Timid's arrival — to be untrue. When he first emerged from the washroom calling for help, he found them mid-celebration. A group in the back led drinking chants and their own versions of stereotyped, chanting sea songs. A grizzled man — with a silver earring and a beard to rival Barend's — leaned forward and wrung his hands in the center of a storytelling circle. Two old friends lounged by the fireplace in a comfortable silence more familiar to Barend than the sound of his own name.

He ruined all of that. Himself drenched, he had tugged a water-logged body across the splintery floorboards and into the hallway in sight of the dozen staring faces. They gave him a free meal.

Now, Barend sat in front of his clean plate and tried to explain himself once again. "He said he'd be okay," Barend testified, "that he'd done it before."

The voice attached to the hand on his shoulder gruffed. "And you believed him?"

"I had no reason not to," Barend answered. "He told me fairy tales, and they came true. He said I needed saving, and I did. I saw his flesh and bone crumble away like a thawing glacier. And I saw him do other things that normally don't happen, when we needed them to happen."

The voice gruffed again. "A man of many miracles then."

Barend shook his head and looked at the linen-wrapped body. "I don't think they were miracles. He was just lucky."

A pipe passed Barend's nose and blessed him with a memory of a scent he used to call a friend. A match slid against the bartop's wood grain and came to life for its happy moment in time. The man standing next to Barend made two puffs and walked to the bench at the main dining table, trailing smoke behind his black woolen overcoat that identified him as one pay-grade above the rest of the scruffy rabble. The man wore no cap, but one sat on the table and hadn't been touched by anyone else. Barend supposed that this man was, in a way, a sort of captain.

A silent moment passed before the large barkeep, Bertha, seized their attentions. "Lads," she said, "I'm sorry about your mate there, but he's got to go outside."

Barend sparked up and nearly shouted, "Outside? In this?" He swept his arm across the room and gestured at the battened up windows.

"Yeah, in this," she barked back, throwing her handtowel onto her shoulder and leaning over the counter and over Barend. "This isn't a crypt. Take him out back or I'll throw you both out."

A group of hands gently ushered Barend off his stool. "Take the feet," one said to him. The procession led itself, partially backwards, out the rickety rear door of the Saddled Salmon and into the windlashed snow. His hands full of cloth and bootless feet, Barend's tears and snot fell unhindered into the night air.

A young lad — perhaps a fledging stablehand— emerged from the inn with directions to take the body behind the goat barn. Although folks had been hard at work clearing the new snow from most of the land around the inn, the rear of the barn had only a small footpath carved against its wall. A moment after they set the body down, the boy returned with two shovels.

Barend sagged against the barn's wood panels, the sound of his huffs joined by ignorant and uncompassionate bleats. Though the wind couldn't quite curl its fingers around to reach them here, the cold still induced shivers. An ice packer with a bushy mustache and suspenders handed his jacket to Barend. Barend liked Mr. Bushy Mustache and Suspenders. Mr. Sort of Captain took one shovel for himself and put the other to Barend's chest. He liked Mr. Sort of Captain too.

Not entirely devoid, the seafloor's various denizens kept Timid companion on his slog. First, a mound of rock. Second, a decaying whale skeleton half-swallowed by the soft sand. Third, fourth, and fifth, more rocks. He said hello to each of them. Occasionally, things did get scared off before he had a chance to say greetings, but nothing came towards him.

Before now, Timid had imagined the bottom of the sea to be much more full of horror. Perhaps the stories of grotesques hauled up by nets were total exaggerations and nothing more than illusions in tangled seaweed. Or perhaps this wasn't the same sea that Timid had grown up on.

Feeling in strangely-high spirits, he didn't interpret the first body as a bad omen — more like the sight of a familiar tree on your daily walk home. The second body filled him with a childlike eagerness. The third was Ezira's. And although each was incapable of responding, Timid greeted them too.

The Malachai's planks painted his feet green with algae. A fragment of the dark moved silently. Timid sang.

O' high on the watch, abandon yer reckon,
Way, ay, sail the Fool's Wind.
O' low below deck, abandon yer mutton,
Way, ay, sail the Fool's Wind.
If I don't come home, my mistress will kill me,
Way, ay, sail the Fool's Wind.
And stay away from my wife, she thinks I'm with ye',
Way, ay, sail the Fool's Wind.

Ghosts danced around him. Like a clock's inner workings, they pulled and shoved and yanked and tossed. The horizon marked a boundary between two different blues, one overhead and the other stretching under his feet. Birds cackled and fought with each other for prime positioning on mast tips and yardarms. Ezira wore his squid-marked cap and judged progress from his symbolic perch on the rear aftcastle.

A voice called out from over Timid's shoulder. "Why are you joyful?" the nautilus asked.

Timid turned to see the creature floating over an empty, broken deck. "Because I made it. I wasn't sure that I could."

The nautilus blinked at him. "Why here?"

Timid had multiple reasons, some more based in logic than others. "Because it's home. And because I thought you'd be here."

"And what do you want from me?" the nautilus asked.

"I want to know what's happening to me," Timid answered. "And why."

The nautilus slowly swam around and regarded different aspects of the ship. It sent a tentacle into a hole in the deck like a dog licking the marrow from a bone. It touched Brawlin's body and seemed to sniff his hands, ignoring the splinter of wood that protruded from his abdomen.

"There is no why," it said, "other than that you didn't deserve what I gave to these people. You've earned everything I've given you, and you've done well with it. I thought you might do more, as the tide fights against me now. Although the others have done even less."

"Others?" Timid asked. "There are more like me?"

"Yes," the nautilus answered, "though not by my doing. You have met some — the ones with flame — who have done too much. More have come, and have done too little. You have done... some."

Timid thought about what that might imply. "Would you like me to do more?"

"It matters little, I can find another. You no longer have debt with me."

"Debts?" Timid asked, confused. "When did we have a debt?"

The nautilus stared a blank stare with its large eye. "Do you not remember?" it asked. "You seemed to understand. I spared you from this and you tried to repay me — and would have, if not for circumstances outside your control."

Timid's mind jumped back to two weeks ago, when he gave the missing poster to his commanding officer at the Boars.

"So I spared you again, from the riverbed. And you repaid me again, this time in fact."

Timid imagined Barend sitting in a rocking chair with foam on his red mustache and an empty mug in his lap.

"We are at an equilibrium," it stated.

Timid didn't reply. He felt ashamed for not understanding it sooner. He had never been free to come and go from this place. A line of credit had been extended to him, and he had now paid up.

"You seem confused," the nautilus said. "Was that not a satisfactory answer?"

"That makes sense — now," Timid answered. "But I only came here to ask about what's happening to me, I didn't mean to actually end my life."

The nautilus was obviously trying to understand. "Hmm, but what is done is done. I do not control the tides of time."

"Well," Timid laughed, "that's too bad."

The nautilus didn't get it. "What is too bad?"

Timid stumbled over his words, unsure of how to explain a joke to a creature who lived at the bottom of the ocean. Maybe it didn't understand jokes. "It's too bad because…" he paused and let the word drag on. He looked around. Broken bodies and frayed ropes bobbed in the slight current. He made eye contact with Brawlin, who didn't have any eyes. "Because I wasn't done saving."

The nautilus blinked slowly, calculating — and perhaps seeing through — Timid's implication. "Do you wish to incur further debt?" it asked.

"Human debt, you mean?" Timid clarified.

"It does not have to be human," the nautilus answered.

"Well then," Timid said, "I figure why stop now? I was just getting started."

CHAPTER 34

A room full of people, unable and unwilling to sleep, made its way through the early hours of the night. A man with a bushy mustache and suspenders spoke of nearby creeks known for bountiful trout spawns. A man with a weathered face and kind-yet-commanding eyes puffed air through his pipestem in silence, his overcoat and cap drying on a nearby rack. A red-bearded man — nearly a foot shorter than the others — warmed his fingers against the licks of heat from the fireplace.

The other men, although not ill-tempered, did not seem entirely sociable. It takes a certain kind of person to thrive in the gills of a mountain pass for a whole summer with no one for company but others like themselves. Most had loved ones in the nearby rivertown of Sevast — but as seasonal fathers and brothers, they tended to weave loose familial ties. The two greenhorns — workers on their first season — were already a bit in over their heads and remained quiet, wondering to themselves how often this crew stumbled upon a dead body they had to help bury.

Barend wished the story-telling and sea-song-singing would return and stamp out the bleakness. That thought's road led elsewhere — to Barend's harmonica. Music, he had always found, did what words could not. Two decades as an outsider in Goodhaven allowed him to self-teach several pensive and gloomy melodies, often at subdued volumes to avoid irking his large and surprisingly strong neighbors. He retrieved it from the bunk room and spit-shined away whatever dust and dirt had collected on its silvery surface.

The Saddled Salmon's saloon possessed no stage, but harmonica players often don't need them. A harmonica is a companion — another member of the group — more than a true performing instrument. Many a harmonica player has staved off loneliness around a hunting or fishing camp, even with only one seat at the fire.

Barend set up shop in the corner nearest the warm hearth, fingers still a wee bit stiff. He dragged a second chair closer for his feet and sat well-postured to draw a breath. The brass reeds fluttered, turning people's heads as a soft, slightly-out-of-key melody bounced off the walls and danced with the window shutters that rattled in the wind.

He played without a specific song in mind for a few minutes. To him, it seemed that nobody else was in the room — or if there was, that they didn't move. It ended quietly and the room fell silent. You don't applaud harmonica players, even if it might cheer them up.

Because they had in fact waited respectfully for Barend to finish his first tune, the ice packers now moved about the saloon to grab another round or do their other, more personal, business. Barend sobbed again for the first time since the burial — which actually hadn't gone so smoothly. What little surface soil that does exist on the side of this mountain was buttressed by permafrost not yet thawed by a warm season. They did scrounge up enough dirt to cover the body but were left with a mound rather than a pit. No doubt someone would have to come fix their mistakes on the next rainy day. But for the circumstances, Barend thought he and Mr. Sort of Captain did okay.

He didn't want to play harmonica anymore. He had never played for a real audience other than Odek and Timid, and so he thought lots of misguided thoughts — maybe these fellas didn't want their conversations to be bothered, maybe nobody out here played harmonicas anymore, or maybe he just wasn't any good. But, looking around the room, he saw dozens of expectant eyes. Some crossed their arms and leaned back, others tapped their toes anxiously, and even the proprietor gave him a silent nod from behind the counter. The wind cut out abruptly, as if someone finally shut whatever door in the clouds had been letting it out. He felt as if he were out on a stage, in front of an eager crowd.

He didn't know any songs about grieving, or about saying goodbye to someone you knew for a short time but felt an unspoken kindred with, or about leaving a magical forest where your best friend was a tree that you grew up with and also wasn't always a tree. In reality, harmonica songs don't even have words so they technically aren't about anything and can be used in a myriad of situations. So he played a song about a cowboy coming home.

Cold dirt fell into Timid's mouth and eyes. A great weight pressed upon him, and though he had breathed underwater just fine moments ago, he felt now that he was drowning.

Luckily, his wiggling about like an earthworm forced things loose. The weight on his right arm — the one still intact — gave way to a blast of winter. He clawed handfuls of dirt from his face until he could draw a frigid breath.

The first sound he heard — that wasn't his own panting or the wind's howl — was a strange screaming sound. He thought that he had awoken outside a barbaric laboratory where cruel doctors forced surgeries upon tongueless patients. Turning his head and wiping his eyes, he saw the rear of a small barn from which the screaming escaped.

He quickly scratched at the mound of dirt covering his neck, body, and legs. By the time he could finally sit up, his arm was exhausted and begged for a break — and his fingers felt the familiar, stiff numbness that meant life was leaving them. On the other side, his half-arm was still raw at the stump and useless. But, as the nautilus had answered just before it sent him back here, he would find new uses for it.

His dirty, bare feet hated the icy staircase and left blackened footprints as if they were a firebrand on bare skin. The inn's rear door fought against being opened — perhaps it too was hardened by the cold — and made quite the commotion when it finally gave way. Entering the inn's back hallway, no person greeted him — but a soothing refrain echoed from the saloon and bade him closer. He inched his way towards the swinging double-doors at the hall's end.

When he took the final step across the threshold and into the firelight, he wasn't sure what the yelling and cursing was about. He turned and looked behind him, expecting to see a snow monster that had just crawled out of some mountain cave, and found nothing but an empty hallway with dirty footprints and a frosty door left ajar.

But the inn's patrons did see a monster — one plastered with muddy soil, wearing mud in its hair, and missing half an arm.

Barend's harmonica clattered against the floorboards. "Timid?" Barend said aloud, more in observation than in true question.

The monster smiled. The room's curses quieted to a murmur.

"Howdy," said the monster.

CHAPTER 35

With a wool blanket draped across his shoulders, Timid sipped the hot tea that the proprietor handed him. Men sat around him in half-circle and the fire hugged him from behind.

Barend had finally stopped apologizing and sat still next to Timid on the hearth. Timid knew that more questions were coming, ones he couldn't silently ignore. The proprietor returned, this time with a rag and a small tub of water.

"For your arm," she said. "Better get that mess out sooner rather than later."

Barend extended a hand, but Timid waved him off. "It's alright," Timid said, "I'll do it myself."

He soaked the rag and touched it to his arm's raw end, sending out a sting of pain so fierce he thought his teeth would crack under the pressure. He heard one of the men say, "Give him something to dull it, something hard," and a moment later he was handed a flask that smelled of spiced liquor. He never liked the stuff, but circumstances being what they were, he choked down a few mouthfuls at the risk of throwing it up and losing the image he was hopefully projecting.

The questions came. "What happened?" and "Did you see anything?" were easy enough to not answer, but he couldn't ignore when Barend looked him in the eyes and asked, "Where did you go?"

"I don't know," Timid answered. "I know I tell you that a lot, but I really don't know. It wasn't here, but it was the same place as last time — and the time before. Some strange ocean."

The room was easy to read — and unfortunately that little bit wasn't going to be enough. It's not like he asked for the attention; he normally shirked any chance to be the conversation's center. He never told the stories at the campfire, he only absorbed them — like the fires he didn't start and the meals he didn't cook.

Maybe he just needed to start small.

"For a while," Timid began, "I didn't think I'd make it back. I tried to make peace with that, but something wouldn't budge. I remembered you, Barend, and this place. And I guess I couldn't let go."

While not the whole truth, it was close enough that he didn't count it as an untruth. Barend, knowing more about the root of the story, pressed on.

"Did you get any answers?" he asked.

"Not any that these folks would believe," Timid answered. He gasped through his teeth as he poked and prodded at his dirty, exposed muscles with the rag. The whiskey hadn't set in yet.

Barend nodded. "We can talk about those later then, eh?" he suggested.

"Aye," Timid agreed.

The other listeners, whether ice packers or inn workers, caught the hint that Timid was done explaining himself. How much could they expect, after all, out of a man who had just returned from the dead? Most often, if you approach a wild animal too quickly, you only scare it off.

The Saddled Salmon did its best to put on a normal face. Bertha took new drink orders. Ice packers seated themselves in scattered bunches, whispering rumors similar to the one they found themselves mixed up in. A small boy brought him a small plate of baked potatoes and roasted goat. Someone had cut each up into small, bite-sized pieces. Pity did wonders for a broke man's stomach.

Barend stayed near and silent, sitting with his feet on the hearth and knees to his chest. Occasionally, he would wipe the back of his hand across his nostrils or cheeks. Everything besides his voice said "I am sorry."

One of the ice packers approached the fire and put his hands to it. Timid knew without asking that this man was in charge. His clothes had few holes, if any, and his gaze seemed to go where it pleased. Most of all, none of the other crewmembers gossiped with him. But more than anything he reminded Timid of a seafolk fable.

Old pant-less Captain Hooper, the trickster and the mooner,
who sailed the Shrieking Sea on a four-hundred-pound grouper.
And if you ever asked him where he would go,
he'd never tell you 'cause he'd never know.

Thankfully, this man had pants. And eventually he spoke, apparently stone-cold sober.

"I would have thought it a parlor trick if I wasn't a witness every step of the way," he said. "I put my fingers to your neck and I piled dirt onto your face. Name's Willem, thought I at least owe you that."

"No hard feelings, Willem," Timid said. "In fact, it was decent of you to give me something proper."

The three men stayed by the fire for a few minutes — without words — watching others lose their edges in mug bottoms and empty flasks. A few of the workers, older and longer in tooth, retired for the night. A storytelling circle came together at a shared table.

Willem puffed at his pipe and turned to regard the room. "They don't realize that they're at the middle of your story, not its end. They'll share this with others, aye, but sooner or later they'll forget about you."

Willem pointed at someone. "Mikhail there, the greenhorn, he forgets to wipe his arse half the times he uses it. He'd be more useful to me full of stones and tossed as an anchor — and I don't even have a boat." Willem cackled, unbothered that it was at his own joke.

"Stories live in pairs," Willem said. "Give them another one."

He left the two outsiders to join his subjects, quieting their voices and abridging their sentences. He pulled an empty chair to the table's head and sat beside it, leaving its armrests standing alert like protectors of a vacant throne. When Timid took the seat, the remaining mouths closed.

"So Timid," Willem asked, putting on a bit of an accent, "your friend says y'er a sailor."

Timid nodded.

Willem continued. "Every sailor I ever crossed has told me tall tales — of things that don't got no explaining." The boss scanned faces, obviously seeking out examples.

One came up. "I heard of harpies," Mikhail offered.

"Harpies ain't real," barked a man with a bushy mustache and suspenders. "Buncha men alone on a boat for two months making shapes out of heavy fog."

"Well what about sea serpents?" Mikhail asked, embarrassed of the fun made at his expense.

"Or ghost ships?" asked a new voice. Heads turned to see the stableboy leaning against the kitchen's doorframe.

"I don't know about harpies or sea serpents," Timid began, "but I've seen a ghost ship."

Eyes blinked at him from all directions. Willem dragged a match against the table's wooden underbelly and set his elbows down to steady himself for the long haul.

Timid cleared his throat as he'd seen Swait do around their first campfire, leaned forward like Barend whispering an unspoken fable in a raucous saloon, and narrowed his eyebrows to look a bit more like Willem.

"You see," Timid continued, "plenty of ships go missing at sea — crews unaccounted for and their widows informed. Every wife, mother, and child lives in fear of that knock on the door. But just as a fishing line lost in the water doesn't make dinner, neither does a lost ship make a story. What makes a story…"

He lingered on the thought and drew back one corner of his mouth to put on his best sailor voice.

"… is when one of them comes back."

CHAPTER 36

At the western edge of the Shrieking Sea exists a barrier isolating the isle from the rest of the world. Seafarers of both our age and the ones of past know it as the Fool's Wind. Stretching far enough south to anchor itself in the world's icy cap, and far enough north that nobody dares go farther, the Fool's Wind looms over all sailors like jailhouse bars — telling them where they may and may not go.

You see, the Fool's Wind is no wind or current of air. It is a current of the sea, twisting in on itself like a thousand snakes sharing the same bed. It does not pick and choose its victims — it eats every and all alike, pushing them around and about until they get caught in the next storm or run out of food and turn on each other. Some say the Fool's Wind has a natural end — that if you follow it for one whole year, you will finally reach its center and find yourself circling a giant drain in the ocean floor.

Curiously, too, is that the Fool's Wind is to thank for naming the Shrieking Sea — and therefore the Shrieking Isle itself. As you may well guess, when a ship is lost, it is often somewhere inside the Fool's Wind. And when a ship is lost, people die.

And when people die — yes, even when grown men die — they scream.

By circumstance, many of the isle's most bountiful fisheries are tied closely to the Fool's Wind. And thus the margin of error — especially for inexperienced navigators and sleepy helmsmen — is naturally slim. That is how I became familiar with its edges and how it began to pluck my dream strings into a nightmarish wail.

Starting at a young age, I scrubbed decks and pulled nets on a fishing vessel named The Malachai. My captain, Ezira, had followed a similar path but was nearer the other end, already familiar with the cracks and crevices that I could not yet fathom. Our crew of a dozen men included those both more and less experienced than myself, but none younger. They were a mixed bag, but it should go without saying — though I will say it now — that as sailors we were all naturally superstitious.

Our curious spyglass always watched for less law-abiding members of our profession, and on one particularly clear day we caught sight of something on the western horizon. A ship, it was, with all its sails pulled in. Knowing that we had placed our nets on the brink of safe territory, this was an oddity. And so we purposely sailed to the limit of where Captain Ezira dared to go and inquired of our watchman.

"Ezira," I remember the watchman calling down, "it's the Black Dog."

The name had significance to us, of course, but for two reasons.

Firstly, and of this you may know, is that a certain number of curses plague the Shrieking Isle — and the legend of the black dog is one of them. Generations of islers, even stretching far back to the first colonists, have run across stray black dogs lurking patiently in the shadows of the night as if waiting for their next meal. Particularly on Black Tides, when the moon has abandoned us, must we keep watch for these creatures. Because with the legend comes a pattern, one confirmed by the test of time, that goes like this:

The first black dog you spy shall bring you suffering,
the second shall bring relief.
But after that, shut your eyes and hold your breath,
because the third black dog you spy shall bring you death.

The other reason to fear this ship — and the reason I am telling you this story — is that Captain Ezira knew of it. Sailor circles are small, you see, even more so for those folk on the top rung. And while the lot of us share a beer or a game of cards in port to pass the time, captains find a closer brotherhood in each other. So Ezira knew the captain of this ship, and knew that the Black Dog had filed its last manifest six months earlier — and had never come back.

You might find yourself scrutinizing our next behaviors, but remember that we did not have the benefit of hindsight — and that sailors are prone to bouts of curiosity. We had not yet answered whether the Black Dog had gone missing by choice — which is sometimes done by those who abandon the friendship of legal ports and turn to piracy. I should also explain that venturing into the Fool's Wind is not always a death sentence. With good weather, a team of men can keep their bearings long enough to spit themselves back eastward to the Shrieking Sea. And, as I've already mentioned, fate gave us blue sky horizon to horizon.

We started by going below deck and bringing the night shifters up to speed, a common courtesy when plans carve drastic turns. I had the unfortunate task of waking a man named Brawlin — who always woke on a grumpy streak, even towards his friends

— and being first hand on pulling our net. A shift as first hand does a wonder on your back, you see, more so than farther down the line — and so the youngest usually gets stuck there.

Thus, I let myself rest while we approached our sister ship, and cannot provide you with details of how we came to overtake her. But I was there when we called out to her, and when we got no response. And I was there when we laid our gangplanks down and set foot on her deck. And I was there when we heard the harsh, unforgettable sound of a dog's bark.

Being recently promoted out of deck swabbing, the white lines of salt and green webs of algae on the deckboard edges immediately told me a story of abandonment. I saw my crewmates hiding their noses beneath shirts and rags from some unseen stench, and I did the same before it hit me — but still, between the cracks of my fingers and through my own stale odor I smelled the filth and rot.

Understand that we didn't want to dive into the mysteries of this ship. There's something higher than our wants, though, that we answered to. The understanding among our kind is that if you're the one who goes missing, you hope someone does this for you.

This ship, being a bit higher class than ours, had two levels below the main deck. Holding out our own whale oil lamps and working quickly so that dusk didn't creep up on us, we searched each cabin and cupboard we came across. But the only sign of life was the low snarl and sharp yaps leaking out from a deeper, darker corner.

Eventually we came to a heavy, locked door with an iron bar laid across it. It didn't look like it had always been a brig — not many working ships have those — but someone had tried hard to make it one. Ezira ordered us to take the bar off, and someone more brave than I stepped forward. I held a lamp, hoping that would be enough so that I wasn't volunteered for any other jobs — but Ezira called my name and ordered me to thrust my arm into the opening door's wake. As always, I did as he asked.

I'll tell you — though I'm not proud of it — that I didn't look. My crewmates gathered around and largely pushed me out of the way so that when I did finally enter the room, there were five or six of us gathered around this frail, nearly skeletal, salivating black dog. A chain wrapped around its throat and attached it to an iron loop bolted to the hull. It ceased barking but bared its yellowing teeth at our hands. I could barely look at the thing, though the smell was what drove me out of the room. That is when another crewmate, Yarly, approached us with a token of evidence.

Yarly held, by one finger, a severed hand. Small holes of rot peppered each side of what skin still clung to it. I emptied my stomach and others came to examine the commotion. We eventually concluded, correctly I still assume, that it had been voluntarily amputated.

The question of the dog's fate remained. Someone proposed putting it out of its misery. But how would we do that? Gouge it with a saber? Or leave and let it starve off? Others thought mercy meant taking it with us. And I secretly agreed, you know. It was a grouchy critter, for damn sure, but even the kindest men go mad in cages.

I think death weighed heavy on Ezira that day. I think he could paint a better picture of what had happened on that boat. I don't know if he knew more stories about empty ships and black dogs than us, or if he just wanted to hold tightly onto the one breathing thing left there. He decided to give it five minutes to get across the gangplanks.

I didn't help. I went topside and crossed back over to the Malachai and tried to get the stink out of my clothes. Others kept searching the ship, and apparently found things in quite a strange state. Meals half eaten, boots missing their partner, empty barrels of water — that sort of thing. We waited for the minutes to tick by, and eventually heard the hollers grow closer. They practically dragged it up the stairs by the chain, and I remember hearing its unkempt nails clatter against the deckboards. But the gangplanks — steepened to a slope by the difference in height between the two boats — posed a problem. Someone would have to carry it — someone with a great set of sea legs under him.

It wound up in the hands of Georgie, a lean veteran of a few different ships. He offered a piece of brined beef as a bribe and managed to scoop it up by the belly. It growled and thrashed but, like many of us, Georgie had earned his life's pay wrangling nets full of worse than that. And we thought it went rather smoothly — he scuttled down to the Malachai and dropped the dog on our deck. But his hand dripped blood and he showed us a fissure on his knuckles.

Other than the bleeding being hard to stop, we didn't think much of it, you know. Happens all the time. I was the odd man out in that my hands didn't look like an old chopping block. So we carried on, some of us taking care of the dog when we could throughout the day. Ezira ordered us to put out all sail eastward and we let the empty ship drift out of our minds.

But as with most stories, night didn't make things any better. Georgie couldn't sleep, you see, something had caught a hold of him. He sweated through his hammock until drops hit the floor and he chattered his teeth so bad I thought they'd burst. And he kept trying to get up, and one of us would have to shove him down onto his back again. I remember that at one point we all huddled around him — me holding a lamp, Brawlin's hand on Georgie's head, Ezira standing on the stairs, and that black dog watching from the dark's edge.

When we awoke, Georgie was gone. Nobody saw him get up, not even the night crew. And then we found a trail — a streak of sweat and blood — from his bed to the stairs, from the stairs to the ship's railing, then up and over.

We barely had time to think before the sun fully rose and the dog bit someone else. Again on the hand, this time of Davin, a young deckhand new to the ship. Reminding me much of myself in age and health, I hated the look on Davin's face. Shame, embarrassment, pain — but mostly fear. Fear of the long day of cold sweats and madness that might lay ahead of him.

Davin's incident gouged a rift between the men, inflaming every emotion in each person — some with their hatred for the dog, others their fear. It was then that we spoke of the omen for the first time. Many of us had been on edge since we learned the ghost ship's name, waiting and hoping that the legend never reared its head. There's another superstition too, you see, that a curse gets its power from your belief in it. But now our lips could not stay sewn shut — not after catching a glimpse of the horrors that might've been in store for us. And you might be wondering why we didn't just stop the curse and kill the creature then — but we asked ourselves a similar, stranger question: why didn't the last crew do that?

But we did know one thing that the last crew did do, and that eventually led us to clean our sharpest machete as best we could. Because the little punctures we found on that decaying, severed hand the previous day looked an awful lot like the ones on Davin's hand now.

So with eleven men and twenty-one hands, we still had to decide the fate of that damn dog. Lucky for it, you don't vote on ships — the captain decides. And if you disagree with him, remember that mutiny is a strong word. Ezira, however, did allow some disagreement on his boat. Mostly about weather predictions or where the fish were going to be, and mostly to keep him sharp. Here, though, things were different. He announced that we would chart course west — back the way we came — and that meanwhile the dog would roam free.

By the time we spotted the lost ship again, it was only a shadow against the setting sun. Believe it or not, I'd say luck was on our side. Because if it wasn't another clear day, we'd have never found it — or worse, we'd still be out there with it.

As we chased it down and threw hook onto railing, Ezira announced his scheme — someone had to put the dog back. Who, though, was up to the Dead Man's Wager. It's a game, of sorts, rooted deeply in the history of sailing men. The captain holds a number of lengths of twine, one for every crewmember including himself. Typically, each is cut from the same spool and is roughly the same length — except for one, slightly shorter piece. Each crewmate draws one from the captain's hand and gifts the last one to him. The sailor holding the short string loses — and most often must perform an unfavorable deed.

We lined up, and down Ezira came — hopping down the line towards me as my friends pulled their strings from his closed fist. I'm sweating, you know, can hardly find my breath. And Ezira gets to me, looks me in the eye and holds out his hand — and I pulled out the shortest string I've ever seen in my life.

You know that feeling in your body when you realize something terrible? Feels like molten iron dropped into your stomach? I almost vomited. I'm damn sure they must have seen it. I tried my best to keep a straight face, because some of the men hadn't yet pulled, but all that ran through my mind was that I've been so scared of that dog this whole goddamn time. And now I had to carry it up this steep, rocking plank without it so much as nipping my hand. But no matter how much I hated that picture in my mind, it was better than the alternative. Because, if you don't yet understand, the penalty for not going through with the Dead Man's Wager is execution.

I'd seen it before. We tied a first mate's feet together and hands behind his back and tossed him over the rail, then we all lined up and drew pieces again.

So I was confused, to say the least, when Ezira walked to the railing and tossed his string overboard. And then he turned to us, stretched his back in an arch, and said, "Well, wish me luck. Now where's that damn dog?"

I don't actually know if Ezira saw who pulled the short string, or if he did in fact pull a shorter one. All I know is that I leaned over the edge and dropped mine into the water, too.

Eventually, Ezira wrangled the dog and found — oddly — no anger or snapping teeth. It let him carry it across to the stinking, rotting hull where we found it. Maybe it thought we were helping it. And maybe we were, because by marooning the dog on that abandoned ship, we spared it from our more gruesome intentions. And I think that's what Ezira was thinking to himself — that if he let something happen to that animal, we'd owe the sea something worse than a hand and a single soul.

I'm still not sure if the curse was real, or if it existed only in our minds. In the end it doesn't matter — I'm still scared of it. Mostly because I don't know how to count my sightings. If the curse says that the first sighting brings you suffering and the second brings relief, then the ship named The Black Dog fits that pattern so far. And this story is one — of several — of the reasons why I am not eager to return to the sea. If I do, however, I hope I never see that ship again — because for those of you keeping track, the third sighting brings you death.

CHAPTER 37

Like a poorly-framed painting, a tilted square of yellow sunlight adorned the wall opposite Timid and Barend's shared bunk. Nothing had ever offended Timid's eyes so much.

Barend reached behind himself and scratched his lower half, bumping against Timid's. The escape from such barbarous torture required standing up — a crucible of mental fortitude that Timid, at the moment, lacked the ability to pass. He flipped through the pages of the imaginary journal in his brain, trying to piece together the puzzle of why his head weighed a thousand pounds. Something about a man with a pipe? Was that man a wizard? Was this a demonic hex cast upon Timid's mind? Drawing from his reserve of fairy tale lore, he now realized what mischief that sorcerer must have been up to. Timid would get up and walk outside to discover his horse stolen and his precious gemstones missing.

Disregarding fantasy, the only thing weighing Timid down was a long night of blood loss, free beers, and shared flasks. Unfortunately, none of them had contained water. His groggy meander to the washroom would be familiar to many, but not him. Even when the Malachai had been docked in port and the crew let loose on the local taverns, he remained underage for the vast majority of his sailing tenure. Besides, he lived on the ship whether or not it was tied up.

Though the inn's patrons remained still, a chorus of shuffling and sizzling escaped from the kitchen. Timid crossed the hallway as quickly as his dehydrated body would allow, trying to prevent the smell from angering his grumpy stomach. It had many good reasons to resent him, but perhaps he could avoid it realizing that breakfast was unaffordable.

Entering the washroom triggered a cascade of memories. The repurposed trough-turned-tub sat alone in the room's center, apparently cleaned by someone since Timid had last seen it. A half-full bucket of water waited near the rear door and an unmistakable red hue spotted the floorboards beneath his feet. Each of these prodded him, inching him closer to the edge. And somewhere below, too, was an ocean. He looked down, and his half-arm throbbed.

Timid remembered the blue of it all. A color to him, now, that meant loneliness. But he hadn't been truly alone — he had seen the nautilus again and spoken to it again. He did agree to another bargain, but he wasn't sure on what terms exactly. And Timid remembered its explanation for what was happening to him — for why he had melted away in front of the fireplace. From what Timid understood, transferring from one world to the next is an imperfect process. Each time he pushes that curtain aside and goes beyond, he leaves a bit more of his physical self behind. As simple — and as confusing — as that.

But that brought benefits, too. He held now an attachment of sorts with the all-connected vein of water that ran between the two worlds. Both the snow on the ground outside and the water sitting quietly in the bucket were acutely aware of him, just as he was of them and as the water trapped inside the charred mass in the middle of Goodhaven had been.

He grabbed the metal bucket's handle and hoisted it up to a waist-high washbasin. He poured it in, sediment and all, and plugged the drain with the provided cork. When he submerged his hand, he might as well have been full of holes. His skin soaked up water and pushed it through his body like his own blood, letting him taste its silt as it ran down his tongue and into his throat.

A splash of water to the face calmed the waves in his stomach enough that he could survive a trip to the bread-scented saloon. Pops and crackles jumped out of the fresh logs in the fireplace and the snowshoes hanging beside the front door reminded him that he still had to walk down the mountain.

The other guests woke up one-by-one, and Timid found himself recognizing their faces and names. Pipe-owning-man was Willem, one of the younger boys was Mikhail. And when each of them reached the saloon, they either regarded Timid with a smile or gave him a friendly clasp on the shoulder. Timid wished that he could remember more than the foggy outline of what happened in this inn last night.

Barend stumbled out, too — obviously worse for wear but equipped with a well-seasoned set of drinking legs.

"ARRRGH," Barend yelled at Timid in his best pirate stereotype.

A flock of synchronized "ARRRGH"s rained out from the other men in what appeared to be an orchestrated effort.

"Barend," Timid called out, waving him over to the bar counter, "we need to get going."

"Aye," Barend answered, attempting in vain to tame his beard. "You seen Crazy Joe?"

Timid picked through his brain. "I have no idea who that is," he finally said.

"You don't remember Crazy Joe?" Barend asked, awkwardly clambering up a barstool much too high for him.

"No," Timid answered. "Why?"

"'Cause he's our ride."

Timid stared at his confusing friend. "What? What do you mean?" he asked.

Barend stared back. "He's taking us downhill to Sevast," he answered. "He said he leaves early, so we better find him."

"Oi, Barend, you got us a ride? That's unbelievable!" Timid hopped up out of his chair and looked around the room. "Where is he, what's he look like?"

"Oh he's not here," Barend said, "or you'd know. Probably out back hitching up the wagon — that's all he talked about last night."

"So we're riding in the wagon, then, eh?"

Barend laughed. "Hope so, because I ain't riding that mule."

The mule was very dirty. Crazy Joe was very dirty. The wagon was very dirty. Soon Timid and Barend would be very dirty.

"We sure do appreciate this," Timid said, hopelessly searching the cart for the best place to set his belongings.

"Aye, 'tis a small task," Crazy Joe responded. With a warm smile. He patted the mule on its back, assuring that the harness fit snugly against its skin. "Downhill for t'e most part anyway, Doctor Speed here won't barely notice y'all."

"That's his name?" Timid asked.

"Aye," Crazy Joe answered, giving the mule a tickle under the chin as it looked back at him.

Barend took the bait. "He fast then?" Barend asked.

Crazy Joe laughed. "Hell no, slowest darn t'ing you ever saw."

Barend didn't quite get it. "Then why is his name Doctor Speed?"

Crazy Joe laughed again and spit on the ground. "Well, son, you gonna ask if he a doctor, too?"

For a split second, Barend did imagine the mule standing on its hind legs, taking someone's pulse. "I guess not," Barend answered, "and I guess I won't ask why they call you Crazy Joe."

"Well that one I can explain," Crazy Joe said, "'tis a family name."

The men finished harnessing the nonplussed creature and loaded the wagon without much help from the shorthanded Timid. Crazy Joe revealed that he and Doctor Speed had come up a few days ago, hauling a full load of feed hay for the inn's stables. Remains from decades of similar or identical trips coated the wagon's floor, soggy and clumped with boot-trodden mud. Timid thought of the long night he spent in Lepori's wagon speeding through the Living Forest and how that seemed like a lifetime ago. And in a way, it was several.

Barend clasped Timid on the shoulder. "Let's go say goodbye to the boys," Barend said.

They entered the Saddled Salmon's rear door once again — which for Timid was something of an uncomfortable revisit of his own history. Barend released another "ARRRGH" into the saloon and got many more in return, though some were hindered by cheeks half-full of fried potatoes.

Willem put down his fork and stood to shake their hands. "So you're off then, eh?" Willem asked.

"Just about," Barend answered, "thought we'd come send regards."

"We'll be sorry to not have your stories tonight, Timid. And Barend's harmonica."

Timid didn't remember much harmonica. "You played?" he asked Barend.

Another man piped up. "How about one more, eh, Barend?" he said. The rest of them chirped in support. Barend tried to wave them off.

But then Timid joined in. "C'mon, mate, I wanna hear," he said.

To a roar of cheers, Barend removed his harmonica from his pocket. He pulled up a chair and sat in it backwards. "So what'll it be?"

"The one about Timid!" someone yelled.

"Me?" Timid asked the room.

"Aye," Willem said, "it's a good one."

The harmonica bled life into the room. Mugs and bottoms of silverware stomped against the table. A man with a bushy mustache and suspenders sang in a familiar call-and-response pattern.

I once met a man, they say his name was Timid,
He was twice the sailor I will ever be.
They say he's the only man, that the sea wouldn't drown...
And the rest of the building, except for Timid, joined in to say,
O' I wish that I was him and he was me.

As much as Timid felt the odd man out, he wasn't. Everyone smiled and looked for his reaction. He didn't have much of one. But apparently the song kept going anyway, as Barend took another breath and Mikhail wrapped his arms around Timid's shoulder to make him sway in tune. They all sang this time.

O' Captain, O' crew, the stormwind's a comin',
Tonight's a Black Tide, with no moon.
O' Captain, O' crew, I think we've met our doom,
Unless that man Timid shows up soon.
O' Captain, O' crew, the waves are a drummin',
That's the sound that tastes of salt and brine.
O' Captain, O' crew, I think we're going down,
Unless we find Timid just in time.
I once met a man, they say his name was Timid,
He was twice the sailor I will ever be.
They say he's the only man, that the sea wouldn't drown,
O' I wish that I was him and he was me.

CHAPTER 38

The wagon proved to be a particularly creaky one. Maybe it, too, was exceedingly bored by Doctor Speed's pace, which seemed entirely unaffected by the downward slope.

Barend's harmonica passed time for all of them. But Crazy Joe particularly enjoyed it.

"You got a certain way with that," Crazy Joe said after one distinctly spirited ending. "Play it like a hog."

"Hog?" Barend retorted. "I object! This is a fine brass instrument, and I treat it with the respect it deserves."

Crazy Joe laughed in a way that made him seem actually crazy. "Hehehehe! Don't take it as an insult, little feller. Quite the opposite."

Timid patted Barend on the back. "The Brass Pig — how's that sound for a stage name?"

"Won't need it," Barend said. "I ain't playing no more. Won't have everyone think of me a hog."

Here, the road grew a thick belly as it approached a drinking hole in the river. Crazy Joe pulled the reins to convince Doctor Speed to stop — which took almost no effort at all. Timid hopped down.

"Hey Barend, think of it like this," Timid said. "I don't reckon he's licensed to practice medicine, but this mule has already taught me something about myself."

"Oh yeah?" Barend snorted. "What's that?"

Timid scratched the mule under its chin. "Names aren't curses."

Here I interject again, for what must be the last time, to give Timid and Barend some breathing room. By the providence of Crazy Joe and his molasses-esque steed, Doctor Speed, they did make it to the river village of Sevast — which sat nervous and still, awaiting the delayed first shipment of fish over the pass. After that, sleeping under the stars for a few more nights proved easy in the warming spring air, although a pesky fog rose with the moon and coated their blankets in a piercing dew. But during the day, quiet streams and sun-soaked pools harbored hungry-enough trout. And because a seafolk can always figure out how to fish, a few fins left the water for good.

The men enjoyed the safety and comfort of populated roads, though Barend sometimes forgot his manners. Eventually, after a few too many debates about how far they had left, they spied the open gates of Corical.

Also known as the Stone City, Corical's walls and palace towers rise higher than any other buildings on the Isle. This is no surprise, as it is home to the Isle's regency and its richest families. Together, daily trade caravans and farming carts haul a diverse array of goods inwards to the city like water down a drain. Whatever is needed to sustain the Stone City's population, the largest — and hungriest — on the isle.

But any city of Corical's size has problems. Class inequality kills more than any disease. Children in the outward slums fall prey to their own empty stomachs by the dozen each day, while those in the Inner

Circle thrive in stone mansions with servants, personal guards, and privately boarded horses. Money runs in the streets of Corical — just not equally.

Crime, too, is born from numbers. But unlike gold or silver, criminality is not confined to one class nor the other — each simply prefers their own poison. Rich socialites might seek influence in the political court, or have a penchant for black market items — which range from fanciful artifacts to foreign houseslaves. But because the less fortunate don't have the means to dabble in such high circles, they turn to petty theft, violent robberies, or underground gambling to make ends meet or — for the ones with more lofty goals — to climb up a rung on the ladder.

Peace, therefore, is hard fought. While the City Guard exists in an official capacity, they work in tandem with sanctioned enforcers. The Boars are one such group, who already have a hand in this whole affair. As it goes, that is where Timid shows his face first, to salvage what he can from his reward. But while he is recognizable in appearance, he carries with him a refashioned spirit. He has saved lives — of both the real and imaginary sort. He has spread tales — and not always using words. And, most importantly, he has gained the unspoken confidence of a man who has entered the Living Forest and returned.

"Do you have any proof?" Commander Varah asked. He leaned back in his chair until it stood only on its hind legs.

Timid shook his head. "No, sir. Only the witness."

The commander pawed at his notes. "And what should I tell the City Guard, hmm? That a seafolk says their sources are foul?"

"I don't know, sir," answered Timid. "I think you should at least tell them to stop sending people in there. I've not told you the whole truth, I know you've figured that much out — but there never was any girl. I'm just sorry I lost Swait before I learned it for myself."

Commander Varah stared down the bridge of his nose. "It's going to be hard for me to explain this to the other men if you won't even explain it to me."

They sat in an office in a tower in a fortress in a city. The office was Commander Varah's, the tower was just a tower, the fortress was the Boars guildhall, and the city was Corical. All that wandering about in the wilderness and Timid hit his intended destination right on the money. It could be viewed as a miracle if you didn't know how roads worked. This room turned out to be rather cozy compared to how it could have been. Desks overflowing with loose parchment lined nearly every inch of wallspace that didn't have a window cut into the stone. To the comfort of Timid's psyche, a mild fishy smell saturated the office — courtesy of two whale oil lamps hanging from the ceiling by chains, though Timid never saw any matches to light them with.

After enough silence, the commander sighed and sat forward again. "I still can't wrap my head all the way around this, but I do believe you, Timid. I don't know why, but I do. Maybe because I don't peg you for a storyteller. Can you draw me a map? So we can at least have something to give the City Guard."

"Yes, sir," Timid nodded. "Will that be all for now?"

"Don't you want your payment?" the commander asked. He tossed a jingling cloth bag on Timid's side of the desk.

Timid took the coinpurse and weighed it in his hand. "But..." he said, "this looks like full pay."

"And why wouldn't it?" Commander Varah retorted. "You did what we asked of you and went through hell to do it."

If you set your eye to him, Commander Varah did not look particularly experienced. Perhaps he had shot up through the ranks because of a noble heritage, but Timid didn't know for sure. However, his reputation as a fair and competent leader was the convincing factor when Timid decided to join the Boars rather than the City Guard. But even then, Timid had expected a mercenary guild's figurehead to be a bit rougher around the edges. Compared to Swait and the other old Boars, Varah appeared unseasoned and devoid of scar — except for a thick casing of melted skin on his fingers and palms.

"Look, Timid," the commander continued, "I know this will be hard to swallow, but I don't think we'll have much use for you anymore. If I had my way, I'd give you some of Swait's purse too. But that's not the contract you signed and someone would catch it in the books. I'm sorry. You'll have to turn in your badge downstairs."

Timid looked blankly across the room at the commander. He probably could have gained some sympathy by pointing out all the trouble he could have avoided if he had ever received a badge in the first place, but he instead nodded politely and dismissed himself from the commander's office. As the door shut behind him, Timid suppressed his instinct to raise the full bag of copper and jump with joy like a child in the rain. He channeled his excitement into a more controlled motion, and walked as directly as he could towards the guildhall's front entrance — where he had told his witness to wait. And, thankfully, Barend had not yet wandered off into the neighborhood's labyrinthian sidestreets or irked one of the Boars' more grumpy mercenaries with unsolicited smalltalk. Barend actually seemed to be in a small shouting match with a pack of crows — one of the more unpleasant of Eadron's creatures. They naturally irked Timid, but although some seafolk believed them to be a harbinger of bad things to come, he regarded them as a friendly reminder that not all gods are perfect.

And as the two men slipped back into the depths of the city, someone else emerged out of it. A courier from the City Guard parted the guildhall doors and tacked a piece of parchment to their message board. The date was scribbled in the top corner and a list of names fell halfway down the page. Among them was "Timid Stormwind, suspected pirate."

CHAPTER 39

Selah lay flat on her bottom bunk and traced the familiar stains and knots on the frame above her. One of the girls would likely arrive home soon, and in these final moments of peace she liked to drift away to somewhere unknown and uncharted. A smoky char tinged the air, a remnant of her multiple attempts to light the hearth their room shared with its adjoining partner. Blood ran down her fingertip from a puncture left by a botched stitch.

She blinked a bit too slowly and reopened her eyes underneath blue sky. She sat up among long blades of grass that flowed in the breeze like waves on the sea — or at least how she imagined waves to be. Even standing up betrayed no signs of anything other than a grassy horizon. Her pulse raced.

Was this a dream? She usually didn't recognize her dreams while they were still happening, and she pinched herself to no result other than vivid pain. Was she dead? Well, she couldn't come up with a way to test that.

So she walked — and walked and walked. If she made any progress towards anywhere, she couldn't tell. Nothing infringed upon the pristine horizon. Every blade of grass was an identical twin of its brothers and sisters. A blinding sunlight beat her over the head and refused to set even as the minutes melted into hours.

Her long, brown hair trailed behind her — because if you're walking aimlessly in an endless plain, you might as well face the wind and keep the hair out of your eyes. And the walking came easy. Like she could do it forever.

Selah figured herself hallucinating when she saw a tiny speck of red in the distance. It grew and grew and grew — and eventually she noticed that it bobbed up and down like a quivering insect.

She cursed her blistering feet and sped up. She thought it to be moving slowly away from her, or else she'd have caught it much sooner. And as she drew up upon it, she imagined herself as a predator. With nowhere to hide in this world, she could catch anything if given enough time. And this was easy prey. It was an old, naked man.

Luckily, the grass grew tall enough to obscure his nether regions — but Selah imagined that it must have tickled. A long beard hung to his chest, wiry and gray from time and neglect, and his balding scalp flaked in patches under the scalding sun. He held a lit torch — the source of red — above the grassy plain as he shuffled slowly and steadily towards some unseen destination.

"Hello?" Selah called out from behind. "Can you hear me?"

That did nothing to distract the man from his path. Selah walked up beside him and tapped him on the shoulder.

"Hello, excuse me," she said, "I need help."

The man cornered his eye and found her with it. "Where are you going?" he asked without slowing.

His voice sounded familiar. Like her father. Like her boss. Like every man she had ever known.

"I don't know," Selah answered. "I don't know where I am."

"Then I can't help you," the man said. He turned his eyes forward again and seemed to put this strange woman out of his mind.

Selah kept pace, an easy feat for someone her age. "Well, where are you going? Can I come with?"

"Yes," the man answered. He kept walking. His back arched forward like a tree carrying the weight of winter — or many of them. His decayed posture forced his shoulder to bend at a high angle so that the flame could safely glide over the grass.

A memory flashed in Selah's mind — an old saying passed around churches and their schools: "Heavy to one, feather to another." Intended to instruct children not to judge others for their problems, it also gave old geezers a way to avoid menial labor.

This old geezer didn't appear to be pulling a charade in order to offload his flaming stick.

"Can I carry that for you?" Selah asked.

The man looked at her and smiled through a sparsely populated row of teeth. He held the torch out to her. "Be warned," he said, "it has magic powers."

Selah retracted her hand. "What kind of powers?" Living in Corical, she had learned to be suspicious of men proclaiming to have special abilities.

"It leads you out of this place," the man answered. All the while, he kept walking.

Selah scrunched her eyebrows. "Then why wouldn't I want it?" she asked.

The man shrugged. "Some come looking for answers."

"Well the only answers I need are where I am, why I am here, and how I can leave."

The old man looked at her like a friend happy to be reunited. "You are somewhere that too many have been. You are here because I like you. And you can leave by carrying the torch."

Another memory pinged Selah from her childhood. During a mass prayer at the Church of Stridelong, a priest described the god of human spirits as the perfect man — aged and experienced, master of fire and survival, lean and unclothed. Selah never understood why he had to be unclothed.

"Are you Stridelong?" she asked.

The man thought for a moment, then nodded. "Yes."

Selah pondered the implications of that. "Am I dead?"

"No," he answered, "but I nearly am."

She didn't want to be the bearer of bad news, but that looked to be an accurate assessment. "What are you dying of?"

This time he took a moment to think. "Too many mistakes," he said after a dozen more steps. "Ten thousand papercuts."

Selah wondered what sort of mistakes could kill a god. "What are you doing wrong?" she asked.

"Seems like many things. Being too generous. Being a poor judge of character. With time comes experience, but I didn't learn until it was too late."

Selah shook her head. "I don't understand," she stated. "How do those things kill you?"

The man tried to hand her the torch again. "Take this," he ordered, "before it runs out."

She obeyed and wrapped her fingers around the torch's ancient, wooden handle. Immediately, her feet moved on their own — filled by a fount of infinite energy.

The old man stopped abruptly. "That's my last one," he said in a much weaker tone. "Use it wisely. Please."

Her legs kept marching. "No, no!" she shouted over her shoulder. "Take it back!" But her body wouldn't turn, and her shoeless feet wouldn't stop.

The man muttered an apology. Selah couldn't tell if he directed at her or himself. She flailed her arms and fought against her legs, which pulled her like two horses reigned to a sleigh. But, with so little experience, she wasn't yet accustomed to holding the torch. An unmindful swing brought it to the tips of grass and set them alight.

Heat and flame spread in a deafening fury. Fueled by the wind, the fire uprooted everything in a spray behind her, much like the wisps of her own hair.

"Stop it," she cried, "put it out!"

The man stared at her through bubbling skin and blood. "I can't," he said, "I can only start them."

Selah woke her housemates with a curdling scream that could have soured milk. Delilah threw her blankets off and jumped down to wrap her arms around her hyperventilating bunkmate. Maria and Simi sat on their bunk and checked the room for murderers and demons — but found none. Delilah rocked Selah in her arms and whispered reassurances.

"A nightmare?" Maria offered to the room. Footsteps climbed the hallway stairs.

Simi put her feet on the floor and offered an extra blanket. "Did you dream about your mother again?" she asked.

Selah only sobbed. Delilah began to sing.

Here, starling, here, starling,

Let out your cry.

Send it to me,

And let it fly high.

CHAPTER 40

The Barking Goat Inn bustled with its usual crowd, which was none. Most people found themselves repelled by the wailing creature perched on a post outside the inn's front door, but budget lodging rates were bait enough for Timid and Barend.

Barend barely contained his curiosity about the goat that obviously lent the inn its name. "That your goat?" he asked as they exchanged enough of their newly-acquired riches for two beds.

The inn's proprietor obviously heard this often. She glared at Barend from under her thinning eyebrows.

"Yes," she stated plainly. Though she didn't appear all too old, her skin sagged off her face as if weights had been attached to it with clothespins — perhaps from a lack of sleep.

Barend rubbed his chin, somehow lost deep in thought in an otherwise shallow pond. "But wouldn't it be less annoying if it was tied out back? I nearly didn't want to even come in here."

They still heard the goat while inside — really it could be heard from quite a ways in every direction. A frustrated sigh escaped from the woman and she put on a face often used to deal with children.

"If I tie it out back," she said slowly, "it chews through the rope and walks out front again. I am not deaf."

Barend laughed. "Well, it's a wonder nobody has snuck up at night and put a knife to it. It might be hard to sleep with that racket."

"They wouldn't be the first," the woman said under her breath.

"What do you mean?" Timid asked. "Someone has tried to kill it before?"

"Not only that," the woman said, "they've succeeded. That's my fourth goat."

"And they all do that?" Timid asked.

"Aye," the woman answered. She set her hands on the countertop and leaned forward. "Now I don't confide in every bloke who comes in here, lest word gets out that I'm a loon, but I'll tell you. I think it's a curse."

The two men looked at each other, saw that the other was willing to burn some time, and then returned their gazes to the woman behind the counter.

"What kind of curse?" they both asked.

The woman leaned even farther forward, perhaps in her best impression of an old croon, and began in a squeaky, soft voice. "Every so often, one of the neighbors — or a guest aboard for a long stay — decides they've had enough. It might seem harmless to slaughter a little farm critter, especially because they tend to leave the meat for me — but there are more vindictive forces in this world that apparently think otherwise. You see, I only ever bought one goat."

She licked her chapped, dusty lips and bathed in the confused looks radiating from the two men.

"Now," she continued, "I'll tell you the rest of it and let you put your own thoughts together. One of the butchers was a guest here. Paid for a week in advance, but after each of the first few nights he goes on and on about not getting a lick of sleep. So, next night the goat goes quiet. The man comes out of his room in the morning all bright, talking about finally getting a good rest. Later that evening, the man goes into his room and doesn't come back out again, far as I could tell.

"Eventually, I get to bed and I'm enjoying my own sleep, you know, just as relieved as any other. But lo and behold, the bleating and hollering returns — only this time it's coming from somewhere here, under the roof. I have a look around, 'cause I don't want it inside neither, and what do I find? It's in that man's room, behind the locked door. I get my keys and let it out, and it clops its little hooves out the front door and up onto that post."

She pointed her skeletal finger at the front door. "That's still it outside," she said.

Barend downed an audible gulp. Timid looked over his shoulder and through the skinny crack in the door that the wind insisted on keeping open, and made eye contact with a small, black goat. Its four hooves fought each other for space to stand as it sang from its precarious perch. And if Timid had known what he was looking for, he might have seen the two Boars that were waiting for him outside.

There were actually three Boars in total, but the third was just now arriving at the City Guard's central office. He waited patiently in line, whistling a short tune about a cowboy finding a once-lost trove of gold. The desk-bound guard in the reception hall eventually called him to approach, and he obeyed.

"I'd like to collect a bounty," the Boar said.

Timid spent the better portion of ten minutes trying to pull a rope out of a well using a single hand. His ultimate mechanism involved a foot and was rather entertaining to observe. As he finally grabbed hold of the prize at the rope's end, water sloshed wastefully over its brim and spoiled the dry dirt behind the Barking Goat Inn. As always, a nearby goat conducted a fierce debate — and its new opponent seemed to be Timid's shorter, more easily ignitable companion.

The mid-spring sun pressed gently on anything under it, which included Timid. A long walk from one side of Corical to the other seemed a marathon without water, but alas his creaking, stiff joints would once more feel greased. He plunged headfirst into the bucket, and — because the water went up past his ears — he didn't hear the men approach. They put a knifepoint to Barend's back and pushed firmly.

"Don't move a muscle," a voice whispered in Barend's ear, who found himself compelled to follow the instructions of sharp, phantom voices.

Timid finally finished his bird bath and noticed first that the argument between man and goat had ended, and second that the goat was champion — once again by forfeit. When he turned to prod fun at Barend, Timid saw the four men.

One wrapped an arm around Barend's neck and poked a thin, curved knife toward his belly. Another, with a ragged City Guard uniform that showed silver mail through its holes, stood closer to Timid and held a hand to the hilt of a sheathed sword. The other two stood behind this man, their vanguard, wearing smiles polished by the power of numbers.

"Timid Stormwind," the guard said, "you're a wanted man."

Timid recognized one of the Boars standing behind the guard. It was a young man much like him; someone he had worked alongside mopping floors and washing dishes. Timid clicked his tongue with a putrid disappointment in the betrayal. This was undoubtedly who had recognized him.

"C'mon, Kilgore," Timid said, "it doesn't have to be this way."

"Eat what you kill," Kilgore said. "You know that."

A dusty lash of wind swept the empty street. Somewhere nearby — maybe in the middle of it all — a tumbleweed rolled idly by.

Timid thought about moving, and they could tell.

"There doesn't have to be much trouble," the guard continued. "The bounty calls for taking you alive enough to hold a trial. Now, you come with us, and do so peacefully, and we'll leave your friend without a new hole in his gut."

The man holding Barend grinned through broken teeth and twisted the knife in an act meant to display gratuitous cruelty.

At this point in time, Timid was more akin to a sickly farm goat than a properly regimented fighting man. He had no knife or weapons of any sort, his only clothing couldn't protect him from any weather beyond the perfectly ideal, and his heels and toes screamed at him through blisters and tender flesh angry at being stuck in old, often wet boots. Add in his new disfigurement, and it would be fair to say that Timid's options were limited.

But his seemingly unquenchable thirst for fresh water drew his gaze back to the bucket at his side — and down into the depth from which it had ascended. An otherwise dark and black sheen reflected a small halo of light, filled at the center by the shadow of the face staring into it.

It is hard to blame someone who always looks for another way out rather than taking things head on. For most, the other route may lead away from death instead of towards it. But time and time again, Timid's path bent back on itself and headed right back at cold inanimacy. And right now, this option presented itself to him again.

The well seemed about twenty feet deep before it hit water. He spied no sharp outcroppings or stray materials on the way down, but the world under the surface remained obscured. Further unknown to him was whether a dive would end prematurely at a shallow bottom with a broken neck — a fate surely irreversible by the forces that shepherded him back and forth across life's border.

Timid also considered whether the nautilus would consider their bargain fulfilled. If the only person saved by Timid was someone held hostage in ransom for Timid's own life, that may not be exactly the sort of deal that the creature had in mind. And if these bounty hunters meant what they said, Timid had a better chance of preserving Barend's life by accepting their offer.

But perhaps they, too, were unaware of certain facts and did not piece together that one of the sleeves at Timid's side was dangling free — empty and lifeless.

The leading man confirmed this when he grew impatient and shouted, "Put your hands above your head."

Timid complied as best he could by raising his right hand in the air.

"Both of 'em," the guard commanded.

"All of the hands I have are above my head," said Timid. Helpfully, the wind chose this moment to show itself, swinging the hollow fabric like a pendulum.

A slow smile made its way across the guard's lips. The three others chuckled behind him like cubs mimicking their mother.

"Aw shucks," the guard said in feigned disappointment, "I was hoping to try out my new toy." He held two of his fingertips low to his side, where a small red dot of firelight appeared seemingly out of nothingness.

CHAPTER 41

Burgush entered the back door to a small repair shop, ducking through the frame built only for those of normal stature. The shop could fit about twenty people shoulder to shoulder if they crammed themselves up against the equipment and projects that stood out like islands — both above and below a sea of green skin and red eyes. And for his fifth such crowd this week, word had spread.

Burgush figured that the shop was successful from the stench of whale that floated about and the steady shadows that didn't flicker and dance. Whale oil torches are luxuries saved for those on more than a salary of pennies. He didn't know who the owners were, but the simple fact that this gathering was allowed to take place here meant that Burgush had unexpected allies. And it served as another reminder that not every human was an enemy.

Burgush stood about where the room's head would be if it had one. "Good evening, ladies and gentlemen. Thank you all for coming, and after a long day I'm sorry that we don't have seats, so I will try to keep this short.

"Something is happening — something that does not bode well for you and I. Flames burn us in the streets. Who is to say that it won't spread to our houses? Our families? Our children? If circumstances were a bit different, we wouldn't be able to do anything about it. But it seems fortune has not entirely fallen on one side, and — for once — we may hold part of our destiny in our own hands. A great providence has been gifted to us, one which we must use wisely — and I do mean we, not I.

"But what I need is your trust. Although I have filled my ranks with our kind, I cannot stay your executions — because a lawful decree says that justice must be handed down fairly to those who deserve it. And because that has not been rightfully enforced before now, it is our right to strike back — and we must do so while the iron is hot.

"Our new revelation is that our city's officials have deemed it fit to extend my reach beyond the gallows and into the streets. I may now sanction the arrest, trial, and sentencing of the lawbreakers in our community. Do not be fooled — I intend to wield this power equally, sparing no soul because of the color of the flesh it inhabits. I do say this to warn you, but also to make you aware that your complaints will no longer fall on deaf ears.

"Another matter deserves discussion: our long-neglected congregation. If you have felt yourselves abandoned by the forces above, I implore you to reconsider your faith. Yes, those with so much are being given more, but now one of us has received a gift no other can match — and by our bond of blood that means that you, too, deserve to be blessed. If you fall ill or suffer injury, let others know and word will reach me. And if you know of someone who receives something they should not — perhaps like a fire that they did not themselves stoke — let others know and, again, I will make sure justice is handed down."

Rows of toothy smiles bade each other quiet, kind words. Burgush turned to his side and left without further ceremony.

To his side walked a cloaked figure, unseen by anyone but him. It, too, smiled.

Do them too often, and wagon rides grow boring. Timid found each becoming less pleasant than the last — and if this one felt of steel bars and angry men, he wasn't looking forward to the next.

Everybody seemed to be in a foul mood, as if they were all being paid to be grumpy. In fact, some of them were. The armed escorts were certainly instructed to make the journey unpleasant, but Timid didn't see why the circumstances alone wouldn't suffice. Plus, all the birds on this road were crows, and he began to wonder what he had done wrong to offend their kind and deserve their scorn.

He sat on an old, splintery wooden bench. They didn't quite know what to do when a prisoner required only one handcuff, so after a great debate they settled on shackling the extra to Timid's ankle. In all, he was terribly uncomfortable — mostly because the chain's insufficient length forced him to hold his wrist to his calf in a hunched posture more fit for a quick stretch than an overnight trip to Shrieksport.

Falling darkness brought the caravan to a halt. Timid had a feeling he'd be sleeping where he was, and he was right. At least the guards had the kindness to enclose the wagon's cage in cloth, trapping some of the heat — and all of the stench — inside.

And the relative safety of a thin, wind-whipped cover subdued Timid's swarming mind, which couldn't remember if tonight was a Black Tide. By Timid's memory, they were at least a few days past the last White Tide — when Celesta hung her beautiful brightness in the night sky for everyone to see by. But only five days separated a White Tide from its dark, hideous sibling — the last of which had plagued Timid's return to Goodhaven with a thick fog of black. Superstitions run abound in the Isle, but it's a hard fact that the smaller a group is, the more vulnerable a Black Tide leaves them. If, instead, the caravan had been camping under a moonless night, the guards might have posted the prisoners as watchmen around the ring of firelight — perhaps even armed with hastily-pointed sticks. Any travelers attempting to stay over in a small, roadside village on such a night would face the same conscription. Without as many lamps to keep the night away, lonely communities get swallowed — sometimes literally. And in that way, the cycle feeds itself. Every time a lamp is extinguished, its neighbors are forced closer to the line of black at the edge of town. So when Timid craned his neck painfully to see out a hole in the cage's cover and saw a pale sliver of moon, it appeared to him as stunningly intense as a lighthouse beacon. Horror breeds in darkness, and he would rather stay out of it.

As lucky as Timid found himself with the pace of the calendar, he felt the opposite about the quality of his companionship. He tried to count, but couldn't find a dozen teeth between the four other men in the cage. Common, typical, petty — they didn't have much going for them. Two of them knew each other, and annoyed the others with idle chit chat.

Any rest Timid tried to gather did not find him easily. A distinct lack of water laid on Timid like a heavy beam across his shoulders, squeezing all of his energy out into the night air. Worse than all that, and scaring away the crows, were the toads. An incessant and unbearable cascade of moans and croaks oozed out over much of the Isle, and here turned out to be no different. The high alpine air and busy city streets almost let him forget about the damn things, but once again he found himself deep inside their territory. For a short while Timid considered the possibility that perhaps all the toads in the world had congregated at this moment in time just to play a trick on him.

If those ingredients weren't enough to make an unhappy person, an encroaching fear of the unknown pricked his mind like falling drips from a broken faucet. Nobody had told him why they suspected him of piracy or what evidence they had to show for such a charge. He was guilty, yes, but didn't feel it. In a way, he felt a different person than the one who had accompliced in the crime. In fact, that person had died. If this Timid was on that ship instead of the other, the fates of all men involved would have been different. But even after all his adventure, fortune, and misfortune, he still held the same name. And this time, his name was more than a curse — it was a noose around his neck.

Eventually Timid did succumb to peaceful sleep, but not alone and not unaided. It seemed that everyone, man and toad alike, were lulled by the gentle sound of a harmonica rolling over the nearby hills, from somewhere just out of sight.

CHAPTER 42

Burgush removed his blood-soaked gloves and lay them on the jail's basement desk. The guard sitting there, an Oruk, peered over the top of his papers and recoiled. "Sheesh. How did it go?" the guard asked.

"Smoothly," Burgush answered. "Though I swear every neck is different. Still getting the swing of things."

The two Oruks let out wide grins, fully revealing their protruding canines. "I never thought I'd see someone killed for stealing Oruk wages," the guard said, "but what a wonderful world it has become."

"Better get used to it," Burgush said. "I'd say 'enjoy it while it lasts,' but this time seems different, doesn't it?"

The guard nodded. "It does, Burgush. I had a kid ask me if I was the Hangman on the way to work today."

"What did you say?" Burgush asked.

"I said 'I wish.'"

Door hinges and keys jangled on the landing above their heads, and chains and heels shortly followed. Burgush massaged the meat of his hands and headed upstairs to the guardhouse's main landing. "See to it that the axe is cleaned," he commanded behind him, "I've got to process the new lot."

Despite his relative public fame, Burgush still had his clerical duties. He had to certify that each new prisoner actually was the person on the bounty ledger, which could be a bit of trouble if someone claimed to forget their name. But men without names needed no food, so they usually remembered it within a day or two.

Burgush gave the new arrivals a glance up and down, ultimately deciding that they didn't seem very dangerous — they didn't even have all of their limbs.

"Welcome to Shrieksport," Burgush said. "Who's who?"

The escorting guard pointed at each criminal in turn, rattling off their name and crime. Most were boring, low-level criminals, one was a horse thief, and at the end of the line was "Timid Stormwind, pirate."

A few Shrieksport guards looked on, and found a mocking pleasure at this fresh bit of irony. "Where's your hook, pirate?" one called out.

The pirate stared forward, silent and blank. Like his extra sleeve, his hair was wet with blood and tied in a knot. A small laceration etched its way across his eyebrow, a familiar sign of a surely accidental collision with a bootheel.

"Who's confessed?" Burgush asked the escort as they exchanged papers.

"All 'cept the pirate," the man answered. He looked around the room and noticed the obvious — that every guard except him was an Oruk. "Hey, you greens really run this joint, huh?"

"Aye," Burgush said. "Problem?"

Burgush owned fifty pounds and six inches on the human, and a little less on the other Oruks.

"Nah, mate," the man said, "just odd. We got a few of you folk up in the city, but damn, not like this. Prolly for the better, to be true. Y'all can take a lickin'."

Burgush looked at the escort — the only human in the room without chains — and wondered if the man simply hadn't heard what was going on in Shrieksport or if he was just one of the few who didn't care.

"Throw the pirate in with the other holdouts," Burgush commanded to no one in particular.

The human tapped Burgush on the arm. "Watch out for that one," the escort said, "can't trust those seafolk."

"I know," Burgush said.

Counting his lucky stars, Timid came up short. On his way to somewhere deeper, darker, and worse, he passed cells for the confessed and noted their beds and blankets. The three other holdouts sat in a single cage-like cell, already much too cramped. A far cry from the typical criminals that Timid had just traveled with, each new face possessed its own unique oddity.

Frightening Timid the most was a frail, small, young woman curled up in the corner, snarling at the others. Her long hair matted against itself to form oily cords, which likely reeked of unkempt odors if anyone dared get close enough. Timid had always called the more refined version of this hairstyle "barbarian hair," so he couldn't come up with a properly worse name for whatever hers was. She wore no conventional clothing, but instead wrapped herself in an eclectic assortment of crudely tanned hides.

Less strange, but still strange, was another woman — eyes, mouth, and even teeth covered in black makeup. Her hair — also black — lay neatly in a short braid directly behind her head, and her wrists, lips, and ears barely showed skin through an impressive array of piercings. Perhaps indicative of a constant state of ornament-induced pain, she flared her nostrils in an odd pattern and seemingly couldn't control the squint of her eyes. Her clothing was surprisingly nice — formal and unsurprisingly black.

The third appeared harmless and bored. He made bubbling noises with his lips while he tapped on the iron bars above him. He was entirely bald and devoid of decoration, except that his plain white clothes bore a small, crescent insignia of the moon goddess, Celesta. He welcomed Timid with a polite half-smile and eyebrow raise.

The cell door clanged shut behind Timid.

"Go ahead, sit," the bald man said, pointing at the cell's remaining, empty corner. "Don't be afraid of her, the bites eventually heal." The bald man held up a hand marked by a red arc below his pinky. "I'm Vorn, it's nice to meet you."

Timid didn't sit. "What's going on here?" he asked.

"What do you mean?"

"All the guards are Oruks," Timid said. "I was raised here, and that was definitely not the case even last year."

The bald man nodded slowly. "A slow wave of change seems to have finally come to a crash. Strange, but not entirely unexpected. Started with the Hangman, come to think of it. We get executions just about every day now, and they're quite the show."

"He hangs people every day?" Timid clarified.

"No," Vorn said, "the name is sort of a holdover — he never hangs anymore."

Timid didn't understand until Vorn made a chopping motion with one hand against the other.

Timid finally sat. "And I thought the noose gave me nightmares," he said.

"Well, what did you do?" Vorn asked. "They do kill for a lot nowadays, but not everything."

Timid glanced around the larger room to see a guard standing near the door. "If you think I'm going to confess to you, you'd be very wrong."

"Okay," Vorn said, "I'll start. Illegal medicine — distributing, mind you. Suddenly everything we did violated some code or obscure law. Never thought helping the poor was a crime, but hey, who am I but a lowly vicar, eh?"

The bald man looked at the others, silently asking for a volunteer. The very piercing-forward woman in all black leaned forward and put on a sly smile. "Collecting souls for Thakros," she said with a giddy jump and wide eyes.

Vorn nodded, seeming impressed. "Hmm, more creative this time. Thank you, Akta." He then turned to face the angry mess in the corner. "Janella? Our new friend here would appreciate it if you shared."

The woman managed to sneak out two words between growls. "Tax evasion," she said. But from what Timid knew of the Isle's uncivilized folk, she likely didn't use money or even know what taxes were.

Vorn counted on his fingers. "So, let's take stock. Distributing illegal substances, that might be death penalty — unless you can pay the fine, which I can't and the church won't. Tax evasion just got added to the list of death-worthy crimes, I think because that's a real surefire way of getting those high-class suckers. Janella, I think you're just collateral damage in that. And I have no idea what 'collecting souls for Thakros' means, but keeping in mind that he's the spirit of death, that doesn't bode well for our woman-in-black here."

Akta physically recoiled, putting her hand to her chest and seeming offended. "I do not interfere with the living, you ignoramus. I usher those who cannot find their way to the afterlife further along their path."

Vorn ignored her for the most part and faced Timid next. Vorn beckoned him to put his goods in the pot, too.

Timid gulped air. "Piracy."

Vorn clicked his tongue. "Ouch, sorry."

"Pirate?" whispered Janella. For the moment, she paused her snarling. "You're a pirate?"

"Allegedly," Timid answered.

"Right," Vorn said, "but she's gonna want to hear your story. And trust me, she'll love it."

Timid bit his lip, a method to train himself from wearing his thoughts as a mask. He hadn't exactly pegged these people to be so swiftly welcoming, like old friends gathered in a familiar home. And even if the only thing they had in common was their distaste for immediate confessions, that was at least something. Just about as much as he and Barend ever shared — loneliness and proximity.

Vorn read the silence and shrugged. "Then don't. But you're still seafolk, right? They always have stories, and I bet she hasn't heard many of them."

The feral woman in the far corner showed a set of eager, hopeful eyes. After only a short moment, Timid said, "Well, do you know anything about ghost ships?"

CHAPTER 43

Timid woke in a pile of moldy straw, forgetting for a moment that he wasn't in the back of another wagon. Near him lay three others in a similar predicament. But beyond all the hushed rustling, heavy breaths, and unhappy stomach groans that came with a shared space, a distant sound of air-blown reeds floated in through the barred windows and vents at the top of the room. It reminded Timid of a cowboy woken by a stray band of morning sun leaking through farmhouse shutters. But the light in the jailhouse — corrupted and dulled on its arduous journey underground — resembled sunlight in few ways,

Already awake, staring at him with an agape jaw, was Akta. Her piercings jingled as she nodded her head in a quick, smiling rhythm.

Timid bid her good morning, to be polite, but otherwise tried to avoid eye contact — which was difficult.

"I had a dream," Akta said. "Of magic."

Timid had encountered such fools before, one of them being himself. "You had a magical dream?"

"Yes, I am worthy," Akta answered. "We are all speakers." She looked at the ceiling and flattened her palms as if she were catching rain. A thick, uncompromised smile spread over her face.

After Timid's tale of black dogs and bloody deckboards, they hadn't let him go to bed before he told one a little more conducive to pleasant dreams. And so, because it might have been his last chance, he told them of the place where the trees walk and the grass listens. But some censorship was necessary — though not in order to deceive, but to ensure that they didn't take him for a mere spinner of tall tales, as the Isle already had those by the barrel. But now Akta reminded him that his story, at its core, was a story of being worthy — and he, too, once upon a time, had his fair share of odd dreams.

The talk of Thakros, the mark of Celesta, and the untamed nature seeping from the crazed woman in the corner — each reminded Timid of his own secret association with that other world. His skin might have cracked and crumbled for lack of water if not for the omnipresent bond that Shrieksport shared with the ocean. And now he realized that his bargain, for all he knew, would go unfulfilled. Somewhere, maybe not far, was a sea creature left with one half of a broken promise.

Shrieksport jail's interrogation room hungered for renovation, especially after all the sessions it hosted nowadays. But because Burgush found thrills elsewhere than torture, there wasn't much to improve besides a simple desk and set of chairs. Still, the stench of rotting wood and body odor made it equally unpleasant for both the inquisitor and the subject. At least the cheap torches in here didn't smell like whale carcasses.

Burgush scanned the pirate's bounty sheet. With so little else to show, he needed a confession. Letting the holdouts marinate in their cell typically cured them of much resistance, so perhaps this morning the pirate would have something to say.

Zacharai appeared at Burgush's shoulder. "I've been watching this one," the hooded figure said. "He stands out."

Burgush gruffed. "He's seafolk, they're all like that. Half this town is."

A door opened to welcome Timid into the small, cave-like room. He recognized the gigantic Oruk inside as the one called the Hangman.

A guard's hand pressed firmly on Timid's shoulder, forcing him to sit. Soon after, he and the Hangman were alone.

"You've got something I want," Burgush said.

"I do?" Timid looked down, miming confusion and empty pockets.

"Yes," Burgush answered. "Your blood. But I can't take it from you, you have to give it to me."

"By confessing to piracy?" Timid clarified. The night spent in a cell with three seemingly innocent people had sharpened his foul mood to a point. "Aye, I could do that. Or, and this is much better for me, I could stay my course — because that you don't have enough evidence to justify chopping my head off. And as a matter of opinion, here, I don't think you have enough to charge half the people you haul up to the block if you're trying to do so with me."

Burgush kept his straight face. "Why didn't you tell the authorities that your boat had sunk? Eleven missing people, wreckage washing up weeks later, and you didn't say a word —

just fled town. Eleven people, sailor. And if I understand your folk well enough, those were your best friends, weren't they? So maybe I don't have proof enough to lay your neck in front of my axe, but I sure as hell am right to drag you in this room and demand an answer."

Timid's throat welled up. Because the Hangman was right. He'd first told himself that he did it because they weren't friends anymore, and because he no longer owed them anything. Then he learned that he slept better if he told himself that justice had been delivered and that gods bestow worthy fates. But that didn't exactly help him now if sitting across from an executioner told him anything about the fate that he deserved.

Burgush continued. "However, if you'd like to make my job easier, I can offer you something in return — and I do believe it to be a fair price."

"Oy?" Timid mocked. "And what's that?"

"You seem unaware, so I will ask. Do you know why Shrieksport has changed in the way it has?"

Timid shook his head.

"It is because divine providence has been delivered to us." Burgush revealed a small, ceremonial knife and slid it down his forearm. Skin parted and blood leaked onto the desk. Burgush calmly gathered a drop of blood on his forefinger and pressed it to his tongue. He held his arm above the desk so Timid could watch the skin reconnect itself, with thin bands of green spreading across the gap like sailors letting out a ship's sails.

"I have tried it on others," Burgush said, "but it only works if I have first taken their life. Their blood becomes my blood, you see. Do you have a loved one? Someone who may be in need of your blood?"

Again, Timid shook his head. His mind raced, trying to comprehend the miracle that had just taken place underneath the Shrieksport jail.

"Because if you give me your blood, you will save others. Innocent lives, who have never done anything wrong but been cursed with sickness and bad luck."

Timid cleared his throat, in the way that you have to after you cry. "Could you do something else for me, then?"

"Depends," Burgush answered.

"Could you release the others that haven't confessed?" Timid asked.

Burgush crossed his arms and leaned back in his rickety chair, which had to work as hard as it could to support his enormous weight on just two legs.

"C'mon," Timid pleaded, "I get it what you're doing. They aren't the ones you're after. Plus you don't have much on them anyway, from what they say."

A hushed whisper appeared in Burgush's skull, audible only to him. "Refuse," Zacharai growled. "That is too harsh a price to pay for what is rightfully yours."

Burgush ignored it. "That may be agreeable," he said.

In that moment, Timid saw that the man — the Oruk — sitting across from him would do almost anything for just an ounce of blood once he got the scent of it.

"And I get to choose how I die," Timid blurted out.

Burgush laughed. "Why would I do that?"

Timid smiled and told a story. "C'mon, how often do you get to kill a pirate? It could be the biggest show of the year. You could even tell people that I selected my method of execution. They'd find you merciful — all while they watch you take a life."

That, at long last, got the Hangman's imagination running. A crowd chanted his name, filling each and every crack and crevice it could to catch a glimpse of him.

The voice in Burgush's head faded away to another place. "You fool," it spit at him.

"And which method would you choose?" Burgush asked the one-armed man.

Timid leaned forward, looked the Hangman in the eyes, and said, "Drowning."

The end,

for now.

Stay tuned for

*A Grave that Cannot
Hold Roses*

The Ballad of Timid
Stormwind Book Two

About R.P. Ashe

R.P. Ashe is a self-published fiction author, at-home bartender, and amateur chess player — among other things.

R.P. wrote his debut series, *The Ballad of Timid Stormwind*, as a love letter to the art of oral storytelling when — after being just a listener for long enough — he finally found the courage to step up to the plate.

He spends most of his day as a young professional in the busting metropolises of upstate New York, and in his spare time you can find him unsuccessfully fly fishing far from the city lights.

www.ingramcontent.com/pod-product-compliance
Lightning Source LLC
Chambersburg PA
CBHW021108110726
47900CB00007B/2084